THE CASELLA BROTHERS

THE CASELLA Sin

C.B. FREY

Cover Designer: Coffin Print Designs

Editing and Proofreading: Hummingbird Editing

Interior Formatting & Design: Quirky Circe.

Rating: R18+

*May we always find comfort in knowing that
like the tides of Falcon's Keep, love will endure,
even when everything around us changes.*

The Casella Sin is a standalone, dark romance book part of an interconnected series. It does contain situations that could be triggering for some readers.

If you don't enjoy taboo/forbidden romances, this may not be the book for you.

This book contains explicit language and explicit sexual content.

It is intended to be for readers 18+.

For a full list of triggers, please visit the author's website at
https://www.cbfreyauthor.com/

<u>This is your last warning.</u>
<u>It contains dark content, which may be</u>
<u>triggering for some readers.</u>

Playlist

Easy to Love ❖ BRYCE SAVAGE
Chemicals ❖ THE DARK
I Wanna Be Yours ❖ ARCTIC MONKEYS
Dopamine ❖ AMERICAN DREAM MACHINE, LOVELESS
Drinking with Cupid ❖ VOILA
Mind of Mine ❖ LØ SPIRIT
Sinner ❖ SHAYA ZAMORA
Comatose ❖ SKILLET
Nobody ❖ TOBY MAI
Good Enough ❖ LØ SPIRIT
Therapy ❖ VOILA
Superhero ❖ FALLING IN REVERSE
Talk to a Friend ❖ RAIN CITY DRIVE
Last Resort (Reimagined) ❖ FALLING IN REVERSE
Hospital for Souls ❖ BRING ME THE HORIZON
Blasphemy ❖ BRING ME THE HORIZON
Skinny Love ❖ BIRDY
Drown ❖ BRING ME THE HORIZON
Bad Life ❖ SIGRID, BRING ME THE HORIZON
Soul Tied ❖ ASHLEY SINGH

Deathbeds ✧ BRING ME THE HORIZON
Unravel Me ✧ SABRINA CLAUDIO
One Last Time ✧ THE PLOT IN YOU
Doomed ✧ BRING ME THE HORIZON
Paralyzed ✧ LANMVRKS
Glass Heart ✧ CASKETS
Fire Up the Night ✧ NEW MEDICINE
Ghosts ✧ Colorblind
Let Me Be Sad ✧ I PREVAIL
When Everything Means Nothing ✧ FIT FOR
A KING
Anymore ✧ LØ SPIRIT
Left Behind ✧ THE PLOT IN YOU
Hollow ✧ LØ SPIRIT, DABIN, KAI WACHI
Still Worth Fighting For ✧ MY DARKEST DAYS
Gone or Staying ✧ SLEEP THEORY
By the Sound ✧ CASKETS
Be Somebody ✧ THOUSAND FOOT KRUNCH
Empty ✧ LETDOWN
Lay By Me ✧ RUBEN
Breathe ✧ LØ SPIRIT
Lifetime ✧ THREE DAYS GRACE

PROLOGUE
Rafael

If I keep running, I'll make it. They'll give up. I just have to *keep fucking running* Don't fucking stop. Not for anyone and not for anything. My stomach churns and my legs start to ache as I heave the air from my lungs, the black sky mocking me. Like I didn't have enough demons inside me, I needed to add to it.

A gun fires behind me, piercing the air, the bullet ricocheting off a car beside me, and I thank whatever gods are on my side that it didn't hit me. They must be out of bullets now, having unloaded everything they had when they were chasing me with their cars, but I can't stop to find out.

I need to keep going.

I need to lose them.

"*Maledetto bastardo*! I'm going to tear your fucking fingers off!" one of them yells as they gain on me, the heavy thump of his footsteps getting closer. The streets are small and there aren't many places to hide, so I had to be clever and lead them to a place I've become very familiar with over the last few months.

"He's heading for the port!" another one yells, figuring out my escape plan.

Turning left, I run up the old path, past the rough houses and boats, and climb up the sketchy ladder, clutching my pocket. I finally make it to the concrete bridge that barricades the sea from the city and realise there's nowhere to go from here. There should have been a boat waiting for me and slowly, as the feeling of betrayal begins to wash over me, I grit my teeth and steel my spine.

It's me against them.

I turn to face them, their faces in visible agony as they work to recover their breath.

One of them steps towards me, he's probably the same size as me, just a little slower.

"Give it back." He holds his hand out, waiting for me to obey his command as I weigh my options, but there really are none.

If I give it back, they'll kill me, and if I don't…they'll kill me.

He pulls out a large hunting knife and the other man beside him grins. "Don't make me use this."

"Come on, then." I tear part of my shirt off and wrap it around my right hand, preparing myself for a fight.

"I vouched for you." He lowers the knife an inch. "I told him you'd be a fucking asset to the team." The hurt in his voice is evident as his brows come together.

I knew my actions would land me here, but I wasn't about to join the devil in his dealings. Not when I could potentially make a name for myself. What's the best way to piss off a mobster?

Speak ill of his name? Maybe.

Fuck up on the job? Maybe.

Steal his most expensive possession?

Check.

"Not my problem." I shrug, which makes him angrier.

He lunges at me, and I swiftly dodge it, sliding backward as we circle each other.

"You know this only ends one way." His eyes narrow in on the bulge in my pocket, his primary goal to get to the stolen item, but there is no way I'm giving it up. Even if it means I fucking kill him. Adrenaline buzzes through me as he swings his right hook. It lands on my jaw, making me stumble toward the edge of the bridge, the water sloshing against the concrete below. Blood flows into my mouth from the impact and I spit, spraying the red saliva into his face, throwing him off balance for a split second. Tackling him to the ground, and just as I'm about to lay into him, hands are on me, pulling me off and throwing me down hard. I can almost hear a crack as his foot connects with my ribs, the collision making my head swim and my lungs collapse.

"I'm fucking tired, Raf." The man with the knife stands, towering over me, shooing the other man out of the way. "Just remember, I didn't want this."

I will my legs to work, to get up, to get me the fuck out of here, but they remain still. Immobilised by the pain and shock my body is enduring. But instead of clutching my ribs, I clutch the item in my pocket.

I refuse for this to be it. There's no fucking way I did all of this just to end up here.

"Do it like a fucking man." I spit the blood from my mouth onto the ground and stare up at him considering my last wish. I need to use everything at my disposal if I want to make it through tonight alive and I'm not above fighting dirty. "You really going to kill someone when they're on their back?"

He huffs, taking a step back, and I work to get myself up on my feet, but before I can plan for my escape, the thick blade cuts through my gut, slicing its way deep into my core. A warmth spreads quickly, along with a frantic tide of adrenaline. A fog of fear clouds over me, sharpening every fucking sound.

I'm going to die.

This is it.

He leans in with his hand still on the handle of the knife and whispers, "Enzo will want your heart for this."

Grunting, I push him off. The steel of the blade is smothered in my blood, the crimson now glinting in the moonlight.

"Tell him to come and carve it out himself," I manage to grunt out before throwing myself off the bridge, the cool night air rushing past me in a howl. The instant my body hits the water, it rips the air from my lungs, the jarring impact like a violent embrace. The iciness envelopes me as the bridge blurs into a distant memory. The endless black swallows me slowly, pulling me into its depths.

I hold my breath, my entire body pulsating with the need for air. My arms burn as I use every bit of energy I have left to swim to the surface. As I break through, their voices are muffled through my ragged breathing. I scan the surface for anything to cling onto and to my luck, I spot an old rowboat secured to the dock.

Maybe someone in the sky heard my pleas.

Maybe luck has nothing to do with it.

But maybe…it's just not my time yet.

"*Da dove viene?*" A voice echoes through my skull as I struggle to open my eyes. The swash of the sea thrusts my body against the wet sand. My head is heavy and my body is drained.

"*Ha perso molto sangue,*" the voice says again, the words jumbling inside my brain as I open my eyes to a bearded man. I lick my cracked lips, tasting the salt on them.

"Let's take him to the morgue," he says as they lift me, the pain in my side growing stronger the longer I'm awake. Groaning, I run my fingers over the large gash and stare down at my hand, the sand now mixing with my blood.

"Don't fucking touch it, *idiota,*" the younger one curses as they carry me through dark woods. I've never seen them before in my life and I have no way of knowing how long I've been in that dinghy, nor do I know where the fuck I am.

When we get to the morgue, the stench of rotting flesh assaults my senses and I almost gag before I'm laid on the cold silver table. They cut open my shirt, pressing a thick gauze onto my wound. My screams reverberate off the walls as something pierces the side of my neck, the thick liquid oozing through my veins. The sting only lasts for a moment before my eyes grow heavier as each second passes.

"Go to sleep." The guy who looks to be my age stares down at me, continuing to press the gauze down harder, and I give in unwillingly, closing my eyes.

It seems like minutes pass and I'm awake again, only this time I'm in a bed. Looking around the room, I spot a dresser and a writing desk, and I can tell by the shape of the window and the size of the room that the house must be large.

Fuck.

Lifting the blanket, I notice I don't have the same clothes on. I flinch at the pain when I move, clutching at the fresh bandage over my wound when the door opens and the same two men walk in. They are clearly related as they share the same dark blue eyes and a strong jaw. The older one looks at me with caution before he speaks.

"What is your name, son?"

I pause, not wanting to give these people my real name because I don't know who they are. They could be on *his* side for all I know.

"You first." I clutch my side as I step out of the bed, ready to make a run for it.

He looks to the younger man and back at me. "Please," he says in a thick Italian accent, "we are not here to hurt you."

The younger one steps forward with my jacket in his hands, "This is yours…" He extends my jacket to me, and I snatch it from him, diving my hand straight into the pocket and coming up empty.

The older man reaches into his slacks and pulls out the item I nearly died for. "Will you explain how you managed to get your hands on this?" He holds up the Fabergé egg I stole from Enzo and I freeze. He steps forward, places the egg on the bed, and extends his hand to me in greeting. "My name is Dante Della Torre, and this is my son."

CHAPTER ONE
Nera

The Call of Falcon's Keep.

Do you ever dream of what it would be like to be someone else?

To be free of all that you carry within yourself?

The freedom that comes from absolving yourself of all the expectations being placed on your shoulders?

Well, there isn't a chance I can ever experience that, and my family made sure of it when I received a text from my brother summoning me back home. It's not enough to be so far away from them because even with the distance, reality creeps toward me, inch by inch, day by day until it's staring at me in the face, waiting for me to break.

"Nera!" Bec shouts from beside me over the music and I snap out of my daze to stare out into the crowd of seedy men, waiting and watching. The lights flash, blurring my vision for a moment, when my hand connects with the cool metal pole, sending my body into the routine I've been practising for weeks.

Sometimes I wonder if my friends are ashamed of how I make extra money on the side, but the only explanation I have for them is that it makes me feel in control.

"Why do you do it when your family is already comfortable?"

Elodie's question is the one I always think about before I step onto the stage, and it makes me question myself every single day.

What would happen if Dante found out?

"Get off the stage if you're not going to show us your tits!" someone from the crowd roars just as my leg hooks around the pole. Closing my eyes, I tip my body back, throwing my weight onto the pole and swinging as the beat of the music thumps through my body.

It's busier than usual tonight, meaning trouble is always looming, and although I'm comfortable with the security we have in this establishment, it makes me nervous when the crowd become rowdy. The man standing in the front row, looking at me like a piece of meat, is beginning to show signs of said trouble. Ignoring him, I continue with my routine, my knees slamming onto the floor as I lay back, swaying my shoulders to the beat.

He points to me, whispering into the ear of a waitress and she nods when he places bills into her bra, smiling.

My eyes scan the room and land on Kyle's. He nods over to the private rooms, and I make my way off the stage. Just as I walk past him, he grabs me by the arm.

"If you need me, I'll be right out here."

I give him a small smile and open the door to the room, but when I enter, I wish I hadn't. Three men sit side by side, waiting…for *me*. I've given private dances before but never for more than one person at a time. I hesitate before taking my place in the middle of the room, trying to keep my exterior calm and collected.

It's a given fact that when you sign up for a job like this one, there will always be someone out there judging, and although it bothers me sometimes, I try not to let it get to me.

"Just another slut with daddy issues." One of them laughs as I stand there awkwardly. "Go ahead, take it off, baby. We want to see what we paid for."

I want to walk out of here, but I don't because I crave the control.

"You couldn't be further from the truth." I smile through the pain of his words.

"What was that? I didn't hear you over the sound of your dirty pussy juices running down your whorish legs."

My jaw is locked as I take a breath and take note of the knife handle poking out of his pocket.

"I was close with my father."

The three of them look at each other and snicker.

"Why are you here then?"

"That's my business. Did you pay for a show or to talk?" I ask as I remove my navy lace bra and almost immediately, all eyes fall to my breasts, their words getting stuck in their throat, and I chuckle.

Simple creatures.

Living in America has taught me many things. For one, everything seems insignificant because of how many people there are in this country.

Competing.

Grinding.

Trying to make something of themselves.

Life in Italy seemed a lot less…cut-throat.

Although it wasn't always the safest, the happiest or most prosperous, it *was* home. But now, I'm closer to my friends here than my family in Italy.

"Did you end up finishing that term paper?" Elodie asks, hooking her bag over her shoulder as we head up the steps into the business building on campus.

"I had a late night last night, so I didn't get a chance to, but I think I should be able to get it finished during lunch today."

She looks at me, clear disapproval on her face.

"Don't look at me like that."

"It's not safe, Nera, and you know this. Why do you still do it?"

To feel like I have a sliver of control over my life.

I ignore her words and continue walking toward our lecture hall when I spot Jeremy and suddenly, everything goes cold. The ice slithers up my spine and lodges itself inside my throat, making it hard to swallow. Elodie follows my gaze and slips her hand into mine, comforting and calming my mind.

"Don't engage," she warns, picking up our pace and practically pulling me through the corridor.

"Nera," Jeremy drawls, his army of brutes standing beside him with sly grins.

"Piss off, dickhead." Elodie pulls me harder, causing me to drop my phone.

Shit.

My hand slips out of hers to pick it up when my space is invaded by Jeremy's obnoxiously large bicep.

"Allow me, *bella*." He picks up my phone, handing it to me, and I shiver at his proximity. I've always hated that pet name and the sound of it coming from his lips now sounds almost like a threat.

Elodie comes between us, shielding me, but I place a hand on her shoulder, moving beside her. I'm not afraid of

Jeremy, just ashamed of myself because of everything that happened between us.

"Are you just going to avoid me forever?"

"I'm not avoiding you. I intentionally don't want to associate myself with you anymore, but I'm wondering why you won't take the hint?" I clutch my phone harder in my hand, hoping the shake in my voice wasn't noticeable.

"Are you still angry?" He talks in a low voice with a foul grin.

"Angry!?" Elodie yells, closing the distance between them. "You're a piece of work, Davis."

"I wasn't talking to you. Why can't you stay out of other people's business?"

"It's fine, Elodie, I'll be right behind you." I motion for her to get to the lecture hall, and she hesitates before looking between me and Jeremy. He's tall, typical jock build, and has a cocky personality to go with his disgustingly charming face.

"Keep your hands to yourself, Davis," she cautions before she gives me a look and walks off to the lecture hall.

"I'm serious. I don't want to hear your voice or see you anymore. Just stay out of my way, okay?"

His army of loyal followers burst into laughter at my words and he smiles. The dimple on his left cheek appears, and the blue of his eyes swirls with a challenge. We've almost finished the semester, meaning our degree is almost at an end. I'm eager to never see his face again, while also devastated that I must return home to Italy, leaving my friends behind.

Leaving the life I've grown accustomed to.

He leans into me, and I grit my teeth. "What will you do if I don't?"

When he pulls back, a lock of hair falls to the front of

his face, and although I once considered him to be attractive, it all vanished in one night when I caught him with someone else.

"Don't push me."

His expression changes as the dimple disappears and lines settle between his brows. "No one will believe you."

My heart sinks because I know he's right. With the influence his family has on the school and the social standing he has with the teachers and with practically every other student, there is no way in hell anyone would believe me. The worst part is that he knows this. He is protected by it, and it's because of *this* that graduation couldn't come quickly enough.

CHAPTER TWO
Rafael

The Blindness of Loyalty.

It's been a few weeks since my return to Italy from London, and everything that's happened weighs heavily on my mind. I watch the trees swaying in the wind outside, the sun cascading beneath the horizon.

My fingers find the necklace hanging around my neck, a symbol of kinship and trust, shared with me innocently, from someone I grew to love over many years.

I look up at the burnt garage, years of hard work taken down within seconds, and the rage I still work hard to hide begins to simmer again. I told myself to be patient and to learn to be balanced in everything I do, but each time I think about this place, another side of me breaks free, wanting to tear down the one person who took everything from me.

Exiting the car, one that was left to me from *him*, I stride to the garage. The ground is littered with burnt timbers, the sun streaking through the barely existing roof. The night I left, when I was young and stupid, is one I will always regret. It plagues me, and I fear this will never change.

La famiglia non è la persona a cui sei imparentato, è chi è venuto e non se n'è mai andato, anche quando i tempi si sono fatti duri e le notti erano buie.'

Family isn't who you're related to, it's who came and never left, even when the times grew hard, and the nights were dark.

My fingers trace over the carved writing on the concrete wall and something inside me breaks a little more. I haven't been here since that night.

I couldn't…because I blame myself for it.

Tyres roll to a stop beside my car, and I watch as Dante exits the black Rolls-Royce. His long strides eat up the distance between us, and when he looks at me, all I see is sympathy.

"I know what's happened has brought up the past for you, but I want you to know you don't have to deal with it alone." He places his hand on my shoulder, a gesture of his support and comfort even though he isn't the type to show it.

"I'm no stranger to it." I chuckle, my gaze returning to the words etched into the concrete by the person taken from this world too soon. The air becomes ice cold when I shut my eyes, taking me back to that night. The wind surrounds me as my legs work to outrun them. My young limbs without a clue as to what was coming next.

"I need your help." Dante's words pull me back and I nod. "We have a lot of work to do."

"Have we found Enzo yet?"

His expression sours at the mention of the name, his dark eyebrows coming together when he speaks. "The moment I do, I will carve him up myself."

"I think Nicholas might beat you to it."

"The Casella brothers might have jurisdiction in London, but not here—this is *my* soil." He slips his hand into his jacket pocket and withdraws his phone. "Things need to change. We can't continue to live separate from the mainland."

Dante's father—Dante Senior—dreamed of being disassociated from the rest of the mafia families in Italy for his family's protection. As the years passed, their allies and resources began to run dry, the suppliers choosing to band with the strongest family in Italy.

The Petruccis.

"They won't let you return to the mainland unless you swear your life and wealth to them."

"There might be another way," he admits, tucking the phone back into his pocket, and when he looks up at me, I know he's ready for battle because that's what it's going to take to gain his family's allies back. "I'm going to need you to do something before we take this on."

"My focus is finding Enzo," I say curtly, not wanting my attention to stray from the person who murdered my half-brother and almost killed Darcy.

"Rafael…" Dante fidgets with the bulky rings on his fingers and I see hesitation hidden behind his eyes. "You're the only one I trust with this. I promise you retribution, but I need you to do this for me."

I can't deny Dante. Not because I fear him, but because I owe him and his family for saving me, for taking me in and treating me like one of their own when my own blood had cast me away.

I nod. "Who do you want dead?"

He pauses, the creases between his brows relaxing when he speaks next. "This isn't an assassination. I need you to bring Nera home."

I haven't seen Nera in years. The last time I saw her, she was just a child, a true daddy's girl who could do no wrong in her father's eyes. I didn't have much to do with her, barely even spoke to her before she was sent off to live and study in America. It makes me wonder why Dante would want her back in the country, but that's where I draw the line of my involvement in his relationship with his sister. He barely speaks of her to me or others, and I can only assume the reason is that he wants to keep her out of this world.

"Why now?"

"Just like me, she has a role to play as a Della Torre," he admits, looking at the floor, clearly not wanting to resort to bringing his sister home.

"What role can a child play in this?" I question.

"She's not a child anymore."

"What about your father's wish?" I pull out a cigarette from my pocket and flick the lighter in my other hand, watching the flame light the tip as I breathe in the poison. My finger brushes the carved letter on the front of the lighter.

"Do you think a dead man's wishes matter?"

I guess not.

"When?"

"In a week. I need her to be here for the Falcon's Keep revelry."

The revelry. Two nights in twelve months when the Della Torre's open the port, allowing the richest people from the mainland to enter an exclusive party, paying thousands just to attend. It's one of the best revenue streams Dante has created, making so much as half a million euros in one night.

"What about Enzo?"

"We have been combing his frequently visited places and known residential properties. He'll turn up."

"Nicholas will have my head if I don't follow through with my promise."

"A Della Torre never breaks their promises."

His words sting as they leave his mouth because I know I'm not a Della Torre by blood…even though he would say otherwise. The red stream rushing through my veins runs in three others but remains tainted with abandonment, leaving me to wonder where I truly belong and who I truly am.

CHAPTER THREE
Rafael

Raven-haired Principessa.

I stare at the food on my plate, still not used to seeing such an abundance of nutrients together, and mentally, I'm back there in his garage, pleading for more after scoffing down the only food we had. The flight to the US was easy, but unlike my brothers, I don't fly first class, nor do I have my own jet.

"Is everything to your liking?" The waitress pulls me from my thoughts, and I give her my best smile and nod.

"Yes, thank you." My smile turns sly, and she responds with a laugh.

"Do you need anything else?"

"Hmmm…" I trail off, undressing her with my eyes as I scan her from head to toe when my phone rings. I excuse myself, pulling it out to answer as the attractive waitress returns behind the counter.

"Does she know she's leaving the States?" I ask Dante and his silence is enough of an answer.

"You expect *me* to tell her?"

"Whatever you do, Raf, just get her here, okay?"

"What if she doesn't want to come back?"

"I give you permission to *make* her."

He hangs up and I return to enjoying my meal when I

notice a woman with raven hair exit the building across the street. I watch as she laces up her black combat boots, the waves in her hair cascading down past her breasts when she stands, her large coat covering most of her body. I swallow the food in my mouth at the slow realisation of who she is.

Nera.

She's tall. Taller than I remember her to be.

Checking the watch on my wrist, I wonder what she could be up to at this time. Placing the last bit of food into my mouth, I slide out of the booth when she enters an Uber.

I guess we're going to find out.

My heart thumps in beat with the bass as I make my way through the establishment, the bottom of my shoes sticking to the floor, and although I should be disgusted, I feel right at home. Surveying the area, I take note of the brute bodyguards by each exit when a woman in nothing but a thong approaches me, holding a notepad and a pen.

"Can I get you something, handsome?" She smiles, eyeing me.

"Single malt, whatever is your strongest." I slide the dollars into the thin strap on her hip, grazing her skin, and she grins as she scribbles on the notepad in her hand.

"I get off at four if you're interested in a nightcap." Sliding the paper on the table in front of me, she winks and makes her way behind the bar. I'm no stranger to attention from women, and although it helps with getting my cock wet, I've never chosen to take it further.

The lights dim and a spotlight appears on stage, and the next song begins as a tall *cigna nera* takes her place on stage in a black bodice and thong with sky-high heels. A stark contrast to her appearance from earlier.

"Not this tease again!" yells some drunk in the corner, slurring his words. She pays no attention to him as she rolls her hips to the music, and it makes me wonder if her brother knows she moonlights as someone else when the sun sets.

"Get off the fucking stage!" The man hurls an empty beer can at her, but she dodges it. I wait to see how she's going to handle it when the buff security guard marches over, gripping the man by his arm to have a word with him as Nera continues with her show. I sit back, taking all of her in—her long, dark hair, her plump red lips and her prominent collarbones accentuated by her slender shoulders. It's been years since I've seen her, and the shy little girl she was is gone. Instead, the woman on stage is unapologetically confident.

She's *definitely* not a child anymore.

I shift in my seat, uncomfortable that blood rushes to my cock at the sight of her sensual curves. Her breasts are slick with sweat as she grinds her hips and throws her head back, the glitter on her skin shimmering in the dim light.

The waitress finally arrives with my drink just as Nera finishes her show and I down it in one go, not wanting to waste more time in this place. I'd much rather be on a plane back home, searching for Enzo.

Standing, I head toward the back when I'm stopped by the brute.

"Whoa, only the dancers are permitted to enter."

"Let me through."

"I said, only the dancers." He grips me by the shirt and

shoves me, making me chuckle. Just as I'm about to rearrange his face, Nera walks by and into a private room, stealing my attention. Without another word, I head over to the private room with the security guard on my heels.

"Hey man, what's your problem?" Grabbing me by the arm, he stops me from entering.

"Touch me again and you'll be eating through a tube for the rest of your life," I warn, and his face falls, quickly removing his hand from my arm.

"You can't go back there, not unless you pay."

He thinks he can stop me.

I don't explain myself to him, because I don't have to. Taking a step back, my foot connects with the door, and it snaps open, violently banging against the wall.

The brute doesn't heed my last warning as he grabs me in a chokehold, but little does he know, I grew up fighting. Not in the ring, like a rich boy, no, I grew up in the fucking pits. There is no remorse, no restraint, and no sympathy in the fights I've had in my life, and what this man doesn't know is just how much I'm willing to follow through on my threat. I'm quick with my movements, so he doesn't see it coming when my hand connects with his balls and I crush them, pulling hard until his girlish screams can be heard over the thumping of the bass. He releases me and I turn around, my fist connecting with his jaw, making him fall flat on his back. I waste no time to get on top, launching my fists into his face, bruising him, cutting him, making him bleed. He can't beg me to stop even if he wanted to as his eyes swell up beneath my force.

Other guards begin to make their way over, having heard or seen the commotion, and it doesn't take much effort for them to reach the same fate. Ignoring the bulging eyes of the customers and employees, I turn and walk into the room, eager to take Nera and get the fuck out of here.

It seems they haven't heard a thing in here because the seedy fucker has his hand in his pants as he watches Nera dance, her bodice now discarded on the floor beneath his feet. A red haze overcomes me as I stomp into the room, startling the man.

"Hey! You can't be in here, I paid for this!" he exclaims like an entitled piece of shit. Nera's eyes clash with mine and I don't know if she recognises me, but I don't wait to find out as my bloodied hand closes around the man's throat.

"What the fuck man?" His voice shakes, the stench of fear emanating from his every pore.

Bringing his face closer to mine, I stare him straight in the eyes. "You have three seconds to leave before I make you piss sitting down for the rest of your miserable years."

He's out of the room quicker than I expected, and just as I'm about to get what I came for, I look around the empty room and catch sight of her heels just as she exits through the emergency door. Following her, I keep calm. She either knows who I am and is trying to prolong the inevitable or she has no idea and is terrified. I begin jogging behind her, up the street, and she looks back, visibly working to run in her shoes. She turns into a dark alley, and I slow to a walk, approaching the bend. When I turn, her elbow connects with my nose, sending the pain straight to my eyes as I groan, clutching my face with both hands.

"Fuck!"

She tries to escape, but I'm quicker. My arm curls around her waist, hurling her back into the brick wall.

"Get your hands off me!" She fights, pushing against me.

"Nera, stop." My hands clasp around her wrists, holding them together in front of me, causing my gaze to fall to her breasts, now pressed together.

"Raf?" She relaxes and I let go of her wrists, her arms immediately covering her chest. "W-what the hell are you doing in the States?" She runs her eyes over me.

"Dante sent me." I don't bother skirting around the subject, because I am here to do my job.

"No, I still have time."

I sigh, removing my leather jacket and handing it to her. "He wants you home for the revelry."

Her face drops, staring back at me like she knows something I don't.

"I-I haven't even graduated yet!" she protests, turning around to slide her arms through the jacket, the material now covering her delicious skin.

What the fuck?

She's Dante's sister!

"Our flight is tomorrow morning. You either come willingly or I'll have to—"

"What? Throw me over your shoulder and take me home?" She scoffs, walking back toward the establishment.

"Nera," I warn with a toughness in my voice I reserve only for those who deserve it.

"I don't want to hear it."

Catching up to her, I grip her by the elbow, thrusting her body back into mine.

"I'm not going back without you, so unless you want Dante to find out about your…hobby…"

She glares at me, knowing her brother would be furious

if he ever found out, so she agrees, placing me one step closer to completing my task here and returning to find Enzo.

CHAPTER FOUR
Nera

The Allure.

The suitcase overflows with unworn clothing as I shove another pair of pants on the growing pile. I can't believe he's not going to let me graduate. It was the one thing my father had made him promise, the one thing I wanted to achieve before I packed up my life here and returned to Italy.

"This is *not* what my father would have wanted." I turn to Rafael, who is now leaning against the wall, his black shirt clinging to every ridge of his strong body. I forgot what he looked like. Partly because I never spoke to him growing up. He'd be with my father or brothers and was rarely ever in the house I grew up in.

"Dante wants you home," is all he gives me.

"But why?"

Pushing off the wall, he strides toward me, placing the last item of clothing I had on my bed into the suitcase. "You can ask him yourself, *Principessa*, when we hit the shores of Falcon's Keep."

A shudder rolls down my spine at the mention of the island where I grew up, and although I should have fond memories there with my family, I don't. I pause, waiting for him to zip up my suitcase, throw me over his shoulder and take me back to the dreary island, but he doesn't. Instead, he waits for *me*.

"How is my mother?" There is hesitation in my voice when I ask because a small part of me doesn't truly want to know. He looks away, the moonlight drifting through the window splashes across his high cheekbones. When he looks back, his grey eyes are filled with sympathy. I don't know why I expected the answer I was hoping for. It's been the same for the last five years.

"Not much has changed since you left," he admits, zipping up my suitcase and placing the wheels on the floor. Dante would never allow me to stay in a shared house, so he leased one for me close to the college my father and I chose together before he passed.

The air stills for a moment, my thoughts bringing me back to the last moments I spent with him, and my chest tightens. I haven't thought of him for years, too focused on achieving the only goal I set out for myself and now, a small bit of guilt claws its way through me as I realise I haven't even been back there to visit or pay my respects to him.

"What time is our flight?" I ask, hoping I'll have time in the morning to say goodbye to my life here.

"Eleven."

"I need to tell Elodie." I reach for my phone with the intent to call her but my screen remains blank.

Dead battery.

Shit.

"Be ready to leave at eight." He takes a step toward my bedroom door with my suitcase in hand.

"I need to pick up something from my friend's house in the morning." I give an excuse to stay a little longer, not wanting to leave without a proper goodbye.

He pauses, taking a breath in, his eyes boring into mine as he considers my request. "Fine. Be up early. I'm not missing the flight."

The years have been extra kind to Rafael. As I stand here and take him in, I notice his boyish looks have been replaced with high cheekbones, a strong jaw, and full lips. The only similarity he shares with the boy I once knew, is the void behind his beautiful steel eyes.

"Rafael?"

His expression softens, waiting for my question.

"How's Dante doing?" I ask, more from a place of curiosity than empathy, because my brother hasn't spoken to me since I left Falcon's Keep.

He takes a step toward me, his jaw tensing as he brings his hand up to scratch his chin. "Dante…has been trying to do what he can with what he has."

"That's vague."

He smiles, his white teeth coming into view, the piercings on his nose twinkling in the dim light. "I don't remember you being this direct."

"That's because you never spoke to me."

"Hm." His eyes graze over me and when they land on mine again, I struggle to ignore the shiver that runs down my spine, all too aware of his proximity. To my dismay, he turns on his heels and takes a few steps toward my door. "Goodnight, *Principessa.*"

He walks away, leaving me to question the direction my life is about to take.

The tapping of my shoes on the floor echoes through the hall as I wait for Elodie, and all I can think about is asking her to come with me. I look over my shoulder at Rafael, leaning on the driver's side of the black sedan, and my heart races at the inevitability of my situation.

People file out of the auditorium and I search for Elodie's bright blonde hair. When she comes into view, I hastily make my way through the crowd, and she gasps when I grab her by the wrist and pull her to the side, away from the crowd.

"What's going on?" She checks me over. "Are you okay?"

"I…" I swallow, the words not wanting to come out of my mouth, unsure of how she's going to take it. "I have to leave."

She pauses, and just when I think she will slap me, she laughs.

"I'm serious." I look over to Rafael, who's still in the same place with a cigarette between his lips, and she follows my vision, her body tensing when she sees him.

"Who's he?" she asks, looking back at me. "Nera, what is going on?"

"I have to go back to Falcon's Keep." The words taste bitter, but I say them anyway, not seeing a way out of this.

Her eyes widen. "What!? Graduation isn't for another few months. What about the ceremony? What about your future? What about all the effort you've put into your degree?"

I slide my hands into hers. "I know, but I don't have a choice."

Disgust piles onto me when there's an unwanted caress at my hip, across my lower back, and I know who it is without looking up.

"*Bella*…what are you doing on this side of campus?"

Elodie squeezes my hands so hard, that the rings on my fingers almost meld together as Jeremy's gaze lingers far too long on my chest. Just as I'm about to push him away from me, his eyes are torn away to something behind me.

"Is there a problem?" The deep timber of Rafael's voice livens up the now empty hall. When I turn, Jeremy takes a step back as Rafael drops the cigarette butt onto the floor, putting out the ember with his boot. He's dressed in all black, the top buttons of his shirt undone, offering a view of his dark chest tattoos and the silver cross he wears around his neck.

Jeremy scoffs and turns back to me. "Did you hire a bodyguard with all your slut money?"

Heat rises to my cheeks at the mention of my night job, and Rafael smiles.

"Do you think belittling a woman for earning her keep will make up for your lack of character and respect?"

Jeremy opens his mouth to answer, but before he can, Rafael speaks again. "It just proves you have nothing of substance to offer in terms of equality." He takes a step toward Jeremy, circling him like prey. "Or support."

He stands behind Jeremy, breathing down his neck. "Typical qualities of a *boy*," he whispers, and when Jeremy turns to face him, my stomach flies into my throat at the sight of Rafael towering over him, the dark markings on his neck a harsh contrast to Jeremy's bare skin.

"At least I have a promising life ahead of me. What do you have in your future? Prison?" His snarky tone makes Rafael grin, and I can't pull my eyes away from what's unfolding before me.

"I cannot foresee the future, but I know what lies in my past." His ominous answer has Jeremy lost for words as Rafael stares at him, waiting for him to break his gaze.

"Whatever, man, I don't have time for your riddles." Jeremy's hand lands on Rafael's shoulder, aiming to push him, but Rafael doesn't waste a second, grabbing a hold of his hand and walking him back into the wall.

"Whoa, man, what are you doing?" Jeremy's voice wavers. "You're hurting me."

I watch as Rafael twists his hand backward, bending his elbow and shoving him face first into the wall, Jeremy's cries resounding through the hall.

"Please! Alright! Fuck! Okay!"

"All it takes is a little bit of force and I dislocate your shoulder, possibly tear some ligaments and sever your chances of playing any sport for the rest of your life."

"No, no, no, please, no," Jeremy begs as Rafael holds him pressed against the wall, the muscles in his arm tightening.

"Apologise."

"Fuck! Sorry! I'm sorry!"

My hands come up to cover my mouth when a loud snap sounds. Rafael takes a step away from Jeremy, watching him cry out in pain.

"What the fuck!?" he screams, gaining the attention of a few straggling students. "My shoulder!"

"I'd say I hope you've learnt your lesson, but I doubt people like you do." He spits at the ground. "*Buona giornata, testa di cazzo.*"

"Time to go, *Principessa*, before I add one more name on my wall."

CHAPTER FIVE
Rafael

Old Habits.

The shores of Falcon's Keep are filled with dead hopes and dreams. It's a place where the nights are endless, sucking you into the void you try so desperately to evade. When I landed on Dante's doorstep after I almost lost my life, I didn't know what to expect. I didn't know that he would be like the father I never knew I needed. But it was only a matter of time before he was taken from me too.

The boat sways on the rocky shores as the sun hides behind the thick branches of the trees, guarding the shadowy building I've called home for years. The years I spent learning to become a part of a family. One I was not born into. The cool metal of the railing beneath my hand vibrates as the boat docks and it becomes difficult not to look over at Nera in the passenger seat of my Camaro. This car ferry is the last one departing from the mainland, and despite Dante's best efforts, most of the trades and relationships his father established have begun to dwindle.

"Tell Dante he's behind on his payments. If he wants the revelry to continue, he needs to pay double." Giuseppe works to secure the ferry to the wharf as he speaks.

Unfortunately, the wealth Dante Senior carried onto

Falcon's Keep wasn't enough to sustain the next generation as he had hoped.

"You'll be paid. I'll see to it."

I make my way to the driver's side and slide into the seat beside Nera, who is now scowling at the phone in her hands.

"We haven't even been here for an hour and I'm already itching to go back to the States." She waves her phone in my face. "No reception."

"It's choppy out here, but you'll get better reception inside." I start the engine, and she sighs. Looking over at her, I notice the pink in her cheeks, her midnight hair and piercing blue-grey eyes stealing my attention for just a moment.

As soon as the bridge is down, we make our way onto the gravel, leading past the beach and onto the road that connects to her house, a term probably best reserved for residential properties in suburbia, as this is not just another house. This is a large manor, nestled between the evergreen leaves, rivers, waterfalls, and mausoleums. The lights of the manor flicker on as darkness settles into the night and Nera clutches at the hem of her dress in my peripheral.

"How is it that when you return to a place you haven't seen in a long time, it feels as if you never left?" Her voice shakes when she speaks, and it makes me wonder what the hidden meaning behind her question is.

Driving past the large fountain in the middle, Dante steps out of the double doors of the manor, preparing to greet us. When we come to a stop, I reach over to unbuckle her seatbelt, and our eyes meet. There's a charge in the air but I can't be sure if she felt it too.

Dante opens her door, not giving her much else.

Stepping out, I watch Nera ignore her brother and walk straight up the steps and into the manor. Dante gazes at the floor, rubbing his face and scratching at his stubble.

"Are you going to explain?" I ask, shutting the door to my Camaro and placing my hands into my pockets.

"I had to make a decision, Raf." He doesn't look at me when he speaks, and I know whatever he has decided must be something he felt was necessary.

"*Signore…*" Stefano interrupts, speaking to Dante. "*Tua madre ti sta chiedendo.*"

Your mother is asking for you.

"Keep an eye on Nera. Until I tell you otherwise," he says to me as he strides up the steps and into the manor. Dante is rarely ever this withheld from me. We've been sharing everything since his father invited me to be a part of their family, down to the women we'd fuck, but ever since he asked me to collect Nera and bring her home, he's been reticent.

Handing the keys to Stefano, I head inside and up the grand staircase, into the wide hall. The walls are adorned with family portraits of the Della Torres dating back generations, and I avoid looking at them, the discomfort returning yet again. No matter how many years it's been, I don't belong here…not truly.

My attention is stolen when the door next to my room creaks open, the soft light filtering into the hallway. I stride past, peeking into the room to see Nera pacing the floor with her phone clutched in her hand.

What is she so worked up about?

I work past the urge to walk into her room and step into mine instead. The bed dips as I sit, removing my button-up and discarding it on the floor. The walls slowly begin to close in, the whispers in my mind becoming louder than ever before.

What are you still doing here?

Dante is dead.

This is not your family.

I've been so deep in the Della Torres' ambition that I forgot my own, and returning to London reminded me of it. Meeting my half-brothers, watching one of them die, reminded me that all of this is temporary. Life itself is fraught, and I'd be doing myself a favour if I just accept that the longer I stay here, pretending to be a part of something, the longer I avoid my true self.

Exhausted, I lay on the bed, intrusive thoughts of Nera's stormy-grey eyes invading my mind.

The rain patters lightly atop the roof of the church, gentle raindrops creating streams down the dark stained glass as I stand before the large cross. Dante Senior made it routine for his sons and me to pray every morning inside this very church before starting our day, and as some routines stuck, this one didn't. It's been some time since I've been in this building, and yet, nothing has changed.

Footsteps echo through the large space as I stare up at the cross, wondering if the god I used to pray to all those years ago even exists.

"Old habits." Dante's voice breaks through my thoughts.

"Tough to break."

"Some, not others." He lifts his necklace to his mouth,

placing his lips on the gold cross. Although we're the same age, he's taller, more put together, and far more educated. He reminds me of his father in a way, and his sister in others.

"The money we gave to the Casellas left a big hole in our holdings," he admits.

"If we couldn't afford it, why did we give it back? We could have waited. I know they wouldn't have missed it."

"It's not our way. We held onto it long enough."

The Casella family played a large role in the set-up of Falcon's Keep and will always remain an ally to the Della Torres.

"Did you know?" I ask, wanting to hear him say it.

"Know what?"

"That I am half Casella and half Guerra?" I question, clenching my fists at the constant reminder of the foreign, sin-filled blood that runs through my veins.

"If I did know, you think I would keep it from you?" He speaks in a low voice. "We share everything."

"Besides the reason behind you bringing Nera back home."

Dante tenses, my words hitting a nerve. "There is only *one* thing I ask of you, Raf. Keep your eyes open at this revelry."

"Always. Do we expect trouble?" I turn to face him.

"Whether we expect it or not, it'll be there."

"Any leads on Enzo?"

"One, but you're not going to like what Stefano has found." His jaw clenches as I hang on to his words, waiting for the news.

"He's recruiting."

"Recruiting?"

"Sources say he's meeting with the Lucchese family."

"*La merda!*" I exclaim, resisting the urge to unleash my temper. "If Enzo manages to get them on his side…"

"I know." He bows his head, not wanting to admit the losses we would face if the strongest family in Italy manages to make an ally out of the Luccheses. "That's why I need you to stay guarded at the revelry. I'm inviting them."

"What role does Nera play in all of this?" I question, still waiting for an answer to my earlier one.

"She'll play her part." He slaps a hand on my shoulder, his dark blue eyes focused on mine. "You're going to make sure of it."

CHAPTER SIX
Nera

The Past is in the Past.

I wish I felt something when I walked into my mother's wing, but I was too little to form a connection with her before she fell ill with Alzheimer's. All I remember is spending time with her on the beach, jumping the small waves with her hand in mine before my father would call us to dinner. He loved my mother, more than anything in this world, which is why he brought our entire family out here. I can't fault him for trying, I just wish he thought about our future.

The sound of thunderstorms rattles the window my mother blankly stares out from, barely noticing me in the room as I make my way to her. She's seated in her usual large brown leather chair by the windowpane, staring out into nothing.

"*Mamma?*" I'm careful not to startle her as I take a seat beside her, placing my hand on hers, and when she looks at me, I know she doesn't recognise me.

"*Posso aiutarti, bambino?*"

Can I help you, child?

"*Mamma, sono io, Nera.*"

She laughs, placing a hand on her chest. "*Chi chiamerebbe la loro figlia Nera?*"

Who would name their child black?

I fight back the emotions as I tighten my hold on her hand, wishing she would remember even for a short moment the little time we shared together.

"*Dov'è Dante?*" She asks for her husband, and I give her a sad smile.

"*Tornerà presto, Mamma.*"

He'll be back soon, Mamma.

I lie, shielding her from experiencing the heartbreak of losing her husband one more time.

"Nera?"

I turn to see Dante standing by the door, his tall build barely fitting in the frame, and I lose all the empathy I once had for him.

"Can we talk?"

"I have nothing to say to you, *brother.*" I stand, my heels clicking on the wooden floor as I try to move past him, but he stops me.

"You can hate me all you want, I'll take it, but *I'm* the one who's burdened with saving the future of our family's name. I'm only doing what I think is necessary," he admits.

"You know…" I clench my jaw, my chest rising and falling faster. "You know *Papà* wouldn't want this."

"Where are Nino and Santi?" I question, noticing their absence as soon as I arrived.

"In the mainland," he answers curtly, sick of me questioning him no doubt. He always hated that I had a mind of my own.

"Why? *Papà* would've wanted—"

"*Papà è morto!*" he yells, clearly frustrated. "He's not here anymore okay, Nera? He's dead and we are *so* close to being forced to make deals *Papà* worked to avoid."

He takes a breath as I swallow the words I want to say.

"Do this…" he takes my hand in his, "*per la famiglia.*"

For the family.

That's the price we pay, unwillingly, when born into families like mine. By chance, you could be born into one with generational wealth, or one that was forced to work under the wing of the wealthy, down to the last drop of sweat. Until one day, you had enough to take your family away from the dangers imposed by the mafia.

"The revelry couldn't come sooner, because once I'm done here, I'm never coming back." Ripping my hand out of his, I storm out of the wing, down the stairs and out into the early morning air. My feet want to carry me to where my father rests, but I don't let them. I can't bear to face the ghost of him, not when I'm doing everything he hoped I wouldn't. Instead, I make my way to the beach. Taking off my shoes, I leave them beside the road, the cool pebbles pressing against my bare feet the closer I get to the shoreline.

The mist floats in the air above the water as I dip my toes in. Closing my eyes, I take a deep breath, the air becoming denser in my lungs, cleaner and *free.* I'm lost in my thoughts and memories of Falcon's Keep until I open my eyes to a silhouette emerging from the depths of the ocean. The powerful figure brings his hands into his hair, wringing out the water, causing it to cascade down his shoulders and chest, covered with dark ink.

The water ripples at his thighs as he approaches me, his gunmetal eyes reflecting the sparkling sea.

"*Buongiorno, Nera.*" His deep voice rumbles as he stands before me, the water gliding down his skin, through every ridge of the muscles on his stomach and down to his dark briefs. I'm not a stranger to the male body, I've been around sports players, but Rafael could not be compared to them. His is rugged, with dark hair sprinkled over his broad chest, down over his abs, leading south to the place I don't doubt is equally as *robust*. A few scars cover his skin, a large one on the left side of his stomach.

I smile, averting my eyes to the faint outline of the moon now slowly disappearing as the sun rises above the horizon. "You're brave to swim at this hour."

The heavy hum of his chuckle vibrates through me, and I lick my lips as my eyes return to his.

"Old habits." His gaze lowers to my lips and down my neck to my chest. I can't decide if he's looking at me like he disapproves of my clothing or if he's thinking something else. "Cold water helps enhance mood and reduces inflammation."

I laugh. "You sound like my father."

"He was a smart man." He gives me a knowing smile, his beautiful, full lips glistening with sea water.

There's a pause as we stand there, the sun's rays beginning to get brighter, and I bring my arms across my chest as the gentle breeze picks up.

"It's nice to see you," I say, looking up at his hard features. "Even though I don't really remember much about you."

"Probably for the best." He drops his gaze, taking a deep breath, and when he looks at me again, my heart races, similar to when you're about to do something you probably shouldn't. An adrenaline rush so intense, it sends a chill up my spine, and I know his stare from earlier wasn't about my clothes.

"You were right, not much has changed."

"Does it ever at Falcon's Keep?" He licks the water off his lips, and it has me wondering if he was always this... *enchanting*.

"I wouldn't know."

"Did you miss *anything* about this place?" he asks, making me think.

Did I?

I rarely ever thought about home when I was in the States, and I don't know if it's because I wanted to escape this place or the ghosts that haunt it.

"Maybe just the cove," I admit, the images of the bioluminescent water by the waterfall filling my vision as I think about the days I spent there before leaving.

"Hm." His jaw tenses as his stare heats my core.

I haven't been this affected by a male's presence since the first day of college. Withering under his focus, I change the subject. "So, what's the theme this time?"

"For the revelry?" he asks as we begin making our way toward the manor. "You know Dante's love for everything dark, dirty, and disturbing."

"Will he be attending?"

"I believe we will have guests from London, so he may be entertaining them all night."

"London?" I question, unsure of who we could possibly know in the UK.

"Distant relatives." He's quick to dismiss my inquiry, so I don't push.

We walk alongside each other up toward the beach, his hand swaying next to mine, so close that if I move my fingers an inch, they'd touch.

"Will Nino and Santi come to the revelry?" I ask, ignoring the other not-so-innocent thoughts.

"Shouldn't you be asking your brother?"

"You know everything he does," I counter, hoping he'll answer, but he doesn't. He keeps walking until we're at the end of the road connecting to the beach.

"Dante's trying." He defends my brother, but I shouldn't be surprised because they are like brothers, more so than Nino or Santi.

"I guess you two are closer than ever now, huh?" I snicker, bending to pick up my shoes and put them on. "He says bark, you say how loud?"

His expression hardens, displeased with my response. "*Stai attento, Nera.* You may be his sister…" He leans in, his lips brushing my ear, the salt on his skin close enough for me to taste. "But you're not mine by blood."

CHAPTER SEVEN
Rafael

Behind the Glass.

As the days pass, the more restless I get. Since I brought Nera home, I've done nothing but watch her walk about the house in her short skirts and with that sour attitude. It's obvious she doesn't want to be here, but it's starting to get under my skin.

This morning was all about planning for my half-siblings to visit, and as much as I want to care, I simply don't. I feel nothing for them. The revenge I seek isn't only because Enzo murdered Asher, no. I have my reasons for wanting to be the one to make him suffer—deep, internalised hatred that never fucking goes away, no matter how much blood I have on my hands.

Enzo took Asher's life in the blink of an eye in front of Nicholas, and I watched as he held his friend, his brother, as he took his last breath. I would have sacrificed myself to kill Enzo a lot earlier if it weren't for my promise to Dante Senior, and I should have. We needed Enzo alive if we wanted to become part of the mainland again, but after what happened in London, there's no forgiveness. The trouble he's now caused extends beyond the borders of Italy and to those who share my blood.

I pick up the lighter, the metal heavy in my hand as I

raise it to the cigarette in my mouth. It's second nature to graze the letter on it with my thumb. The minute the flame is snuffed out, I take a long drag, the toxins crackling through my lungs, a reminder that this body is temporary.

There's a storm passing over the island as I stand under the cover of the greenhouse, staring out into the blackness of the night, the lightning illuminating parts of the forest. It's my favourite place, far enough from the manor and just high enough to see the majority of the island. I come here when I don't have anywhere else left to go and especially when I need to disentangle the never-ending thoughts in my fucking head.

The door to the greenhouse opens and from where I'm standing, I can't see who enters. It's known to Dante and the staff at Falcon's Keep that this has been my place of solitude for some time now, so I know it isn't them. Intrigued, I begin walking over to the entry when her voice takes me by surprise.

"You shouldn't smoke in a greenhouse."

I turn to face her, the grey in her eyes every bit as powerful as the lightning outside.

"You've been back for five minutes and you're already bossing me around, *Principessa*?" I chuckle, purposely taking another drag and tapping the ashes onto the ground.

She purses her lips, irritated. "Don't you have some post you have to *man* or whatever?"

"I'm not a watchdog." I take a step closer to her, blowing the smoke into her face. "Shouldn't you be up in your castle, little girl?"

She scoffs, waving her hand in the air to clear the smoke. "This is *my* home."

"Just yesterday, you were saying how much you didn't

want to be here." Her wet hair sticks to her face, her tank clinging to her body as she stands before me, making my hand twitch with the need to brush away the beads of water clinging to her chest. "Did you finally make up with your brother then?"

Her dark brows come together as she speaks with gritted teeth. "That's none of your business."

"He must have done something truly horrible to cause you to hate him this much." I smile wryly, noticing that I'm getting under her skin when she snatches the cigarette from my mouth. Just when I think she'll put it out, she takes a puff, surprising me. The sight of her with *my* cigarette in her mouth, her wet hair and clothes, elicits impure thoughts. Ones I shouldn't be having for *her*.

"Why do you hate him so much?" I question, wondering if she'll give me anything in return.

She hands back my cigarette and begins to wring out her long hair, the water making a stream down her collarbone, past her breast and into her pyjama shorts. My mind instantly returns to the moment she stepped out on stage in her lingerie, her smooth skin glistening under the lights and the thin strap of string between her cheeks.

Fuck.

"Well, I haven't spoken to him since I left." She sighs, looking out into the night. "Do you ever wonder what it's like not to be tied to family?"

There's a twinge in my chest at her question but I don't show it. Instead, I take another drag, the cigarette finally coming to an end. "Is being tied to family such a bad thing?"

"Some days I wish…" She trails off, returning her eyes to mine. "I guess it doesn't matter."

There's a silence as she leans back onto the stands

before she speaks again. "Why are you in my father's greenhouse?"

I take a step closer to her, invading her space so I can smell the perfume lingering on her damp skin. "You first, *Principessa*."

Her hand comes dangerously close to mine as another bolt of lightning brightens the entire greenhouse, her stare not backing down. "I asked first," she pushes, inching her fingers closer to mine, her eyes dropping to my lips.

She's reckless…like me.

"Because I've spent longer in this greenhouse than you have on this island."

She tries to hide her smile, but I see it, begging to be freed. "You see those dahlias over there?" She nods to the back of the greenhouse. "The very first batch was planted by me and my father."

"So you ran in the rain, with your close-to-nothing outfit, at this time of night for some flowers?" I laugh, but she doesn't.

"Your turn." She stands, peering up at me beneath her damp lashes, her curvaceous body just inches from mine.

I clench my jaw, unwilling to divulge the reason for my being here, but the more she gazes into the depths of my soul, the more I want to give her.

"I come here because it's the only place on this island where you can see Venus."

"It's storming," she counters, making me smile at her wit. "So why are you here *tonight?*"

"*Sei veloce con la bocca.*"

You're quick with your mouth.

I push off the stands and come to full height. "Maybe you'll have a chance to figure it out."

Grabbing the last of my restraint, I head toward the door, leaving her to stew over my words.

I haven't seen my brothers since I left London. I'm unsure what they expect of me and I fucking hope it isn't much because the only thing I will be doing for them is avenging Asher's death.

It's hard not to hold a grudge. Especially when I've lived such a different life to theirs. My fists tighten as I watch them all disembark the ferry, Ezra's dark coat flapping in the sea breeze as a cigarette hangs from Nicholas's mouth.

Expected.

What I don't expect is to see Darcy. The wind weaving through her fiery hair, standing tall next to Nicholas, her husband, and Jackson. The only thing connecting us is a sin committed so long ago by those destined to live a life apart.

"Broody." Nicholas looks around, the darkness of the island swallowing up what light is left by the old wharf.

"Just like you," I sneer.

"Where's Dante?" Ezra asks, his eyes almost morphing with the darkness of the night.

"In the manor, waiting. Follow me."

We begin walking up to the manor, Ezra and Nicholas a few paces ahead as Jackson and Darcy walk beside me.

She slips her arm through mine. "It's good to see you, Raf." She smiles and I must admit, it eases my temper to see her happy with Nicholas.

"Been kicking their asses at rummy?" I ask, reminiscing about our last game.

"Did you teach her how to play?" Jackson questions.

"I wish I could take the credit." I look at her green eyes and smile back. "But it was all her."

We reach the gates of the manor and Nicholas scoffs. "Fuck, Raf, didn't tell us you actually live in a castle."

"You never asked." I punch in the numbers on the security system and the heavy gates creak open. The less they know about me and my past, the better. I don't need their sympathy any more than I need them in my life.

"Like something out of a thriller," Jackson states with no emotion.

"We have rules here at Falcon's Keep." I keep my voice low. "Stay on the manor premises unless you're with either me or Dante."

"Why, got something to hide?" Nicholas smirks and I flex my hand.

"Dante and Raf have respected our wishes when they were in London. We will show them the same courtesy," Ezra says, nodding to my request.

Turning, I open the double doors that lead to the indoor space used for events, but tonight, it has a large table in the middle. Wait staff stand by the walls and Dante sits at the head of the table. Just when I think I'll escape Nera's presence tonight, her heels clack on the wooden flooring behind me. As she walks past, the scent of violet and jasmine is like an assault on the remaining rational thoughts inside my head. I watch as she rounds the table, her tight black dress hugging her hips and ass, the thin, almost invisible line of her G-string resting beneath the fabric, and I wonder what it would feel like to taint her with my stained hands.

I know it's forbidden to lust over someone like her. I know it's unforgivable to even think about her the way I have, and it sure as fuck is a death sentence to act on it.

"Ah, my friends! Thank you for coming." Dante stands, interrupting my thoughts as we all take a seat. Nera and I beside Dante, across from each other, Nicholas beside me, and Darcy beside Nera, with Ezra and Jackson next to Darcy. In the years I searched for my family, the years I spent trying to uncover even the smallest little detail about them, being in the same room with them now makes me feel nothing.

"I assume we're here because there's news on Enzo?" Ezra asks, and I clench my fists beneath the table. His authority stands in London, but not here, and he should be careful with the way he speaks.

Dante notices my reaction briefly before calling one of the waiters over, asking for a round of drinks. "I know your father stepped out of Italy to start something new in London, but mafia ties run deep in our country."

Nicholas leans back in his chair, smiling down at his lap. "Must everyone speak in riddles? Whatever happened to just saying what you fucking want?" He looks up at Dante and my thighs hit the table when I stand abruptly.

"Raf." Dante nods for me to sit and I reluctantly do.

"What my brother is trying to say is that there are families in Italy that have been in the mafia for generations. They have wealth beyond your comprehension, and with their reach and influence, they can be unstoppable if they make a deal with the wrong people." Nera speaks out of turn.

"Thank you, Nera." Dante gives her a warning look.

"So, what the fuck does that have to do with us?" Jackson asks, twiddling a fork in his hand.

"It's not like Enzo could make friends," Nicholas jeers, making my blood boil.

"We cannot go into this guns blazing. We need to be ready for what he might do, or worse, what he might have already done. Surely you understand, given the nine-millimetre scar on your fucking chest." I spit my words, aimed to cut, and Nicholas grits his teeth.

"Just tell us what you know," Ezra interrupts.

"He's been seen with the Lucchese family," Dante reveals and everyone at the table stills in silence, the gravity of the situation finally making sense.

"Lucchese? As in Frances and Tommy Lucchese?" Nera asks.

"Fuck," Nicholas utters, looking at Darcy when the waiters bring out our drinks.

"So what's the plan?" Nera's question is directed at her brother.

"We invite them to the revelry," I answer her.

Laughter erupts at the end of the table. Jackson's fist hits the oak over and over as the rest of us remain silent. "That's the funniest shit I've heard." He stops when no one returns his amusement. "You can't be serious."

He straightens, no mirth left in his expression. "They have the power to wipe us all out. They'd do it for sport!"

"And that's exactly why we need them on our side," Dante says, looking back at me.

CHAPTER EIGHT
Nera

Living with Temptation.

I'm familiar with it. The way things go in our world. The push and pull of power, the thirst for revenge and the constant struggle to find your place in it all. Growing up, *Papà* didn't really involve me, not because I was a girl, no. He loved that I wanted to know things. He fed my curiosity with stories of his past and told me if, one day, this was what I wanted, he would hand it to me instead of Dante.

This dinner is something I didn't think I would experience, sitting at the same table with the Casella brothers, wondering if they'll help us. I knew of them when *Papà* was alive. I just didn't know I'd ever get a chance to meet them. *Papà* always said he was indebted to them and spoke highly of their father, Dominic Casella, whenever they were to come into conversation.

What happened at Falcon's Keep since my father passed away?

What is the secret my brother keeps, even from me, until this day?

"That settles it then." A shiver rolls down my spine as Ezra speaks, a sinister smile spreading across his face. "We give them a party."

"One they'll never forget," Nicholas chimes in as Rafael steals a glance my way.

The entire night has been filled with stolen glances between us, and I've been shifting in my seat any time he catches me. I can't make it too obvious either because Dante is right next to me.

"I'm stuffed." Nicholas stands, and Darcy follows.

"Thank you, again, for being here. Your support of the Della Torre family will not go unnoticed," Dante says, waving to one of the staff. "Julia will show you to your rooms."

"If this revelry lives up to its name, I'll be the first one here next time." Jackson smirks, placing his napkin on the table and leaving the room.

Ezra's silence is deafening as we remain seated, and I nervously run my fingers through my hair.

"Now that the others have left," he picks up a knife, the warm light from the chandeliers shining off the blade, "is there something I should know?"

Dante stops fidgeting with the bulky rings on his fingers, his gaze skimming from Rafael, down to the table, then to Ezra.

"Nera, can you please give us a minute?" he asks, his familiar blue eyes pleading with me not to create a scene. If it were me and Dante, I would do exactly that, but Ezra's presence is enough to scare the most powerful of men. It's not like I won't get my chance to find out. I didn't come back here to follow orders from my brother as he so evidently believes.

I stand and when I make my way out of the room, the doors are shut right behind me, leaving me out in the open space of the foyer. If Dante thinks I'm still a child, he's in for a rude awakening.

Making my way out of the manor, I head toward the greenhouse, the one place I can truly shut out the island.

I'm halfway through the greenery when my heel digs into the soft, muddy sand and I wince in pain as the buckle of my shoe pinches my skin, my ankle twisting before I hit the ground.

Shit.

Taking my shoes off, I rub my ankle, the bruise already forming. When I get back up, I spot a dark figure in the distance and I cling onto my shoes, hanging them off my fingertips as I take a step forward.

"Hello?"

The trees sway with the sea breeze, carrying the salt into the air, and I begin stalking toward the person when they disappear behind a tree. I quicken my pace. No one hides from me at Falcon's Keep. I am the don's daughter and Dante's sister. Surely, they know who I am. "It's Nera," I call out, hoping they will show themselves, but when I look around, I only see the trees, thin grass, sand and mud with the figure nowhere in sight. I swallow at the hollowness of the night and it feels like something is different here. The island isn't what I remember it to be. Somehow, it's darker, quieter, and a lot more eerie than before.

Who was that?

Glancing up the hill, I spot the greenhouse and push through the last part of the forest before finally entering and closing the door behind me. Everything stills, the smell of citrus and earth flooding my senses, bringing a smile to my face at the memories of gardening with my father.

This was my favourite place growing up. *Papà* always used to say the plants can feel what we feel and the way we treat them shows what type of person we are. He always tried to get Dante, Santi, and Nino in here too, but they all had other interests. Santi wanted nothing to do with us all.

He would be happy to escape to the mainland and find some hole to sleep in rather than come back here. Many times, he'd go missing for months, and *Papà* would have to go after him with Dante. Nino was neither here nor there. He'd do the things asked of him by *Papà* even though most of the time, he didn't want to. Like a good soldier.

Dante…well…he was always hard to read. As the eldest brother, I never got a chance to make a connection with him because his interests never aligned with mine due to our age difference.

I brush the leaves of the lemon tree with the pads of my fingers, the moisture still in the air from the heat of the day, when my mind flows back to last night and being crowded by Rafael's strong, hard body. Taking a breath, I close my eyes, remembering the taste of smoke on his breath, the way his dark hair fell over his forehead, and the piercing void behind his eyes. I lick my lips at the thought of his rough hands on my face, gliding down to my neck and chest, and my breath hitches.

He's older.

I shouldn't want to know what his hands would feel like on me.

I shouldn't want it, but the more I stay on this island, the more I want to open myself up to the side of me I try to escape, the part of me I wanted to leave behind when I started college. It was a dream to get a degree and separate myself from my family, but Falcon's Keep calls out to me, it calls me home like a song you've listened to on repeat, a melody so deeply engrained in your soul that it evokes memories of a place you truly belong.

My mind returns to the excitement I felt as he surrounded me, the thrill that buzzed through me when his lips were just inches from mine, and I can't stop my hand from grazing the hem of my dress. As my hand slips into my panties, I open my eyes, staring at the exact spot we were in the night before. Circling my clit slowly, I grip the edge of the stand, the deep timbre of his voice still fresh in my mind from dinner. I imagine what it would be like to have him murmur the dirtiest of words beneath my ear, his breath fanning my neck, as I slip a finger into myself and moan. I pause, suddenly feeling exposed by the entirely see-through glass walls, but a flush of heat coerces me to continue. I push another finger inside myself and prop my leg up onto the crate by the stand, imagining what his fingers would feel like inside me. I know they'd be bigger, thicker, and stronger, and the thought makes me push my fingers further as I grind my clit onto my palm and throw my head back. The strap of my dress falls and the cool night air floats across my chest, my nipples peaking as my breathing begins to get heavier. A thud on the thin glass startles me and I remove my hand to straighten myself up. Searching the outside through the glass, I see nothing but shadows and trees swaying in the wind. It could have been anything, an animal, a branch, but what if it wasn't?

The door to the greenhouse creaks open and to my horror, Rafael walks in.

Did he see me from out there?

Straightening myself, I fidget with a leaf beside me as he walks down the long aisle.

"Better not make this a habit." His nose rings glint in the dim light of the greenhouse and I swallow, nervously trying to come up with something to say.

"My habits are none of your concern." Steeling my fingers beside me, I'm now aware of my wetness still coating them. Hiding them behind me, I hope he doesn't notice the move as he steps closer to me.

"Hmm." He rolls his tongue over his top teeth, his eyes lowering to the material covering my chest. My heart is beating so hard, I'm surprised he doesn't notice the vibrations in the fabric.

"Tell me, how do *you* know about the Lucchese family?" he questions, his eyes now on mine.

I stop for a minute, taking in his spiced cologne, inhaling hints of sandalwood, musk, and jasmine. It makes me want to step in closer and take a deep breath of the pleasant fragrance.

"Frances Lucchese is often compared to legends at our campus back in America," I explain, stealing a glance at the falcon tattoo on his chest, the buttons of his dress shirt now open. "Their family are elitists. I don't know about Tommy, but Frances is dangerous. There was a rumour circulating at our college that he and his men murdered innocent students because they would not commit to their cause."

Something changes behind his eyes, but I can't tell what he is thinking, and when he speaks next, I know I must find out what has happened at Falcon's Keep since I've been away.

"How would you define innocence?" he asks, the question flooring me.

"What?" I laugh nervously, unsure of the direction this conversation is taking.

Heat rushes between my legs as he takes a step closer, his hand delicately exposing the one behind my back and bringing it up to his face.

"Is it purity?" he asks, lifting my hand by my wrist under his nose, and closing his eyes as he takes a deep breath. "Is it a lack of sin?"

The deep steel of his eyes glares into mine, and for a

second, I forget he's my *adoptive brother*. I hold my breath, his full lips just inches from my fingers as my heart beats harder in my chest.

"Sins are like weighted chains," I admit, moving one thigh over another as I desperately try to ignore the throbbing between my legs.

"Would you drown with them, or would you sever the chains binding you to something you might come to regret?" he asks, the desire evident in his tone.

"Would you?" I turn the question on him, knowing exactly what he's asking. I caught him staring at me all night, not a care in the world as to who was watching *him*.

Dangerous.

Risky.

Scandalous.

Slowly, removing my wrist from his hand, I trace the cross necklace hanging from his neck. "Tell me what my brother is hiding," I whisper, slipping my hand beneath his open shirt, the hard muscle mixing with his smooth skin underneath my touch.

In an amused huff, the muscles in his chest tighten as he moves closer, his hand coming up to clasp mine. "Which secret would you like me to start with, *Principessa?*" He lifts his hand to my lips, his thumb brushing them as he stares down at me. "The one you're desperately trying to hide between those pretty, long legs?" My thighs burn as I press them together, wishing for his torment to stop.

Leaning into me, his lips graze my lobe as he whispers, "Were you thinking about me?"

Swallowing, I close my eyes, fighting the urge to pull him closer, to feel his body on mine.

"It's impolite to watch people having an intimate moment to themselves." I fight to regain control through his compulsion, and I think I might make it through without faltering until his fingertips brush the side of my thigh, moving slowly up to the short hem of my dress.

"I can't help myself when you walk around in this… this…piece of clothing that should *not* be called a dress." He lowers his tone, something dark clouding behind his eyes as he levels his gaze with mine. "You shouldn't be wandering out here alone."

His hot breath fans my lips as his palm slowly glides up my thigh, his fingers hooking onto my G-string.

"It's my home." I defend my actions and ignore the pleading between my legs, unsatiated from tonight's earlier actions. I place my hands on his chest and gently step away, refusing to lose myself to basic human pleasures. Not when I need to find out the truth about what happened here. I take a step toward the door of the greenhouse, stopping when he speaks.

"Falcon's Keep isn't what you remember, Nera." Peering over my shoulder, I watch his dimly lit silhouette lean against the stand as he lifts a cigarette to his lips. "The waters are vexed, murky, and will not hesitate to lure you into its depths."

"Consider me warned," I say over my shoulder.

"If the siren's call becomes unbearable, you know where to find me."

CHAPTER NINE
Rafael

FIFTEEN YEARS EARLIER

I know I shouldn't be here. Fuck, anyone could tell you this is probably a fucking suicide mission. Yet, here I am, staring at the blue lights shimmering in the night sky by the Hagia Sophia mosque.

I have *nothing* left.

No home.

No family.

No loyalties.

Some say a man is at his most dangerous when he doesn't have anything left to lose.

I'm not afraid of what comes next because this either propels me forward or kills me. A man on death row has only one way to go and that is up. It's either this or spend the rest of my years begging for food on the streets, taking the scraps of others. I'm sick of living off scraps, sick of pretending like I'm not fucking starving for food, not knowing where my next meal will be coming from.

No one is coming to save you.

The voice inside my head gives me the strength I need, and finally, my feet are moving.

The fleeting thought of moving to Istanbul enters my mind as the beauty of the harbour holds me in its trance.

"How did you find us?"

I stop in my tracks to a man dressed in a fine suit standing before me.

"From a *friend*."

"And what do you want?" he questions, pulling out his phone.

"I want to speak to Erhan."

The man laughs, dismissing my request. "You think Mr Kara meets any old straggler from the streets?"

"I know he came from the streets."

Intrigued by my response, he pauses to take a look at me. "What's your name?"

"Rafael."

"And what do you have to offer, Rafael?" He waits for my answer, and the voice in my head warns me to turn away, a sixth sense cautioning me that something is about to change the course of my life forever.

Good. I hope it fucking does.

"My life."

PRESENT

As the sun breaks the barriers of the horizon, I stare out into the restless sea. Strong, unforgiving, and temperamental today. On most days here, all the dark and sinister things that have taken place over the years loom in the air, and I'm no stranger to it. I've done most of those sinister things, and although I don't regret it, a part of me wonders if this is truly who I am.

Am I meant to be the taker?

Am I meant to exploit the power given to me by Dante Senior for my own sick pleasure?

I curl my toes into the sand, waiting for an answer to the questions in my head that I know won't come.

Not unless I look for the answers myself.

Stepping toward the shoreline, the icy water covers my toes, sending a shiver down my spine as I go deeper, until the water hovers beneath my chest. The sting in my side has me clenching my teeth as the water pierces my skin, into my muscles, and deep within my bones.

One thing I love about this island is that it doesn't matter who you are here. You could be the most hated person in the world and the trees wouldn't care. They wouldn't judge you for what you've done in your past or what you continue to do. On the mainland, however, I am beyond redemption. But I know why Dante wants back in.

I know he wants glory, power, and all the humanly sadistic, self-satisfactory, baseless pleasures a human seeks, and I know I'll help him get it because I owe him.

The revelry is two nights in a year that I can let go and truly release the toxic things I carry, stuffing it all into oblivion until they resurface the morning after. But this year, it'll be different.

Because of her.

Nera Della Torre.

The woman I've become obsessed with. I think about the inexorable pleasure that will come with having my fingers inside her, ruining her. Despite the low temperatures of the water, my cock responds to my thoughts of her last night, in that dress. Fuck, it made me mad with lust to watch her pleasure herself through the glass. All I wanted was to break through it, just to get a small taste of her.

I close my eyes and will myself to focus on what I have planned for today. As my half-brothers, Ezra, Nicholas, and Jackson, are being hosted by Dante, I need to carry on like business as usual.

The work here at Falcon's Keep waits for no one.

Stepping out of the water, I gather my things and head past the road that leads to the manor. Instead of taking the road left, leading to the large gates, I veer right and venture toward the stone path into the forest. It's not that far of a walk, maybe a few minutes to reach the shack by the palm trees. Once inside, I find my working gear and step into the overalls covered with dried blood.

Locking the shack behind me, my feet sink into the muddy sand as I make my way into the forest. There are no signs on Falcon's Keep, partly because we all know it like the palm of our hands, and also because we don't want *guests* loitering on private property. Especially not in the bowels of the island. Walking up the steps, I grab the large padlock on the door of the old concrete structure and dig into my pocket for the keys, unlocking it. The stench of dried blood, rotting skin, and mould waft through the door, and anyone in their right mind would flinch at the smell, but I remain still. Unchanged.

It's become mundane, almost like waking up to freshly ground coffee in the mornings.

I get to work without wasting too much time, gathering up some loose intestines from the floor, and shovelling them into the black buckets I grabbed on my way in. Pieces of skin stick to the concrete floor and I scrape them off with the end of a shovel, the grating sound echoing through the space.

This sort of job was left for the employees of Falcon's

Keep, but ever since we began to run dry, things needed tending to. I don't mind, truly. I kind of feel at home here.

It's dark, damp, and dirty.

I pick up the fresh human liver off the floor with my bare hand and study it. Funny how complex the human body is. If even the smallest part of the entity shuts down, the rest rots along with it. Like humans on the outside, really. The closer you are to the rotten, the more likely you'll turn out the same.

Cleaning up the rest of the mess, I head out the door and lock it back up, carrying the bucket of organs up to the cliff's edge. Normally, I'd say a prayer of some sort, you know, to honour those who are no longer with us, but I'm not feeling very spiritual today. Grunting, I lift the bucket and toss the contents over the edge, now permanently painted red from the years of use.

It takes me some time to make another trip back and forth to empty the second bucket, but once I'm done, I return the overalls to the shack and throw on a white button-up, along with some dark jeans. Lighting up a cigarette, I close the door behind me and head back to the manor. It's no surprise Nicholas is the first to comment on my appearance when I approach the lounge.

"What happened to you?" He laughs. "Looks like you got mugged."

Ignoring him, I nod to Dante, confirming the work for the day is done. Scanning the room, I find Ezra eyeing out a skull figurine from one of Dante's shelves.

"Let me guess…" Holding up the skull, he smiles at Dante. "Female, aged twenty-seven, maybe one hundred and forty or one hundred and forty-five pounds?"

"It's a fucking figurine," Nicholas deadpans and Ezra chuckles. "What's wrong with you?"

"I like guessing games." He steps toward me, crossing his arms, analysing me. "Sweat, probably day-old blood, and…" He pauses, his gaze running down to my bare feet. "Enjoyment?"

"I'm not a sadist," I retort.

"Have you tried it?" A sickening smile spreads across his face and the sheer evil that emanates from him is something I will never get used to.

"The Fortress will be ready in a few days," I say to Dante, ignoring Ezra. "With the extension we've built, we can fit up to two hundred guests."

"Wonderful." Dante toys with the thick rings on his fingers at his desk by the window, his stare fixed on whatever is in front of him.

"Now, even though I could not give a fuck about *your* safety," I look at Nicholas, a permanent fucking smirk on his lips, "make sure Darcy is safe at all times."

Dante stands and walks over to me, placing a hand on my shoulder. "And I want *you* to implore that same fiery protectiveness you have for Darcy over Nera during the revelry."

I stare at him, wondering if he knows about the sinful thoughts that bounce around in my head every time she's near. I nod, aware that whatever happens to her during the revelry won't be by anyone's hands but mine.

The rest of the afternoon goes by quickly, filled with me packing whatever I needed to bring with me to the mainland. Usually, it would be Nino, Santi, and me travelling across Italy to gather the funds for the revelry, but this time, I'm on my own.

And now, it needs to be quick, because I need to get

back to Falcon's Keep to make sure things don't begin to get fucked up with too many cooks in the kitchen. It wouldn't bode well for the others to find out how Dante and I have kept Falcon's Keep afloat all these years, especially not for Nera. But none of that will matter if we can secure some sort of alliance with the Lucchese family.

Shutting the door to my car, I step out onto the front of the ferry boat, watching the waves splash as Giuseppe releases the ropes docking the ferry to the wharf. Pulling out my gun, I check to make sure it's loaded before we head off. Along with collection, sometimes there are those who want to make a name for themselves, to bargain or get their way, one way or another. Can't be seen as weak when you don't have an entourage of men on your side like the Casellas do. The last of our men that helped in London did it out of goodwill to Dante Senior, so I guess he must've done something right in his days as their don.

There's a creak and a clunk that hits the floor of the ferry just as it moves away from the wharf, gathering speed as it heads to the mainland. When I look back, I know I may have gotten more than I bargained for when I see the raven-haired woman before me.

"Going somewhere?" She smiles, straightening her cropped shirt.

Sighing, I run a hand through my hair, wondering what the fuck Dante will say when he finds out.

"Giuseppe!" I call out but he doesn't respond.

"Don't bother, I already bribed him," she shoots back.

"What are you doing, Nera?"

"Following you, of course." Climbing onto the bonnet of my Camaro, she slips a cigarette from the packet she's holding, *my packet,* and places one between her perfect lips.

"I want to see what all the fuss about the mainland is about."

"Just another city riddled with wannabe rich boys, clawing at their fathers' pockets, snorting cocaine, and lost so deep in pussy, they become one." My toes flex, the itch to be near her becoming stronger the longer I stare at her hair whirling in the wind.

She chuckles. "You can't tell me that wasn't you at some stage."

"Interested in my past, *Principessa?*"

"Never." She gives me a sly smile, the twinkle in her eyes giving away every secret she tries to keep from me.

Securing my gun at my back, between my belt and pants, I inch closer to her, leaning on the bonnet of my car. Holding out my hand, I ask for a puff, and instead of placing the cigarette between my fingers, she places it directly between my lips as she leans in closer, her face just inches from mine. The grey in her eyes swirls manically, pulling me in, rendering me powerless.

"But if I was…" she whispers, licking her lips, "would you tell me?"

"What happens if you find things you might not like?"

She pauses, her eyes drifting down toward my lips as I take a drag. "Onions."

"What?" I ask, confused by her response.

She removes the cigarette from my lips, holding it between her delicate fingers.

"We don't acquire a taste for something like onions until our taste buds mature and we take a liking to them." Sliding off the bonnet, she stands beside me, her gaze never leaving mine. "The things I might have considered a sin years ago may not become a good deed today, but I don't think things are black and white anymore. So, no matter what you say, I don't think I could judge it."

She surprises me with her answer. There might just be more to this twenty-three-year-old woman than I originally thought.

"So?" she pushes on, and I smile at her courage.

"Maybe after we've had a few drinks."

"Drinks?" Her white teeth shine in the dim lighting of the late afternoon sun when she smiles. "Are we going to a club?"

"Club?" I scoff. "You're still thinking in black and white."

Her expression changes, wondering where I could possibly be taking her.

"There'll be music. There'll be dancing." Taking the cigarette from her fingers, I place it between my lips and take a drag, blowing the smoke into her face. "But this is an exclusive invitation, so stay close." Leaning in, I take a breath of her perfume. My eyes trace her delicate collarbones, stray droplets of water from the sea clinging to her skin, mocking me. I wish for a moment that it could be my tongue on her skin instead. "And maybe we can explore what it means to dance in the grey *together*."

The Grey.

The minute I entered this place, I knew I was far from home. Not because I felt like I didn't fit in, but because of the sheer luxury. From the glass tables to the glimmering jewels on the ceiling, I just knew whoever owns this place, owns pretty much all of Italy and possibly has a hand in other investments overseas, too.

It *screams* money.

Rafael takes my hand in his as we make our way through the entry, past the bouncers and wait staff, the thin chain on both our wrists shining as the lights flash.

"What is this place?" I ask, looking around. I expected it to be filled with people, clamouring to get to the bar, fighting over who touched who, but there are probably a hundred people here and *all* of them look like they are swimming in money.

"It used to belong to the Albani family, but now, it belongs to the Savelli family."

"That means nothing to me," I admit, wondering why my father didn't teach me more about the history of the royal families of Italy.

"You're about to find out," he says as we head to a grand table, which looks like a crystal sitting at the back of the room. A man probably just older than me comes to greet Rafael.

"Raf, so good to see you again," he says, shaking his hand. "And who's this?" He looks over to me, his too-perfect teeth stealing my attention for a split second.

"N—"

"No one," Rafael interrupts, gripping my hand tighter in warning. "Do you have what I came for?"

The man nods and motions for us to enter a room behind the crystal table. "Right this way."

I look up to see several monitors, showcasing multiple people on the screens.

Real people.

Fucking.

On a screen.

Multiple screens.

"I didn't anticipate the rise in costs this year," the man mentions as his skinny fingers work to punch in a code on the large safe bricked into a wall. The room looks like an office with a desk in the middle, the monitors mounted on the wall behind the desk, and the safe on the left.

"Think of it as *snow* tax."

The safe clicks and I have to physically clench my jaw shut to stop it from falling to the floor.

Hundreds of bars of gold, along with cash, jewels, and a necklace, which looks to be sprinkled with rubies, sit inside.

"Well, you know I love it when it *snows*." He smiles, handing over a duffel bag to Rafael. "Tell Dante, for the extra money he's charging, he better have something spectacular to showcase."

Rafael opens the duffel, and with a quick glance, he nods in approval.

"Why don't you keep it here until you leave tonight?" he suggests, then turns his attention to me. "I'm sure your...*plus one* wants to see what this place is famous for."

I look at Rafael, pleading to let us stay a little longer.

"I expect to find it here in an hour," Rafael stresses and the man nods in agreement.

He still hasn't let go of my hand, the entire time we've been here, and I don't know if it's because he doesn't want me to wander or if it's because he wants me close. A big part of me hopes it's the latter. The moment we leave the office, house music bounces through me as we enter another room, darker and louder than the first. I know the smile on my face is bigger than I've ever let anyone see, and when Rafael looks at me, the corner of his mouth twitches.

"How about we live in that grey area for a little while?" He leans in to speak into my ear and pure excitement courses through me.

"How is dancing in a nightclub living in the grey area?" I ask, moving closer into him, fiddling with the buttons on his shirt, which hangs open.

He gives me a wry smile and spins me around to guide me through the crowd and another door. At first, it looks like a regular corridor, but when he shuts the door behind us, my eyes adjust to the lighting, and my ears slowly return to normal as we leave the reverberations of the bass behind. It's then I realise this isn't a regular club at all. Taking a few steps forward, I glance to my right, through the glass window to find a man and a woman, completely naked, and I swallow my trepidation.

"Are they..."

"Fucking?" he whispers, leaning into my space.

I spot the thin chains on their wrists, like ours, but the

only difference is theirs are gold and ours are silver. The woman's moans filter through the speakers as the man takes her roughly from behind, his thick cock dripping with her arousal.

"This isn't grey at all." I turn to him, his eyes now dark with desire, focused only on one thing.

Me.

"The grey area…" He pauses, the pads of his fingers brushing the skin on my thigh, gradually ascending as he places his other hand on the glass above my head. Leaning into me, he whispers, "…is the one you were thinking about as you had your fingers inside you in the greenhouse back at Falcon's Keep."

Heat rushes to my cheeks and I just know they're red. I knew he saw me, but I hoped he didn't, and I hoped by me not openly speaking about it, he'd just forget.

"You saw."

"The whole thing." He licks his lips, the rings in his nose glinting as he cocks his head to the side. "Tell me what you were thinking."

I want to be brave, to tell him how I imagined his thick fingers thrusting into me as I clawed at his chest, but I wonder what others would think of me wanting—*lusting*—over my adoptive older brother.

"No, no, no." He shakes his head, tilting my face up with his finger beneath my chin. "Don't go…stay here, with me, in the grey."

"You're older than me," I breathe nervously, running my hands up his muscular chest as his body presses against mine.

"By eleven years," he confirms, placing his hand gently around my neck. "Does it not make you want it more?" he whispers, and I lick my lips at the thought of his mouth on mine as his hand moves further down the middle of my chest, his fingers now playing with the neckline of my dress. "Knowing that I can please you in ways men your age could only dream of pleasing a woman?"

I bring my legs closer, but before I can press them together, he pushes his knee between them, the lower part of his thigh pressing against my clit. Clutching his shirt, I take in a sharp breath. "We shouldn't." My voice comes out shaky, but he doesn't seem to care as the back of his fingers graze the top of my breast.

"Why?" he asks, lowering his mouth dangerously close to mine. "Because you don't want to?" His hand drops to my side and slips beneath my dress, roaming up my thigh and grabbing my hip. "Or because it's a sin?"

I'm tongue-tied, trying to control my breaths as his knee presses harder against my pussy, making me desperate to grind my hips on him.

"Because Dante would kill you." It's not a lie, but it's not the real reason. I can't do this with him. I can't succumb to my desires…not here.

"Might be worth it." He smiles as he slowly backs away, removing his knee from between my legs, leaving me wanting more.

More exhilaration.

More pleasure.

More *sin*.

"Wait." I grab his wrist, pulling him back into me, needing to feel like I'm in control, that only I can decide what I do with my life. And right now, I want his lips on mine. Morals and ethics be damned.

His eyes meet mine, surprised by my response as he assesses me.

"I was thinking about what your fingers would feel

like," I whisper. Grabbing his other hand, I place it on my hip, his fingers intuitively curving to grip me. "Inside me." I rise on my toes and press my lips onto his, not waiting a second more for either of us to back out of this.

He gives in, pressing me against the glass, the loud moans of the couple behind it filtering through the speaker. My heart thunders beneath my chest as I wrap my arms around his neck, his tongue parting my lips and sliding into my mouth with need.

Wet, hot, and greedy.

He groans as he lifts me, my legs wrapping around his waist, our breaths mingling in heated whispers as our tongues fight for dominance. I'm afraid if we keep going, I won't be able to stop.

"Raf…"

His mouth moves to my neck, leaving wet kisses as his tongue glides across and up to my ear. "Do you want to find out?"

Oh, god.

He lowers me onto my feet as his hand slips between us, then beneath my dress. I open my mouth to speak, but nothing comes out as he pulls my panties to the side.

"This is your last chance…"

I don't want to back out. I want his fingers inside me. I want to know if it would feel as great as I imagined, and just as I'm about to grab his hand, a door to my left opens and two people walk out with their hair in disarray, holding hands.

"Booth three is free if you want to continue…whatever is going on here." The man smirks and guides the woman out of the hall, completely ruining the moment.

Rafael checks his watch and curses.

"*Merda.*"

Grabbing my hand, he guides me out. "We need to go."

I'm frustrated. I didn't expect anything to happen between us on this trip. I knew better. I know he's my brother's best friend and our adoptive brother. I know nothing can eventuate from this, and yet, I'm being pulled in his direction. I want to know him, I want to find out what he's so desperately hiding beneath that mysterious exterior.

The ferry jostles on the water as we sit in Raf's car and although we're heading back to Falcon's Keep, something inside me sparks with excitement. When we get back, I'm going to do everything in my power to find out what is being hidden on the island.

The entire car ride is silent, neither of us knowing what to say after our heated moment. I watch Raf fiddle with the silver lighter and I wonder what the significance is for him.

"Is that a tic?" I ask playfully, but he doesn't return it.

The metal glimmers in the moonlight as he opens it, flicking it as the flame ignites. "It was your father's."

My brows pull in and I take another look, noticing the letter 'D'. When he looks at me, I can tell it means a lot to him, the way he always keeps it on his person.

"Why would he give it to you and not Dante?"

"I think he felt sorry for me." He chuckles, closing the lid and gripping it tightly until his knuckles blanche.

"But…" I pause, thinking about what to say next when I realise I don't really know anything about his past. "How did you meet my father?"

Smiling, he leans back, the rhythmic swooshing of the waves hitting against the ferry. He undoes the buttons on his shirt slowly and I stare unapologetically. He reveals the scar I saw on the beach that day as he runs his fingers over it.

"When I washed up on the shores of Falcon's Keep with a machete wound and two fucking euros to my name, Dante took me in."

I swallow, reaching out and running my fingers over the thick healed skin. "What happened to you?"

"I got caught up with the wrong people."

"And my father just took you in?" I question, and his jaw tenses.

Obvious discomfort covers his expression as he speaks. "It's not as simple as that."

"What do you mean?"

He shifts in his seat and turns the radio on, rock music now filtering through the speakers. "Like I told you before, things are not what they seem."

"I'm so sick of your riddles." I huff, crossing my arms and glaring out my window. I want answers and I won't stop until I get them. "My father would never take in a stray. He was adamant about keeping the island barricaded from the rest of the mainland. Why would he rescue someone he didn't even know?"

"That's a great question and you're finally thinking in the grey." He's smirking when I look over at him and I'm furious at how my body reacts to his charm.

"I think we've had enough grey tonight," I whisper, swallowing as his gaze runs over my body, making me squeeze my legs together.

"Have you?" His hand climbs up my thigh as he turns his body. "Or do you want to see what it might feel like…"

I release my legs, letting them fall open as he inches up further, teasing me. As much as I would love to wait for him to make the move, to give me everything I imagined when I was touching myself, I don't.

I push his hand away, take my heels off, and lazily remove my underwear, making sure he's watching. Then I climb onto his lap, straddling his thigh between my legs and he smiles.

"Brave." He chuckles, sliding his hands beneath my dress and gripping my hips. "Go on then, *Principessa*, take your pleasure."

Flattening my hands against his hard chest, I study the falcon tattoo. Every inch of him is beautifully tanned, strong, and *dangerous*. A fire ignites within me, the frustration built up to the point where I cannot bear it anymore, and I begin moving my hips over his thigh, rubbing myself slowly over him. He gently moves the material of my dress aside, revealing my bare breast. A moan escapes my parted lips when he takes me into his mouth, my hips beginning to move faster on their own.

"We shouldn't be doing this," I whimper as I grind harder, my arms now slung around his neck, pulling him closer to me.

He says nothing as he continues to lick his way to my other breast, now exposed to the cold, and I tip my head back, rubbing my clit faster over his thigh. His arm wraps around my back and the other remains on my hip, rocking me back and forth as he lifts his gaze to mine.

My breathing becomes ragged as I come closer and closer to my release.

"Do you feel that?" he asks, his hand now snaking into my hair, forcing my forehead to his. "It's the perfect combination of desire and thrill." He takes my lips violently and I whimper, grinding and rubbing, the firmness of his thigh placing the perfect amount of pressure on my clit.

"Rafael," I whisper, breaking our kiss, and he releases me, leaning back.

"Keep going, Nera. I want to watch you come all over my thigh without me touching you, like a needy *troia*."

It shouldn't be this arousing, the degradation of me on top of him, taking my pleasure as he watches me, my wetness probably already soaking through his pants, but I want him to say it again.

I bite my lip, moaning as I pinch my nipples, the intensity of my arousal now running down my spine.

"Mmm..." He undoes his belt, zips down his pants to free his cock and my mouth salivates at the sight of it.

Thick. Hard and long. I groan at the thought of him inside me as he strokes himself.

"*Cavalcami, bellissima troia*," he murmurs, rolling his hips as he watches me work to get to my release, and it's the most thrilling thing I have ever done.

His precum trickles beneath the head of his cock as he fists himself and it makes me want to take him into my mouth just to taste him.

"This..." I breathe, squeezing my eyes shut. "Can't..." I moan, fisting his shirt as I shudder, the thin veil between black and grey now disappearing forever.

When I come down from my high, he has himself tucked back into his pants.

"Can't happen again," I finish and climb back into my seat, the weight of what I just did rushing over me. He ignores me, still smirking in my direction, and when I look over at him, he nods to the wet spot now covering his thigh.

"Are you sure you mean that?"

I swallow, and his hand cuts through the air between us, grabbing my cheeks and forcing my lips to pout. "Lick it off then," he growls, and my eyes go wide. "If you're so ashamed of yourself, lick every last fucking drop of cum you've left from your soaking cunt as you rode my leg like your own personal toy." He releases my cheeks and I blink, my heart thumping beneath my chest at his demand. "Go on, try to erase it." The deep timbre of his voice is like a dare, and everything within me screams to not give in to it, but my body leans forward, betraying me.

Getting on all fours, I bend over him as my tongue darts out, licking my arousal off his pants. The great thing about old cars is the roomy front seat, without the disturbance of the middle console. They knew what they were doing when they made these cars. I continue, closing my eyes, enjoying the taste of myself on my tongue and getting lost in the act when his hand closes around my neck. His steel eyes stare back into mine, mystery, danger, and thrill whirling like a tornado behind them.

"The only thing you'll be able to erase is the purity you cling to, making room for the depravity you crave."

CHAPTER ELEVEN
Rafael

I struggled to close my eyes last night, because every time I did, I imagined her on her knees, licking herself off my pants. She aggravates me more than anything else in this fucked up world. I'm tired of her pretending like she doesn't want the same thing I do. I see her. Every time she lays eyes on me, her chest rises and falls faster, her eyes linger, and she crosses her legs to avoid admitting to herself how much she wants this. I'm going to make her see just how much she wants me, but first I'm going to make her admit it with those pretty pink lips.

The damp air is cool against my skin as I serve the seven-day-old stew onto a wooden board and place it on the floor, edging it underneath the bars with my boot.

"Eat it," I command, and the man grumbles, clinging to the bars in the corner of the room. His clothes have begun to unravel, covered in dirt, a ripped shirt with one sleeve clinging on by a thread or two.

"If you don't eat, you die." I wait, watching him as his soil-covered face meets mine, his eyes pleading with me to let him go.

This is the part I wait for.

For them to lose it completely. To break the thin wall between sanity and insanity from being stuck in a cold, dark place alone. For some, it takes weeks, and for others it takes months, but the requirements differ from person to person. Everyone has their tether to the world, to their sanity, and when you find that golden coin, there's no coming back. I forget most of them, the ones we break, but sometimes, one of them will stick with you for a very long time.

Leaving the cell, I head to the back of the space, through the long dreary corridor of cages, and when I reach the end, the man lunges forward, his head clashing against the thick bars, his guttural growls serving as a warning to not step closer.

"Down," I say sternly and he bares his teeth like a dog, growling as he clings to the bars, his fingernails covered in blood and dirt. Raising my lighter up to his face, his growls grow louder until I light the flame, and his pain-filled screams echo all around me.

What most don't understand about retraining the human mind is that you need to know how to rewire every single neural pathway that has formed over time. In some, these pathways are stronger than others, taking longer to break, and sometimes, it takes less than ten thousand repetitions to turn a human into a wild beast.

What's something that's stood the test of time in both animals and humans?

Fear.

In my experience, there are three types of fear. Instinctual, learned, and phobia. Learned fear is my favourite because after certain experiences, humans are simple creatures, they don't want to experience the same fear, so they do everything in their power to avoid it. Most know about the fight or flight response, but it's not enough to turn someone into a beast. You need to eliminate the fight in them, and the only way to do this is to alienate them, make them suffer until they physically and mentally cannot fight back anymore. And when they're at their end, give them an option to serve you as their master or die.

Some say taking a human life takes some of your humanity away from you, and if you asked me years ago, I would say this would be a lie. Today, I believe it to be the truth and this man before me is evidence.

"Your next meal will be in reach before you know it," I tell him, shutting the lid to the lighter, and he turns slowly to look at me. The best thing about turning someone into a human killing machine is that you don't have to do any of the work because they do it for you. They can understand you even though all they think about is ripping into their next meal.

This one hasn't spoken. Not for months since I burned half the skin off his face, and I prefer it this way. It makes it simpler when they don't question their next assignment. Dante believes we should be keeping them caged up all day and night unless they're on assignment, but even animals need sunlight now and again.

Unlocking the cage door, I slide it open, and the man cowers into a corner as I approach him. Reaching into my pocket, I grab a handful of cut-up raw steak and his attention zeros in on it.

"There's more where that came from, *cane*."

He eases closer to me, picking up the pieces of meat and shoving them into his mouth, the blood trickling down his chin as he chews. Reaching for the metal collar, I clasp it around his neck and attach the chain, coiling it around my hand.

"Let's take a walk."

"I'm not waiting another fucking second." Nicholas pulls his gun out and checks the bullets, flicking the magazine back into place.

"No, we need to wait for the revelry." Dante swivels the largest ring on his finger as he speaks, while Ezra polishes the gold handgun in his lap.

"We cannot count on the Lucchese family to back us in this," Nicholas warns, taking a step forward, clearly frustrated that he's not getting his way.

I know what this revenge means to him. Enzo took his best friend, his brother, and to be fair, I'd want the same.

"If he's been spotted, we should attack and we should do it now!" he demands, the hurt still evident in his voice. Darcy places her hand on his shoulder to calm him and he sighs.

"Dante, what are you waiting for?" Ezra asks, finally looking up from his gun, and Dante stands, turning to look out the window.

I know Dante wants to help the Casellas, but he also has his own family to think about. The decisions he makes now could condemn Falcon's Keep to a dire fate.

"I've sent Santi and Nino to speak with Tommy. I can't risk them, not when we don't know what has happened between Tommy and Enzo."

Nicholas lets out a frustrated grumble and slumps into the seat beside Ezra.

"I promise you'll have your revenge, Nicholas, but I must ensure the safety of my family first."

"Have they accepted the invitation?" I ask Dante, and he turns to look at me, the darkness beneath his eyes more prevalent than before. I know he's burdened with a lot, being the oldest of the family, and I hate to see him like this, but he hasn't spoken to me in a long time. Not like he used to.

"They made it quite clear that they'll be here." His jaw clenches as his eyes clash with mine, a warning flashing across them. "And we will be prepared for their arrival."

NERA

The rock splashes across the water, skipping until it finally sinks into the depths. I spent most of my day with my mother and although she doesn't remember me, I held her hand and told her stories of my time in America. She laughed at some of the things my friends and I had done, like skipping class to hang out with our boyfriends at the time. I enjoyed that it was easy to speak with her without the added pressure of her lecturing me for doing what people my age do.

"Care for some company?" a female voice says from behind me, and when I turn around, Darcy is taking off her boots and socks. I don't know much about her, only what my father had told me about the Brayford family history. All I know is that her family wanted to overthrow the Casellas.

"Sure." I smile when she walks to stand beside me, handing me another rock. "So, how do you know these thugs?"

She laughs at my question, her beautiful wavy hair

blowing in the breeze. "Do you want the long version or the short version?"

"There's a long version?" I take a seat on the sand, motioning for her to do the same. When she's seated, she sighs, fiddling with the rock in her hand.

"Our families knew each other. Mine and Nicholas's. My uncle wanted to overthrow them, and he basically did everything in his power to achieve it. Including stealing their older brother at birth and shipping him off to Italy to use him as a secret weapon when he grew older."

My eyes widen and she looks up at the sea as she continues, "Raf doesn't like to speak of it, but I know it bothers him that his half-brothers got to live a better life than he did."

I glance at the sand beneath my feet in bewilderment. I didn't know this about Raf, and it begins to make sense why my father wanted to take him in.

"You two knew each other back then?" I ask.

"We grew up together, but apart," she answers, confusing me further. "We wrote to each other and became friends. The cross he wears around his neck is the one I gave him when we were little."

There's a pause as I try to make sense of her words before she speaks again.

"I think he's lost," she whispers, looking down at the rock in her hands. "And I don't know how to help him."

I purse my lips, unsure of how to respond.

"I don't know what goes on here, but I can see he's losing himself to it."

She confirms my suspicions about the secret activities on Falcon's Keep, and I'm even more determined to uncover them.

"I haven't been back here in years, and I know

something is different. Ever since stepping foot on the island, I could sense it."

Her eyes meet mine with a warning. "Be careful, Nera. Speaking from my own experience, sometimes it's better to let things be."

She stands, and before I can speak, she's heading back to the manor. I consider heading back too, but I feel a pull from the direction my father lies in rest. I want to visit him, I want to speak to him, to let him know everything I'm feeling, but I can't bring myself to go there because standing inside the place he's buried is admitting that he's gone forever. It means admitting that he's no longer part of the same world I am. Instead, I head to my hideout. The one place I've now learnt is someone else's hideout, too, and I hope to see him there.

Making my way through the trees, the sky begins to darken and I curse myself for not learning from last time.

Shit.

I need to make it to the greenhouse before I'm soaked under the rain. Picking up in a jog, I weave through the forest, glancing up at the soft glow inside the greenhouse getting closer and closer, when I'm stopped in my tracks, my heart thumping loudly beneath my chest. Fear curls its way over my bones, and I force myself to swallow the saliva in my mouth.

I'm frozen as I stare at the man before me, the ripped material barely covering his body, which looks like it's been torn by a bear. Cuts, bruises, and blood cover the majority of his skin. Raising my hands, I take a step back and his top lip twitches.

"M-my name is Nera..." I look around, no one else is in sight. "I'm Dante's sister."

The man doesn't respond, his gaze firmly fixed on me, and I shiver at the craziness in his eyes.

"Who are you?" I ask and he bares his teeth, launching forward into a sprint.

Shit.

Turning on my heels, my muscles fire to run back to the manor. "Help!" The terrified scream rips from my throat, hoping someone will hear me, but being this far from the manor, it dawns on me that I'm most likely alone.

"Dante!" I scream at the top of my lungs, my pleas swallowed up by the thick forest. Glancing back to the man now running on all fours, the horror builds inside me as tears blur my vision, the urgency so powerful it overcomes me.

"Rafael!" My voice tears my lungs apart, my legs desperately working to outrun him.

No one is coming to save me.

Rain begins to fall, wetting the ground and distorting the forest around me, turning it into my very own nightmare. The chill in the air stifles my breath, creating a vice around my throat as the thumps of his footsteps begin to inch closer and closer. My mind reels with thoughts of safety, my only goal right now is to put distance between myself and him. When I glance back at him, he lunges forward, plummeting us both onto the ground.

"Get off me!" I block the snapping of his jaw with my forearm on his neck, his mad eyes darting between mine.

"Down!" The heat of flames lick at my cheek and the man tumbles off me within a second, curling into a ball on the ground, his wailing screams seeping into my chest. When I look up, Raf is standing there with a flamethrower, his face contorted in anger, staring down at the man on the ground.

"Go to the greenhouse." He looks at me with brows knitted together. "Now!" he roars, and I stand shakily, padding around the man now immobilised on the ground, curled up in the foetal position, covering his face with both arms.

I don't know what I expected, but I knew something dark had rooted itself in my home, and now, I'm finally about to get the answers I've been searching for.

Whispers of Desire.

I pace the greenhouse, my stomach in my throat as I think about the man covered in blood, coiled into a foetal position just by Rafael's command, and I'm perplexed.

Who was he and what was he doing at Falcon's Keep?

Staring at the door, I chew on my bottom lip, wiping the sweat off my palms. I consider if I should stay here like he asked, and quickly dismiss the thought. No, why should I stay here and wait for him?

Throwing the door open, I stomp outside and run through the bushes and trees, the mud beneath my shoes squelching and splashing against my ankles. It's beginning to feel like the closer I get to the truth about Falcon's Keep, the blurrier my childhood gets. Was anything my father told me real?

Grumbling, the frustration and anger bubbles up inside me and when I look at the ground, I notice two sets of footprints pressed into the thick mud. I know it's probably dangerous to follow them and I know if Dante found me here, he'd be pissed, but I'm not about to give up on discovering what he's been hiding.

Reaching the old building now covered in moss, I rack

my brain for any memory of this place, only to come up short. Was this always here? The lock on the door is large and chains run through the gate covering the door. There's no way I'll make it in without a key. I pull on the chains, hoping the rust will somehow break them off when Rafael's voice sounds behind me.

"I told you to wait at the greenhouse."

When I turn, he's breathing heavily, his black shirt stuck to his buff chest. Droplets of water fall from his wet beard, and the flamethrower is nowhere to be seen.

Pointing at the building, I step toward him. "Who…the fuck…was that?" I almost yell, the shock evident in my voice.

He plays the silent game, turning to walk away from me without a word, so I grab his arm, forcing him to face me. "Give me an answer!" I demand, the rain now creeping into my eyes from my brows.

I gasp as his hand flies between us, circling my throat. "You don't get to demand *anything* from me, Nera." He walks me to the gate in front of the door and slams me against it. "I wouldn't want to make you regret tainting that effervescent purity of yours," he snarls, turning me around roughly, the bars now pressing against my cheek and chest as he leans into me, his breath inducing a shiver down my spine. "Tell me, did you enjoy the taste of your cum off my pants?"

I want to be disgusted, to turn around and slap him across the face, but I feel the need within me grow the closer his body is to mine. Protected from the rain, thanks to the eaves of the building, he runs the back of his fingers along my cheek, collecting the beads of water from my face as his other hand lifts my short skirt. "Perhaps this time, you'll let *me* taste you."

"If you think this is going to stop me from digging into the things you and Dante are trying to hide…" I trail off as he tears my G-string, the material snapping and landing on the ground.

"Keep threatening me, Nera." He eggs me on, almost like he thrives off it. "Watching you walk around in these short skirts with that fucking attitude makes me want to fuck it right out of you."

My breath hitches when his belt clanks, and as I peer over my shoulder, a thrill ignites within me. His hands grasp his belt tightly as he slides it out of the loops of his pants and holds it out to his side. "You know what I think?" The gates rattle as he thrusts himself against me, the hardness of his cock rubbing against my ass through his pants. "I think you don't know what you want." Whipping me around to face him, his steel eyes accuse me of the truth I've been squashing down, trying to forget. "Falcon's Keep excites you. It calls to you, to the true Nera, who hides behind the *purity* her father once burdened her with."

"You pretend to know what you're saying, but you have no idea who I am." I tip my nose up, glaring, daring him to push me further, and he smiles, his gaze running down my nose to my mouth.

"Oh, but I do…" I grip the bars behind me with both hands, trying to focus on keeping my composure as he weaves his belt through the bars and secures it around my neck. "Because when I look at you, I see a woman calling out for help." Kneeling before me, he gazes up at me, and the sight of him like this has me beaming with power. "I see someone who needs to remember who they are and where they come from."

I bite my bottom lip as his hands ascend my thighs,

lifting my skirt. "You pretend to want something because it's easier for you to focus your energy on that rather than admitting that you'll *never* be that person."

"Fuck you," I spit, angry that he's been able to read me.

"Don't worry, I won't tell," he whispers, his soft breath warm on my skin as he lifts one of my legs over his shoulder. I hesitate briefly, the knowledge that he's my adoptive older brother stopping me from taking his hair in my fist and making him eat his words.

I lick my lips as he teases me, running his mouth over my thigh, to the top of my clit.

"I've wanted to taste you ever since I caught you with your fingers inside yourself." His gun-metal eyes stare up at me and I almost roll my hips, the ache to have his mouth on me growing stronger by the second. Before I can stop myself, my mouth opens.

"What's stopping you?"

The corner of his lip tips up in surprise, his tongue darting out as he keeps his eyes trained on mine. He teases me, the wetness of his tongue just barely touching me as he licks from my wet core to my clit, and I shudder at the instant pleasure that rolls through me.

He groans, sucking my clit into his mouth hard, and I whimper at the sudden lust running through my veins. Closing my eyes, the back of my head hits the gate, and I let a moan escape as he covers me with his mouth, his tongue swirling around my clit. The belt around my neck rubs on my skin, and the sting of his grip on my thigh grows stronger as he devours me. In this moment, I am where I'm meant to be. This is the one and only time this will happen. I will never let him touch me, ever again.

This is it, Nera. If you want your pleasure, now is the time to take it.

For once in my life, I listen to the whispers of desire and run my fingers through his thick hair, and when he grins with my wetness coating his beard, there's a sinking feeling inside my chest. Almost like something within me is telling me this won't be the last time I'll want him between my legs.

"Still want to go back to the States?" He flattens his tongue against my pussy and licks, sucking me into his mouth, and I roll my hips over his face.

"No talking," I murmur as I begin to grind my hips on his tongue, his hand grasping the bars of the gate to steady himself against my motions. The sting from his grip growing stronger on my thigh. The tip of his nose grazes my clit once, and then again. His tongue stills, allowing me to take exactly what I crave from him. I clench my fist tighter in his hair and he growls, grazing my clit with his teeth, making me hiss.

"If you want it, Nera, *take it.*"

Tipping my head back, I go all in, grinding back and forth, moving my hips in a circle, the intensifying electricity beginning in my toes and rolling up my legs. He grips my other thigh, placing it on his shoulder, my weight now pulling me down, the leather around my neck beginning to clamp tighter as the air begins to thin. My lungs scream for air, but the wetness of his tongue overpowers everything else as the euphoria now ascends to my stomach, my vision beginning to dim. With one last roll of my hips, I explode over his mouth, and he drops my leg, my foot connecting to the ground as I stand and gasp for air. Shuddering against the gate, I work to regain my breath.

He plants delicate kisses from my ankle that still rests

on his shoulder, up to my thigh, then stands to full height, releasing my leg. Slowly, he begins to undo the belt, removing it from my neck. The back of his fingers brush the burns the leather left behind on my skin and his eyes grow dark.

"Some things are better left alone." He runs his fingers through my hair, gripping it from the nape of my neck and pulling hard. "But I fear the more I run from them, the more they'll force me to expose their truth."

"And what is the truth?"

"If this continues," he stops, his Adam's apple working as he swallows, "I don't think I could ever walk away from you."

CHAPTER THIRTEEN
Rafael

FOURTEEN YEARS EARLIER

It's already been six months since I washed up on this island, and the more I wanted to head back to the mainland, the quicker I realised I couldn't. I have no allies, no friends, and the one person I have back in Sicily cannot ever be tainted by this world. I would never forgive myself for it. Dante Senior offered me a place to stay, but more than that, he opened up his home to me, fed me, and gave me a bed to sleep on. I had my doubts about him the moment I woke with the blinding pain in my side, reminding me I was alone in this world, but as I got to know him, my thoughts began to change.

"Remember, if you need anything, you call me." Dante tightens his hold on my shoulder and places a gun in my hand. The sun sets beneath the horizon as the steady hum of the ferry's engine drums in the air.

Nodding, I step onto the ferry, the waves crashing against the hull as the horn sounds, pulling me away from the island. I don't know what to expect once I get back to the mainland, but I know it's not going to be in my favour.

I rub my thumb on the handle of the gun and swallow,

my palms now slick with sweat. I barely made it out alive, and if I want to continue to live, I must be smart. The ride to the mainland is only a couple of hours, and I lose myself in my thoughts as the ferry rocks me gently back and forth. When I glance over the rails, I spot the lights of the port in the distance. I don't know what's waiting for me, but I'm ready.

Once we're secured to the port, I stand, working up the courage to face my past.

"Grazie, Giuseppe."

The darkness of the port at this time of day reminds me of the last time I was here, and I do my best to push it from my mind as I make my way back to the shop. It's not far from here, and it's one of the reasons I didn't mind not having much, because as a boy, I got to sit by the port, watching the sailors and the sea.

As I step into the street, my blood runs cold at the sight before me. The place I was raised is now burnt to the ground. The only pieces left behind are ashes in the wind or stuck between the crevices of the earth.

Figlio di puttana!

My muscles fire as I step through the half wall, now barely standing. "Demetrio!" My voice strains as I yell, bile rising up my throat when there's no answer.

He has to be here…

"Demetrio!" I try again, taking the rickety stairs two at a time.

"Please be here," I whisper as a silent plea, more to myself, as I scan the place I once called home. I burst through the bedroom door and cover my mouth with the crook of my arm.

No.

The one person I trusted most is on his bed, clutching

something to his chest. The only thing left of him now is bones and teeth. Tears fight their way through, and one breaks, making its way down my cheek at the sight of his body. Taking a step forward, I pry the knife from his hands and walk out, coughing as my knees hit the floor of the kitchen.

I'm so sorry.

So fucking sorry.

I never meant for any of this to happen.

My shoulders slump, the tears flowing freely now as I come to terms with the fact that I must live without him. The person who raised me, cared for me when I was sick, with the little that he had. It's only when my vision clears that I notice what's surrounding me, and red-hot rage fires within as I step to my feet and slam my fist through the glass cabinet.

Hundreds of Enzo's calling cards are scattered throughout the space.

A warning.

Fuck him.

He's about to find out what blood tastes like and I'm going to drown him in it.

CHAPTER FOURTEEN
Rafael

PRESENT

She's been incessant about finding out the location of the cells we use to house the broken ones, and no matter how much I ignore her, she won't stop. I practically wrapped my belt around her eyes and threw her over my shoulder after I finished my meal so she didn't know how to get to the cells, and now I wish I just let her fucking see.

"Nera's going to find out," I say to Dante, who is sitting behind his desk.

His eyes shoot up, a fear I haven't seen in them before. "How do you know?"

"One of them got loose," I admit.

His fists thud onto the desk. "Fuck, I thought you said you had them under control, Raf. What the fuck are they doing out of their cells!?"

"It won't happen again."

"*Merda!*" He stands, swiping the contents of his table to the floor in a rage, and I grit my teeth at the outpour of anger.

"What's gotten into you, huh?" I walk over to him as

he leans on his desk with his hands, his head between his shoulders, looking down at the floor.

Standing, he wipes his face. "Nothing."

"*Stronzate.*" I cross my arms, waiting for an answer. "We've known each other this long and you're going to hide shit from me now?" The anger continues to bubble inside me, frustrated that he won't share whatever the fuck he's hiding. "Why won't you just tell me?"

"Because! It's not your fucking burden." He glares at me, and my nails dig into my skin as I fist my hands. I've never said a damn word about how I've been feeling the last few months—fuck, the last few years—and now he wants to talk about me carrying burdens? I've lived for this family, and I've said I'd die for this family. I breathed their blood like it was my own because I wanted to feel like I was a part of something. I wanted to desperately belong somewhere, and no matter what I did or how hard I worked, I always felt inadequate.

"Burden!? All I've ever fucking felt was like a burden to your family." I don't mean to say it, but I do.

"What?" Shock evident on his face, he takes a step forward to me. "Dante thought of you as his son…How can you think that?"

I scoff. "You wouldn't understand even if I tried to explain it. We lived different lives. Mine was a lot lonelier than yours."

"I called you my brother."

"And I called you mine, but that doesn't make us blood relatives. You don't get to choose your family."

There's a rap on the door and Nera walks in, glancing back and forth between us, no doubt sensing the tension in the air.

"And that's my cue." Before he can say anything else, I

take my leave. I'd much rather be amongst the ones he calls animals than be in the same room with him right now.

Muttering under my breath, I pass Ezra on the phone outside near the fountain and I ignore his nod of recognition as I make my way up the path, past the shack and into the forest. Everything within me tells me to go into the cells and shoot every single one of those broken souls, but I know if I do that, I'd be sentencing myself and the entire Della Torre line to death. I think about heading to the greenhouse, and I don't know why my feet don't immediately take me there. Instead, I open the wooden doors to the church and step inside, cleaning the sand and mud off my boots on the mat before I walk down the aisle.

Why the fuck are you even here?

The voice sounds in my head again and I gaze up at the statue of Jesus.

Do you even believe in God anymore?

I did once. A long time ago, when Demetrio would teach me about the religion. I was fascinated by the stories he'd tell about Jesus and Moses. I almost smile at the memory of the first time he told me the story of how Moses parted the sea until I remember everything *I* had done.

God will forgive, son.

Dante's voice echoes through my mind as I grasp the cross pendant and press it to my lips. I say a prayer, in the only way I know how when the doors to the church creak open. I don't turn to check who it is because I already know.

"Come to repent for yesterday's sins?" I tease as her soft footsteps become closer.

When she stands beside me, she doesn't look at me. "Is that what you're doing?"

A smile sneaks its way onto my lips at the one thing that fascinates me most about her. The way she isn't afraid of the grey. Not even a tiny bit.

"What was that back at the manor?" She turns to me, and I grind my teeth at the reminder that Dante will no longer share his plans with me.

"Just a small disagreement." I shrug, pulling out a cigarette and placing it between my lips. "Nothing of your concern."

"Hmm." She steps closer into me as I light the cigarette. "You think I'm *concerned* about you?"

"No. I think you came here with a purpose." I take a drag and hold the cigarette to my side, leaning forward to drop my nose to hers. "I think you finally see how much you want me, too."

She smiles, her eyes dropping to my nose, and the sight of her biting her lip makes my cock so fucking hard that I groan. Placing my forehead onto hers, I close my eyes to inhale her perfume. "Don't do that," I whisper.

"Do what?" she speaks softly, grabbing the collar of my shirt and pressing herself against me, my cock practically tenting at her touch.

"Don't bite your lip at the thought of me fucking you."

She giggles, turning to press her ass against me, and takes the cigarette from my fingers to take a drag for herself. "It's fun to tease you."

"Is that so?" Flicking the cigarette from her hand, I put it out with my boot and snake my fingers around her neck, holding her to my front. "Will it be *fun* if I took away the air you breathe as I fuck you inside your house of God?"

She grinds her hips over me, and I growl at her dare.

As I walk us over to the statue of Jesus, footsteps sound just outside the door. Covering her mouth with one hand, I shield us behind it, pressing her front to the stone with my body. The heavy door thuds closed as boots thump on the floor of the church. There's a moment of silence and then he speaks.

"Forgive me, Father," Dante says as he begins his prayer, unaware that he isn't alone.

Nera moves her hips, and my cock begins to dig into her. It hardens beneath my pants, making me want to take it out and stick it deep inside her to teach her a lesson.

Lifting her skirt, I caress my way over her hip to her pussy, my hand still covering her mouth.

Let's see how you like to be teased.

I begin to rub my hand over her pussy, slowly over her underwear, and she tips her head back. I thoroughly enjoy watching her give in to me. She can't make a sound, and judging by the dampness of the material between her legs, it's turning her on even more. She rocks her hips, getting greedier the more I refrain from giving her what she wants. Grazing past the top of her pussy, I slide my hand beneath her panties and tug, the material tightening as it pulls against her clit.

I press my lips beneath her ear. "Don't make a sound, or I stop," I whisper, and she nods, silently begging me for more.

I tug a little harder and she bucks, grinding herself to the friction, and I smile at what she's becoming. A needy little whore, desperate to be fucked. Dante remains quiet and I can only assume he's finishing the prayer in silence as I slip my fingers into her panties to rub his sister's clit.

Not many people can say their first time was memorable, but I'm going to make sure as fuck ours is. Her heat swallows two of my fingers as I push inside her, and she lets out a muffled moan. My hand tightens around her mouth, warning her to stay quiet, and she presses her eyes shut as I push deeper, her body squirming against mine.

The problem with sinning is once you start, it's hard to stop. It's like doing the same thing over and over without losing the endless craving. The more you do it, the more you *want* to do it, and it's no different to touching her, feeling her body against mine, or just looking at her.

She presses her hips forward, with my fingers knuckle deep inside her. Curling them, I massage the delicate spot inside her and she opens her mouth, biting down on my hand, making my dick jerk. Retrieving my fingers from inside her pussy, I slowly unzip my pants and pull her panties down her legs until they're a mess on the floor.

It makes me ravenous when she lifts her leg to prop it up onto the statue, inviting me in. Pulling out my cock, it throbs with the need to be buried inside her warmth. I stroke it, wiping her arousal over my crown before easing the tip in. I squeeze my eyes shut at her tightness, and the sting on my hand returns as she sinks her teeth into me. I know she wants to let it out, to scream or to moan in pleasure as I sink deeper into her. Prying my hand out of her mouth to grip the base of her hair, I hear footsteps recede from inside the church. When the doors shut, she lets out a breath.

"What's stopping you, huh?" she says breathlessly, spurring me on further, daring me to take full control. "Fuck me like you actually mean it."

A deep rumble forms in my chest, and I yank her hair harder, craning her neck. "I was giving you the grace I thought you wanted, *Principessa*. Slow, like the life you pretend to crave." I ram into her, and she gasps, gripping onto the statue. "But if you want to be fucked like a desperate little slut," I pull back and slam into her again, "I'll have you shuddering on my cock until you can't breathe."

She chuckles, looking back at me through her lashes. "Promises, promises." She grins and I'm lost in her eyes, ready to tell her to just have her way with me and leave because if she doesn't, I don't know if I'll *ever* give her the chance again.

The Sin.

My nipples harden as his grip grows stronger on my hip, my body jolting forward as he thrusts into me harder. The dirty sin we're committing inside Dante's most sacred place has me both on edge and excited.

"Or perhaps you prefer it that way?" He curls his hand around my neck, bringing his other hand over my nose and mouth. "How far are you willing to go, Nera?"

I know he's not asking about this moment right now because the tone in his voice hints at something else, something we both know will never be possible.

I push my hips out, meeting his thrusts as he pinches my nose and covers my mouth, the air in my lungs beginning to beg for release. It's not something I ever imagined I would enjoy, but the assurance and care I feel around Rafael makes me feel free enough to try anything he wants.

My pulse thrums in my throat, and my vision begins to dim, the pressure building inside me as he continues to pound into me.

"Yes, Nera, you see…" he buries himself to the hilt,

"without air, your feelings for me float to the surface. You lust for a life that defies everything you've ever been taught. Without air, you'd still find yourself searching for me, like a sailor in the throes of a storm, yearning for the safety of the shore, begging for the waves to carry you back to me."

My pussy clenches over him again as he drives in and out of me. Every part of me buzzes with pleasure. He moans below my ear, deep like the ocean, carrying me into a trance I never want to break free from.

Suddenly, my lungs are heaving for air, the feeling of emptiness rushing over me as he pulls out. Turning me around, he holds me to the statue by my neck. I don't know what's gotten into me, but watching him place two fingers into his mouth to prime them makes my pussy pulse.

"Spread your legs wider."

I listen to his command, doing exactly as he asks, and he slips his fingers inside me. "Good girl. Now let's see if you're all bark and no bite."

I smile even as his hand tightens around my neck, my fingers gripping the edge of the statue. Everything inside me screams with the need to come as he fucks me with his fingers, immobilising me with one hand. I should be ashamed of how much it's turning me on, the way I'm rocking my hips into his hand and meeting his thrusts.

"Don't you dare come," he warns. "I'm not finished yet."

I want to protest, and my body begs to let go. My eyes slowly roll back into my head when he removes his fingers, making me cry out. The desperation in my tone shocks me.

"The next time you think you can strut around and tease me without any repercussions, I want you to remember this moment."

I smirk and his lip curls into a snarl.

"Oh, you *don't* want to take this seriously?" He pries my mouth open, shoving his fingers down my throat, and I gag at the intrusion. He removes his hand, and I suck in the air, flinching slightly when his hand taps my cheek, my saliva mixed with my arousal dripping down my chin.

Rising on my toes, his fingers find my core and as he penetrates me, I focus on his ferocious eyes. "Let me come." I grind my hips again and he smiles.

"A *principessa* should not forget her manners," he rumbles.

"Please," I beg, now desperate for release. "Can I *please* come?"

"That's more like it," he drawls. "Go ahead, come all over my fingers inside your house of God."

The dirty words stir something deep inside me as I close my eyes, my body trembling with pleasure coursing through my spine. Before I can come down from my high, he's inside me, burying himself deeper and deeper as he covers my mouth and nose.

"Seems like you enjoyed that last one." His gunmetal eyes burn into mine. My body hasn't had a chance to return to its base levels yet, my heart rate still soaring as another wave of pleasure builds from within. A sharpness grazes the side of my neck, and a stinging pain zings my body back to life.

Did he just bite me?

"You drive me insane, you know that?" he whispers with quiet anguish in his voice. "So fucking insane that I don't know who I fucking am anymore. You make me want to do things…*sinful*…things…"

Pausing mid-sentence, he whirls me around. Forcing

me down, he bends me over until my shoulder rests on the statue as he fucks me. I'm too breathless to say anything. I feel his cock harden inside me, his groans echoing through the church as he tightens his hold on my hair at the base of my neck.

"Fuck," he roars softly, his cock jerking inside me as he grunts through his release, filling me with his cum.

As I stand, the remnants of him ooze out of me, running down my leg. Fixing my skirt, I reach for my panties and clean my thighs with them as he shoves himself back into his pants.

What we just did is *unforgivable*.

No one would ever understand it, and as that thought dawns on me, so does another.

I want to know more about him.

I want to see him reveal himself to me in a way he hasn't to anyone else before.

I want to unravel him until he's bare before me.

Stepping closer into him, I rise on my toes and press my lips to his cheek as I stuff my panties into his pocket. "A keepsake," I utter as his steel eyes smile down at me.

"Are you going to give me your panties every time we fuck?" He chuckles and I run my tongue over my bottom lip.

"Only if you fuck me exactly like that." Turning on my heels, I stroll down the aisle of the church and out the door, pleased I finally got what I wanted.

Falcon's Keep used to be a place of solitude for me. A home where I could be myself, unafraid of what my brothers would think of me. Or what my parents would say. Now, it doesn't matter what anyone else thinks, because all that plays in my head, like a movie, is the thought that if Dante found out about what we just did, he'd murder Rafael right in front of me.

"*Sapevi che ho partorito in un giorno come questo?*" my mother says, absently staring out her window, and I give her a sad smile. She hasn't been off this island in years, probably since I was born, and it makes me grieve the life she's lost.

"I know, *Mamma*, it was the day I was born." I smile up at her in her chair from my kneeling position, rubbing lotion on her hands. She doesn't respond, her eyes losing any emotion once there as she blinks at the window.

Santi used to say it was my fault that she's like this and any time he wanted to hurt me, that's the insult he'd use.

Mamma lost her mind because you never listened!

His voice is still a permanent echo in my head.

It's true, though. I didn't listen. But it wasn't because I was defiant, it was because I was curious. I wanted to know everything and some things a child shouldn't know. My father knew I'd never stop asking questions, that's why he'd answer them in his own way, feeding my curiosity but also satiating it in another. He knew what to say to me, how to get me to agree with him when enough was enough.

I sigh and stand, the heaviness of my father's death still weighing on me like the Titanic. I should go see him, to tell him exactly what's on my mind.

Footsteps sound from the empty hall outside my mother's room and the door opens as Dante walks in, closing it behind him.

"Knew I'd find you here." He shoves his hands in his pockets, to stop from fidgeting, no doubt. "I heard about the incident in the forest." He looks around the room, clearly unsure of how to approach this with me, but I stare directly at him.

"Oh, about how some crazy person tried to eat me?" I say incredulously, stepping towards him, his eyes now on me. "Are you going to explain to me what's going on here?"

"I don't think you're ready to hear it," he admits, pulling out his phone, the buzzing of the vibrations filling the quiet room. Ignoring it, he shoves it back into his pocket.

"Why did you really bring me back, Dante?" I ask, curious as to what he's planning for me.

"The whole family needs to be at this revelry," is all he gives me, his face more stoic than before.

"You couldn't postpone it? For another three months?" I huff, crossing my arms. "*Three. Months.*"

He shakes his head and looks at the floor, the frustration now creeping in.

"I could have graduated," I whisper, stealing a glance at my mother, still dazed in her chair.

Dante pinches the bridge of his nose. "You think a degree would do anything to keep this life from catching up to you?" he questions, and I open my mouth to speak but he continues before I can get a word in. "You think you can forget everything he ever taught you about the families? About money, drugs, or inheritance?" He steps forward, his voice beginning to harden. "You think it's as easy as getting a degree and fucking off to the next continent, to what? Be with some fucker who has a condo and a trust fund?" I close my mouth, the vein in his forehead now popping as he raises his voice with irritation. "Do you honest to god think that a piece of fucking paper will sever all your fucking ties to this world, Nera!?"

I remain silent, waiting for him to finish, hoping he reveals whatever he's been hiding.

"I'm sick and tired of you pretending you don't belong here." He grips my forearm, and I wince. "Take a look around, Nera, you were born here, raised here, with your brothers who would do *anything* to keep you by our side. You are the heiress to Falcon's Keep."

I furrow my brows and yank my arm free from his hold, my eyes stinging with unshed tears at the truth he's just shown me. I've spent my whole life studying, wanting to become something better than my family, but the truth is, the Della Torre name will follow me everywhere I go.

"The revelry is tomorrow, and I expect you to be there. You will meet with Frances and Tommy." He demands, rather than asks for my presence and I fight a snarl as I push past him into the hallway. My boots thump on the wooden floorboards, creaking as I make it down the stairs.

I spot Rafael in the foyer and look away, heading straight for the front doors as he catches me by my upper arm, spinning me around.

"What happened?" he questions, looking me over. If one more person grabs me today, I swear I'll chop off their fucking arm. Pushing him with all my might, he steps back to gain his footing, his gaze moving to the top of the stairs, mine following his to see Dante.

"Ask *him*." Without another word, I push past the doors and out onto the road, making my way through the tall black gates. I'm in no mood to speak to anyone right now, so I avoid the greenhouse because I know he'll look for me there. Instead, I run through the forest, in the opposite direction of the manor. I can barely make out the path I made for myself when I was a child. It's faint, but it's still there, the weeds and shrubs now growing over it. Reaching the end, I stare up at the wall of rocks and begin climbing, one by one, and as I get closer to the top, the rush of water grows louder, the rhythmic roars like gentle thunder. Stepping over the edge, I stand and take it all in, watching the water hit the surface of the pool, splashing and breaking apart. The gentle, melodic sounds of the waterfall calm my mind as I remove my boots and socks, then my clothes, keeping my bra and panties on. I wriggle closer to the water, my toes submerged in the warm pool. During the day, as the sun is out, the body of water heats up and, on afternoons like this, it becomes the perfect time to swim. Stepping deeper into the water, I kneel and push off, dunking my head in, holding my breath as I close my eyes and focus on the muted sounds. The soft, continuous rush of water above me, along with the faint echo of my heartbeat create a peace of its own.

Breaking the surface, I swim over to the edge and pull myself up.

This revelry will come at a cost, and with the way Dante has been acting lately, I don't know whether I should take the next ferry back to the mainland and run, or if I should stay and figure out what he's been hiding.

I owe it to my mother to stay, to fight and take her with me, but I'm afraid of what I might find.

A branch rustles from below, the sun now setting as the chill in the air returns, and I peer over the edge to see where the sound came from. There he stands, as if he's put a tracker in me, finding me no matter where I am on this island. Rolling my eyes, I return to my seated position and wait for him to climb up. He huffs as soon as he takes a seat beside me.

"You didn't exactly cover your tracks well."

"Thought you'd look for me in the greenhouse, so I

came here." I wring out the water in my hair and stare at the pool, the ripples continuing to create mosaic-like patterns.

There's a pause before he speaks again.

"A long time ago, I thought everything of your family," he confesses, catching me off guard. I purse my lips, unsure of how to respond, so I let him continue.

"They saved my life, Nera."

I look up and meet his gaze, seeing vulnerability in place of the usual hardness.

He casts his eyes to the water. "That night was one of the worst ones I've lived. When I came here and met Dante, I knew my life would never be the same again. He made me feel like I was part of something bigger… something *better*."

Sighing, he lifts his shirt, revealing the scar protruding from his skin, breaking the perfect strokes of his dark tattoos.

"I thought I was cast aside by my own blood, so I sought to make a name for myself and take everything I could from the most powerful people around me. It started with stealing their money, but it wasn't enough. Bit by bit, I longed for more. I wanted them to know who I was, to have a reputation so fucking dark that they heard about me from the other side of the sea and regretted ever casting me aside."

I can empathise with him, with everything he's saying. I reach out, holding my hand out to him, and he takes it.

"But the one action that landed me here was enough to change me forever. Because of this, I lost someone very close to me…someone I called a father, and eventually, that hole in my heart was filled with Dante's grace and hospitality."

I close my eyes and take a deep breath, understanding everything he's telling me. "Why are you still here?" I say softly. "After all this time, why haven't you gone back?"

He opens his mouth to speak, then it suddenly dawns on me. "Do you…" I pause when his eyes meet mine. "Do you feel like you owe him something?"

"But I do."

"You don't." I shift my weight to my knees and face him. "My father wouldn't have done this if he wasn't a good man."

He laughs at my words and shakes his head. "We are not good men, *Principessa*."

"I'll believe it when I see it."

He nods, his eyes moving south to my stomach, the crease in his brows forming as he spots my scar. He looks back at me with the question in his eyes. Pointing to the large scar that runs from below my ribs to my hip, he opens his mouth to speak, but I answer the question before he can ask it.

"They had to remove my kidney," I explain, taking my hand from his, the vulnerability now switching sides. "I had a tumour when I was eleven and it was big enough to have the entire thing removed." I swallow, nervous that this is the first time he's seen me without my clothing.

"Such a soldier, even at the age of eleven." He smirks and I push him playfully.

"It was a hard time, but I was lucky it was localised, so all they had to do was remove the kidney."

He stands and begins to remove his clothes as I stare, in awe of his beautiful physique. When I get to my feet, I admire the numerous cuts and marks on his body as the sun completely disappears, the bioluminescent water coming to life in the darkness.

"Up for a swim?"

"With you?" I shrug. "Only if you go commando."

He doesn't break eye contact as he removes his briefs, his cock hardening right before me.

"Get into the water, before I throw you in myself."

CHAPTER SIXTEEN
Rafael

Scars of Ghosts.
Deathbeds – Bring Me The Horizon

My stomach jitters at the sight of her entering the water. All I want to do is take her against the hard rock, make her feel the need I have for her and how much that need grows every single second she's by my side.

"Are you nervous about tomorrow?" she asks, her nerves clearly readable through her question.

"The only thing I'm nervous about is you," I admit, showing a side of me I have never shown to anyone before.

"I make you nervous?" She giggles, softly grazing the water with her fingertips. "Why?"

"Because when you start asking questions, all I want to do is give you the answers. But I know once I do, you'll run." I step closer to her, the water now up to my waist.

She wraps her arms around my neck, circling her legs around me as I carry us further into the water, like I'm carrying her deeper into the island.

"I promise I won't." She licks her lips, eagerly waiting for me to divulge more information, and I laugh.

"If I'm going to ask you to promise anything, it's not that you won't run…"

She looks at me expectantly but instead of continuing, I take her lips with mine, my hard cock brushing her pussy as she kisses me back.

Breaking the kiss, she stares into my dark soul, the only light being the reflection of her.

"Promise me you won't think differently of me." I lower my forehead to hers and close my eyes, my traitorous heart now wild at the thought of her hating me.

"I promise," she whispers back, taking me into a passionate kiss.

I believe her like I believe in the salt in the air and the sun in the sky. I need her to know I can't be without her anymore. I knew it was over for me the instant I had her. I knew then that I couldn't be with anyone else.

But now that I've had her, I can't bear to disappoint her.

Will she be disappointed in me when she uncovers the truth?

Panic rises within me anytime I think about her discovering what this place is used for. When she knows the deals we've made, she won't want to stay. She'll tear my fucking heart out and take it with her, leaving me to bleed out on the floor.

Wouldn't be the first time I bled out here.

As I gently place her back on a large rock beside the rush of water, she slips her panties off and they float atop the water. My fingertips caress the beads of water on her chest, her breasts rising and falling beneath my hand.

"You're starting to consume me, *Principessa*," I breathe as I hover over her, tugging her bra straps off her shoulders until her breasts are bare before me. "Every fucking touch," I whisper, lowering my mouth onto her wet skin, gathering the fresh water with my tongue. "Every breath…" Grazing her collarbone with my teeth, I fight the urge to sink them into her skin again. "I thought I had already lost myself to this island a long time ago, but the thing that terrifies me the most is how alive you make me feel."

She raises her chin, her eyes begging me to take her hard against this rock, and my mind wanders to what she would look like on her knees.

"You dig into places I don't even recognise."

Grabbing my hand, she guides it to her mouth, her plump lips closing over my fingers as she sucks. Lowering herself into the water, she frees my hand and takes my cock, wrapping her fingers around it. My balls twitch, sending another shot of blood to my crown, the feeling almost painful as I stand there before her, fully erect.

"I think it's your turn to beg *me.*"

I huff a laugh, her hands coming around to grasp my hips as she stares up at me, her stunning features accentuated by the moonlight. "I'm not playing that game."

She yelps when I grip her hair at the top of her head. "Open."

Her knowing smile tells me I'm no longer the one in charge, but I'm okay with that because I'm done pretending this is a game. There are no more rules and certainly no winners. Just us, tangled in something neither of us can walk away from.

Her tongue is like a version of heaven I imagine exists, spreading warmth from the base of my spine up to my neck. She creates a suction in her mouth, her cheeks hollowing out as she swirls her tongue around the crown of my cock. My thighs tense at the intense pleasure, drawing out a guttural growl from deep within my chest.

There's that smile again, hiding on the corner of her mouth.

As I thrust myself deeper, she tries not to gag, holding back her own body's impulses as she opens up her throat.

"That's it, *Principessa*, invite me in until you can't fucking breathe."

I fuck her throat, shoving myself further with each drive of my hips. "It seems you believe you're the one in control." I pinch her nose and she closes her eyes as my cock fills up her throat. Pausing, I enjoy the warmth and wetness as her hands begin to push me away.

"Uh-uh." Clutching the back of her neck with one hand, I pull her to me, her mouth and throat swallowing my entire cock as my balls rest on her chin.

Tearing myself out, she heaves for air, but the only air she should be breathing is the one I allow her to.

"M—" Before she can speak, I push back into her mouth, silencing her.

"You don't get to speak, *Principessa*, not until you suck every drop of my cum with that beautiful mouth and swallow."

She moans around me, the vibrations making me grit my teeth at the sudden shock of desire. My crown rubs ever so wonderfully in the back of her throat as her choking is muffled by the loud rush of the waterfall stream.

The intensity builds, wrapping itself around me, and I groan as she works to get me off.

"Why don't we raise the stakes?"

There's a hint of fear in her eyes as I lower myself into the water and hold her under, taking my pleasure. The water sloshes around me as I pump into her throat, bubbles from the air left in her lungs rising to the surface.

"*Fuck*," I groan, holding myself deep inside her throat.

My cock twitches, the release pulling me into its hypnotic tide when she swallows around me.

I release her and pull her head out of the water as she splutters and coughs. When her beautiful, thunderous gaze is on mine, I see the pure enjoyment she gained from this and I curse to myself.

I am royally *fucked*.

The addiction that's growing within me starts and ends with her, and addictions like this are risky because there's almost no clean break.

This obsession will destroy us both.

FIFTEEN YEARS EARLIER

The only reason I'm alive today is because I refuse to fucking die. Maybe in ten years' time, I will curse myself for coming here, or maybe, it'll be the best decision I ever made. Either way, there's no turning back now. I thought I wasn't afraid of anything or anyone, that was until today.

Erhan Kara. Seeing him sitting there in his dark leather chair, at his black desk, makes me rethink this whole stupid plan. He motions for me to sit and I do. The chairs are comfortable, a lot more than the plastic ones back at the service centre I call home.

"What are you doing here, kid?" he asks, taking a breath of his cigar, his blue eyes brighter than the blue lights that shine across the bridge on the mosque. It was like a knee-jerk reaction, ending up here on the roof of a building in Turkiye. I knew if I wanted to show the

Casellas just how much they'd regret casting me aside, I needed to do it with something extreme.

"I need your help."

He huffs a laugh and sets his cigar down on the ashtray. "My help doesn't come cheap."

"I'll give you my life," I say eagerly, hoping he'll give me the chance to explain my situation.

He shakes his head in disappointment. "Haven't your parents taught you the value of life, kid?"

"I have no parents," I admit.

He stops to assess me, and I try not to fidget under his stare.

"I'll do anything you ask of me. Please, I'll sell you my fucking soul if that's what you want," I plead like the worthless piece of shit I am.

"Hold on, kid," he says, standing from his chair and stepping around to take a seat in the armchair across from me. "Tell me why you're so desperate for my help."

"I haven't eaten a proper meal in two weeks. I survive off bread and butter and spend my days by the dock fishing just to try and sell the fish at the market to make a few euros to afford the bare necessities. I'm sick and I'm fucking tired of living like this!" Frustration is laced in my voice, but I don't care. "I can't do this anymore. I need to have something to live for, something to call mine. I don't want to be another statistic. I want to leave a fucking mark on the world."

"Even if that mark is black?"

"*Especially* if that mark is black." I hold his gaze. "My parents abandoned me, left me to grow up in a foreign country with a fucking stranger while they played house and built a whole empire. I *need* this."

I'm not sure if it's compassion or sympathy I see in his eyes, but I hope I've struck a nerve.

"I'll do anything you ask," I beg. "Please, just tell me what you need me to do and I'll do it."

He leans back in his chair, and I can see the cogs in his mind working as a small smile sneaks onto his face. He snaps his fingers and in an instant, someone walks through the door.

"*Bu çocuğa biraz sıcak yemek getir.*" He directs his words to the older woman who leaves as soon as he nods. I can't understand Turkish, but growing up in Italy, there were a lot of people I met who were Turkish. Some were travellers, coming to the tourist hot spots and others worked for Enzo. That's how I heard about Erhan.

"I'll make you a deal, kid." He smiles and leans forward, his elbows on his knees. "You have a nice warm meal tonight and sleep in a comfortable bed. Then tomorrow, we can discuss the rest."

My stomach rumbles at the mention of food, my mouth watering at the thought of a warm dinner.

"Does this mean you'll help me?"

"Actually," he stands and reaches for his cigar, placing it between his lips, "you're going to help *me*."

TWO YEARS LATER

Cocking the gun in my hand, I pause outside the doors of the bar, my only chance to turn in the opposite direction and forget about revenge. All it'll take is one step after the other, and I can have a different life, move from Italy and start fresh. I consider it an option for a millisecond, then the vision of the garage flashes in my head and my lips curl back into a snarl. I know he's not here, and even though my end goal is to make him suffer, I want all of them who had a hand in this to feel the same excruciating pain I felt when I stepped into that garage.

Taking a step forward, the bouncer checks me, and before he can refuse me entry, my foot lands on the door, snapping it into the wall. All eyes are on me as I step in, and within a second, I identify the five men responsible and raise both my handguns. The scrawny one spits his beer onto the bar top as a bullet fires from one of my guns, landing in between his eyes. Another tries to stand on the other side of the room, but another bullet pierces his right eye, his blood smearing the wall behind him.

There's a shuffle as another reaches into his jacket pocket, hanging on the back of the barstool, and his screams smother every other sound in the room as a bullet lands in his hand, then silence as another enters his forehead.

The bulky one fires his gun, the shot missing me and landing on the wall beside me. Drunk bastard has shocking aim. I fire another shot, the bullet landing slightly off-centre on his forehead, but he's across the room, so I give myself some grace. And finally, the last of them crawls on the floor beneath the tables, the bar now half empty since I step foot inside.

"*Vieni a conoscere il tuo Grim Reaper.*" *Come and meet your Grim Reaper.* I taunt him, as he whimpers, still clambering through the tables.

Kicking the table, it lands on its side, revealing the fucker now on his back, his hands shaking as he struggles with the safety on his gun.

"Any last words?" I ask, but as he opens his mouth to speak, I pull the trigger, the bullet flying into his mouth and out the back of his throat, leaving a nine-millimetre hole.

"Like I'd let you speak to me." I pull the trigger again and his body falls flat against the floor, his eyes wide open.

Looking around the room, I notice there are still a few people who have stuck around. They are no doubt working for Enzo, too.

Good. I hope they report everything back to him.

"Just in case you don't know, my name is Rafael. You can tell your boss I've resigned."

The Influence of Revenge.

PRESENT

I fiddle with the hem of my dress, the low thrum of the ferry horn drumming in the distance. I don't know what to expect in the next couple of days and I'm nervous to find out. Dante and Rafael stand by my left, and the Casella brothers are beside Jackson on my right as we wait for the ferry to dock. All I've heard about the Lucchese family is that they've been around for a very long time. Longer than the Petruccis. Their rule was mainly over America, but now, I hear it extends to France and Spain. Tommy and Frances have been running their business together since it was passed down to them, and from what I've heard through the grapevine, they do it relentlessly.

"Stop fidgeting, you're driving me insane," Dante murmurs, slapping my hand, and I take a deep breath, clasping both hands together at my front.

It's not a big deal. I just have to welcome them to Falcon's Keep.

I want to remind myself that after the revelry, I get to go back to America, but now, I don't know if I want to leave as much as I did when I first got here.

I steal my spine as the ferry docks and Frances and Tommy step onto the wharf. I'm stunned as they stroll over to us and the tall one speaks, his midnight hair in harmony with his eyes. He extends his hand to Dante who takes it, then to me.

"Nera, right?" he asks with a relaxed grin.

Taking his hand, I return his smile. "Yes, and you are?"

"Frances." He tightens his grip on my hand ever so slightly. "Frances Lucchese."

"I'm Tommy." His younger brother steps forward, nodding.

I don't know what I expected, but it certainly wasn't for them to be this polite and well-mannered. A few of their men disembark, dragging another man with a cloth bag over his head and forcing him to kneel before Rafael and Dante.

Frances gestures with leather gloves at the man on his knees. "A gift. Given the invitation was very last minute, we couldn't wire you the ticket price."

I can sense sarcasm in his voice as he stares at Rafael, and then at Dante.

"Thank you, for your…*trouble*." Dante nods as the man is shuffled away in the direction of the forest. Rafael steals a glance at me in warning then follows them, and after the introductions are complete, we head to the manor. Dante informs everyone the revelry will begin at nine tonight, so I head upstairs to prepare.

Pacing my room, I glance at the time on my phone and notice the many missed calls from Elodie. I've been keeping in contact with her but when my roots started to grow back, my ties to America seemed to dull.

Pressing call, I hold the phone to my ear and stand in the one spot in my room where I have reception.

"I thought you were dead. What the fuck?" she scolds, and I can hear it in her voice that she's mad.

"I'm sorry. Things have been…*weird* around here."

"Explain."

"Frances and Tommy are here."

She gasps and there's a ruffle on the other side of the call.

"Lucchese?"

"Yeah."

"Okay, I know you said your family come from organised crime, but they're linked to the Lucchese family?" she asks in disbelief.

"I don't know, but I'm going to find out tonight. How have the last few weeks been?"

She sighs. "Honestly, it's been tough trying to stick to a schedule. Between class, sport, and family, I have no time for fun."

"So no clubs, huh?" I fiddle with the hair tie on my wrist, wedging the phone between my ear and shoulder. "No hot one-night stands I should be aware of?" I hold back a smile.

"As if," she scoffs and there's a pause. "When are you coming back?"

I bite my lip, unsure of my answer.

"You are coming back, right?"

"Elodie—"

"Nera," she warns.

"Yes. It's still the plan." I placate her because I don't have the energy to fight with her today.

"Okay. I'll hold you to it. Mr Foster just walked in and he seems pissed. Keep in touch, okay? Don't go MIA on me."

"Okay, love you, El."

The call ends and I rest my head against the wall, catching the phone as it falls. I know in the moment I hated it—the classes, the speeches, assignments and essays —but right now, I kind of miss it. I miss the denial I lived in that maybe one day, I could have separated myself from this place, but the truth remains rooted in the trees and my heart.

Falcon's Keep is my home.

Stepping into my wardrobe, I shift through the hangers, digging out two of my favourite dresses when I spot a deep forest-green box on the floor. I don't remember putting it there. Kneeling onto the floor, I slide it out, pulling the cream, cotton ribbon and lifting the lid. To my surprise, a small note lays on top of satin packaging, concealing whatever is underneath.

PROMISE ME _YOU_. – R.

Taking the cover of my phone off, I stuff the card inside and place it back on. I hesitate before opening the package and take the six-inch, sky-high stilettos out to place them on the floor. I stare at them in awe. With open toes, a criss-cross front that buckles at the side, and a jewel-encrusted falcon on the heel, they're magnificent. Smiling, I grab the dress I wore to the dinner party with the Casellas, knowing he couldn't keep his eyes off me that night, and begin getting ready for the revelry.

RAFAEL

A splash of blood splatters onto the sand. The man's face is still covered with the cloth bag. We've been here for an hour and all I've done is give this man a whipping.

"Damn, so this is what goes on here," Nicholas says, stepping down into the pit. Ezra and Jackson have been here since the Lucchese brothers came, but even they don't know who's behind the mask.

"I thought we should have some fun with him before he meets his inevitable fate," Frances says, taking a seat on the step, watching as the blood runs down the man's back and onto the sand-covered floor. We keep sand here to remind them how something as granular as sand can be painful, among other reasons. This place was originally made to store produce back when Falcon's Keep was thriving, but has since been changed to house the darker secrets. Despite Nera's best efforts, the only way to get into the Pit of the Damned is if you have a key. We keep it locked tight because it's where the broken ones stay. The space resembles a small circular area, something like an arena. With the exorbitant amount of blood the sand has seen, it's now tinged a dark brown.

"Just put him out of his misery already." Nicholas lights up a cigarette and Dante looks at the floor. My brows pull in, sensing he knows who's under there.

Jackson looks around the room with a question behind his gaze.

The whip lands down hard and fast on his back, creating another crater on his skin. His thick blood oozes out from the wound, his screams suffocating the windowless space.

Frances stands to stroll over to the man, gripping at his restraints, and when he pulls the cloth off the man's head, my heart lurches from my chest. Adrenaline peaks, and as I'm about to swing, Dante's firm grip holds me back.

Nicholas drops the cigarette in his hand and launches forward, Ezra now barely holding him back.

"Motherfucker!" Nicholas spits, hurling himself in Enzo's direction.

Jackson's entire body is frozen, the grip on his phone tightening as his knuckles blanch.

"Merry Christmas." Frances smirks.

"This was your gift?" I question, glancing at Frances, then aiming my next words at Dante. "What was the price?"

He doesn't speak, his gaze firmly fixed on Enzo. Something like this can easily cost a life, sometimes more, and I'm not ready to give the Lucchese family any more than what they've already taken from me or the Della Torres.

"I'm going to fucking kill you!" Nicholas bellows, breaking free from Ezra's hold, his fist cracking through Enzo's jaw.

Enzo chuckles as Ezra pulls Nicholas back. "How's Asher?"

Jackson jolts forward, his hands closing around Enzo's neck, squeezing as his guttural screams fill the void.

"Enough!" Ezra yells, and Jackson releases him. "Dante, explain this."

"I'll see my brother take his revenge first," he says, his face still emotionless.

"No fucking way. *I* get to kill him," Nicholas says, reaching for his gun.

"He's mine!" Jackson's gaze doesn't move from Enzo, and I know above everyone else, I'd let him take his piece first. After all, he lost his brother at the hands of Enzo.

Pulling Dante to the side, I force him to look at me. "What have you done?" I question, and his blank stare is far from the person I know.

"It's done. Now take your revenge, Rafael," he orders.

He's never spoken to me like this in the years that we've known each other, and even though I want to shake him, I know what's done is done and there's no going back. It's time that I take what I've been working toward.

"Death is too easy," I say to Nicholas and Jackson as they pause, the gun in Nicholas's hand resting beside him. "What I have in mind is far more excruciating."

I make my way over to the table of weapons and pick up two large knives, handing one to Nicholas. Standing behind Enzo, I speak low so only he can hear me.

"This is for everything you took from me, and everyone you've ever harmed in my life." Piercing the knife into his spine, he shrieks, the muscles in his arms tightening.

Nicholas stands beside me, gripping Enzo's shoulder. "If you faint, Jackson will keep injecting you with adrenaline until we're done, you hear me?" He thrusts his knife alongside mine into his back, another blood-curdling yell reverberating through the empty space. I begin first, slicing down into the first rib, sawing it as Nicholas does the same. I struggle to grip the blade, Enzo's blood now pouring out like a river as he battles to stay upright.

"That's two," I say, slicing and sawing into another rib. "That's four."

He slumps forward, passing out from the pain, and Nicholas swears as Jackson grabs the adrenaline needle from the table across the room. Jabbing him in the chest, he punches him across the face, leaving the needle in place. "Wake up, fuck face, it's time to repent."

We begin cutting again as he slowly comes back, his screams returning as the adrenaline courses through his veins.

"Just kill me!" He pulls the chains, rattling them. "Please, just fucking kill me!"

"We'll get to that." I clean the blood from my hands onto my pants and continue. "That's six. Are you ready for the finale?"

When I look up, Ezra's smiling, no doubt adding to his sick fucking collection of torture methods, and Frances and his brother look bored out of their minds.

"Are we about done?" Tommy checks his phone.

I don't answer him as I grip one rib, and Nicholas does the same on the other side. Pulling, the loud crack tears through the space, and Enzo cries out in agony.

Crack.

Another rib snapped open.

Crack.

Another.

Crack.

And another.

By this stage, I'm surprised the adrenaline hasn't worn off as he whimpers, barely holding himself up. Rolling up my sleeves, I glance at Nicholas, and he nods. Jackson moves between me and Nicholas, and we all dig through Enzo's ribcage.

I grasp my hands around the soft, spongy organ and yank it out, warm blood spilling out onto the sand, and my shoes, and splattering all over me. Jackson reaches into the middle of Enzo's chest and pulls out his heart, holding it as he stares at it. Enzo goes limp, his lungs now on the floor, covered in sand. I remain still, willing the anger and resentment to subside now that I've taken my revenge, but they don't. They remain embedded within me, the momentary satisfaction of holding his lung in my hands now like smoke in the wind.

"Fickle, isn't it?" Jackson murmurs, still staring at the organ in his hand. "I thought it'd make me feel better."

Dropping the organ to the ground, he flattens it under his boot with a stomp, the blood that was left in the chambers now decorating the sand in splatters of vermillion red.

It's not often someone is subjected to this method of death because it's reserved for people like Enzo, who truly deserve the agonising pain before their soul is taken from them and their body is pulled apart. As the world continues spinning, my next question is: what twisted, sick agreement has Dante dived into with the Lucchese brothers, and how the fuck am I going to get him out of it?

CHAPTER EIGHTEEN
Nera

Distance and Mistakes.

Music thumps through the walls of the Fortress, a building I haven't been in since its extension and renovation. Heading to the bar, I spot Darcy in a skintight champagne dress with jewelled tassels falling from mid-thigh, her blazing hair curly and wild. She waves me over, and I smile.

"I thought Dante would keep you home for this one." She chuckles, ordering hard liquor.

"Unfortunately, when you're a Della Torre, you need to act like one, so I'm here." I shrug, ordering myself an espresso martini and looking around the room. She picks up on my nerves and leans on the bar, facing me.

"He's not here yet," she says, taking a sip from her glass and I sigh.

Taking in my surroundings, I notice everything and everyone reeks of wealth. Years and generations of wealth. The men with their expensive suits and watches, the women with their icy jewellery, the reflections of tiny rainbows dancing through the space as the light reflects off their frost. If you were to look at them, you'd believe it if they told you they were good men because they dress the part, speak the part, and play the part. They hide in plain sight so well that it's hard to differentiate, but I know better. I know this is how they prefer to be seen because it's easier to blend when you conform to what society sees as a goal they want to achieve.

Everyone wants to be rich.

Everyone wants to be able to afford to live without worrying about when their next paycheck is coming. But most of all, they crave the finer things in life. They crave the life itself, lusting after it like it will somehow magically fulfil their happiness and erase their loneliness.

"Ah, there they are." Darcy gestures with her glass to Nicholas, who walks in with Rafael and Ezra, with Jackson behind them. Nicholas places a soft kiss on her cheek as he reaches over and orders a drink for himself.

"We leave tomorrow morning." Nicholas gazes deeply into Darcy's eyes, making the room slightly uncomfortable. "I'm not spending another second away from our happiness. Especially not on this fucking island."

She smiles sweetly, placing her hands on his chest as Rafael clears his throat. "I see the shoes fit."

"Creepy how you know my shoe size."

"If you think *that's* creepy…" He trails off when Ezra steps up beside him. The man terrifies me with just the way he stands, tall and intimidating.

"So, when does the *fun* begin?" he asks, pulling out his phone to check it, but Rafael doesn't answer him. Instead, his eyes graze from my breasts, down to my shoes, and I'm almost lost in a trance as I watch him devour me until the veil is broken.

"Fuck, that's messed up." Nicholas barks a laugh, glancing between us. "Does Dante know about you two?" His question makes my heart rate spike, the fear now compounding with the rush of the thrill.

Rafael turns, crossing his arms. "You say a word and I'll beat the life out of you."

Darcy pulls him aside as he tries to hide his laughter, and Ezra murmurs something to himself before taking a breath and facing Rafael.

"I don't have sisters, so I don't know what it's like, but you're playing with fire, and it's not the kind you want between family," he warns, and I feel a pang in my chest at his words. There isn't a part of this world where Raf and I make sense.

Not one.

"What would you know of *family?*" Rafael growls through gritted teeth. "You left your own brother to fend for himself in a foreign country." He steps forward but Ezra doesn't flinch. In fact, he looks unaffected by Rafael's anger.

"You're right. We all learn from our mistakes." He glances at me, and I remain silent. "But a mistake is made unknowingly. This…" he gestures between us, shaking his head, "is just negligence."

I fight the emotions inside me, denying myself a moment to feel hurt by his words because it's the truth.

We cannot be.

Grabbing my drink off the counter, I push past them with one goal on my mind.

Get so fucking drunk that I can't feel my face.

"Nera!" Rafael calls out after me, but I'm already on the other side of the room, taking a seat at one of the poker tables. I have absolutely no idea how to play, but what I do know is how to play *men.*

The brunet with shoulder-length hair beside me leans in. "It's a ten thousand dollar buy-in," he says, handing me his card, and I smile as I take it.

"Generous." I bat my lashes, hoping Rafael is watching from somewhere in the room. I try to ignore the fact that he didn't stick up for us, but it annoys me to the point where I want to make him squirm. Placing my hand on the man's arm, I lean in and laugh at some joke he made, joining in with the laughter around the table. His baby-blue eyes light up in excitement. He undoubtedly knows who I am because Dante would have notified everyone of my attendance tonight. The baby sister, back after years studying abroad.

"How come you've never been to these before, Miss Della Torre?" he asks, and I ignore Rafael's burning gaze on my back.

Crossing my legs, I tug at my dress a little, lifting the material slightly to reveal the side of my thigh, all the way up to my bare hip. "I've clearly been missing out. Wasting my time in the US."

Someone clears their throat behind me, and I look up through my lashes at Frances Lucchese, now standing inches from me, extending a hand. "Nera, would you like to join me in the VIP section?"

"I'm quite alright here, thank you." At my dismissal, the man beside me goes rigid, gulping as he stares up at him.

Frances smiles, cocking his head to the side. "I like you." He narrows his eyes and reaches into his breast pocket, revealing a gold cigarette case. "Join me outside, then?"

I consider whether I should, only agreeing because if anyone is aware of the underworld and its dealings all around the world, it's Frances. As I stand, dangerously close to him, he doesn't move back an inch, leaving me to squeeze between him and the chair I was just sitting on.

There's a hot flush on my chest, followed by a sprinkle of hesitation down my spine as I step outside into the large wooden balcony, perfectly decorated with modern outdoor furniture. My brows knit as I wonder how Dante was able to afford this, and when I turn back, the few people that were out here now disappear back inside.

"You can really empty a room." I cross my arms as the cool breeze of the night brushes against my skin, like it's warning me of the person in my company.

He smiles, placing a cigarette between his lips, and when his piercing blue eyes fall onto mine, the need to avert my gaze grows. I almost crumble under it, like a brittle bone trying to withstand the pressure, right before it's crushed.

"Dante has hidden you well."

I don't respond, unsure of what to say. Instead, I fiddle with the end of my hair, looking for an opportunity to head back inside.

"It's no wonder," he whispers, stepping closer to me. "A pretty girl like you, on an island like this…"

"Dante didn't hide me. I chose not to come back."

He nods before he speaks again. "Are you here of your own free will then?"

What an odd thing to ask.

I shrug. "It depends on who you ask." I hold my breath as his fingers brush through my hair, the darkness of the night accentuating his alluring charm.

"I'm asking *you*." His lips move, and all I can think about is Rafael. I'm still here because of him, and I don't know why I continue to cling to this dream.

I swallow as he leans forward, my words beginning to jumble inside my head as a cool sweat rolls down my spine. The doors to the Fortress open and Tommy steps out.

"Frances! Fuck, I've been trying to find you everywhere. It's starting." He swirls the drink in his cup and sucks the rest down in one gulp. Frances doesn't seem at all interested in whatever Tommy is talking about, but he drops his hand and reluctantly takes a step back, extending his hand to me.

I'm afraid of what might happen should I reject him, so I take his hand and head back inside, following the crowd of people now making their way into the forest.

It looks different tonight, with the bright flood lights illuminating a sectioned-off space in the middle of the forest and the large braziers filled with fire. The crowd murmurs as they gather around the large circle, most of them drunk off the high of being around others who can afford to attend this party. Some are just plastered off cocaine. I scan the space, searching for Dante and Rafael, and as the forest fills with people, I begin to hesitate.

Being alone with Frances doesn't feel safe.

"Why are we out here?" I ask, wrapping the coat Frances gave me across my torso, covering my bare skin from the cool wind.

He looks at me and smiles without saying a word. The night stills as Dante walks into the middle of the space, everyone's attention now on him, and mine focused on finding Rafael.

"Friends, thank you for attending the first revelry of the year!"

The crowd roars with cheer as I spot Ezra and Nicholas on the opposite side.

"I know the snow tax was an unexpected cost, but this year, we have something new to explore with you." He motions to four cages being wheeled in by men, and my mouth goes dry. The man with the crazy eyes who attacked me is clawing at the bars, his clothes torn as he bares his teeth to the crowd. "This year, we introduce you to the Pit of the Damned, where two broken souls fight to the death. Your wager on the winner of the Pit could win you some serious cash!"

I purse my lips, my hands growing clammy with every second that passes. The roar of the crowd is now a faint hum behind the pulsing in my ears.

Frances leans into me and his expensive cologne mixed with the smell of cigarettes surrounds me. "Are you ready to have some fun, Nera?" he whispers, the sense of danger now growing as I search for Rafael.

"We only have two rules," Dante continues, putting on his best entertainment voice. "Kill…or be killed."

The crowd goes crazy, with people jumping and roaring at the excitement of fresh carnage. The thirst for blood is evident in their eyes, not one of them questioning why these poor souls are here. Not one empathetic thought that these people might have families.

One of the cages opens and the crazy one steps out, covered in dried blood. His pants are stained with what I assume is urine, but he doesn't care because he's no longer human.

"When the fighting ends, and one of these damned souls is crowned the survivor, you will each have an opportunity to bid for your chance to take them with you."

My stomach churns at his words. Since when did we become *this*?

"Rest assured, you will be shown how to manage and control them."

Fucking barbaric.

Another man is released into the pit, his clothes clearly once represented a well-put-together man.

"I think I need to use the restroom." I take a step back when large hands clasp around my forearm.

"I want you to see this." Frances urges me to stay and I nod, afraid that if I say no, it'll ruin things between our family and theirs.

Dante removes himself from the middle, and the men instantly launch themselves at each other, pulling, ripping, and biting. One of them manages to get on top of the other, gripping his hair and smacking his head onto the ground repeatedly.

Frances chuckles beside me, and when I look up at him, I see pure satisfaction in his eyes. "Looks like this might be a short one." He releases my forearm, leaving a stinging sensation behind.

I continue to look for Rafael in the crowd and my eyes clash with Dante's. He doesn't let his gaze linger too long before he retreats into the crowd, leaving me beside this psychotic man.

The two men in the pit continue to attack each other, the blood now covering both their faces, one with a large gash on his cheekbone. I close my eyes, not wanting to watch anymore as the violent sounds of the blows rattle inside my head. The roar of the crowd gets louder with each hit.

"Yeah! Bite his fucking ear off!" someone yells from the crowd, and I open my eyes to someone throwing a knife into the pit.

"That's not allowed! It's cheating!" another person exclaims, but it doesn't matter to either of the men in the pit. In fact, I don't think they saw it land beside them, too consumed by their violent rage.

The queasiness is back. I stare at the man now on top of the one with the gash, and when he leans over, he bites the other man's nose and tears it off completely with his teeth, the blood covering his chin.

I cover my mouth with my hand, unable to tear my eyes away as the man beneath him cries out in pain, desperate to get away from his attacker. His fingers claw the dirt as he manages to crawl to his front, inching his way to the cage they arrived in.

Whirling around, I make my way through the spectators before Frances can grab me again. I head back inside, the Fortress now completely empty. My heels clack on the marbled floors as I step behind the bar to help myself to a drink, so many new questions in my head.

Forgoing the glass, I pour a shot of vodka into my mouth, barely flinching at the burn in my throat. My mind whirls with countless conflicting thoughts, and I hate that I no longer know what I want. My entire being is telling me to confront Dante, but my rational side is telling me to let it go and do what I'm told to keep the peace.

"Thirsty?" Frances appears at the glass doors, keeping his distance.

I don't respond as I take another long gulp of vodka. I don't want to be here. I want nothing more than to be in my bed with my best friend in the States, watching a TV show and worrying about which tutor will take our exams.

"I thought you said you were here of your own free will."

There's that odd fucking statement again.

"Why do you keep saying that?" I question, stepping toward him, and he pauses. "You do realise this whole thing, this entire night was set up just for you, right?" I speak before I think.

"You know that Dante wants to be in your good books so that you don't work with Enzo…" I shift my weight onto one leg, my body beginning to feel lighter as the alcohol takes effect. "You're only here as a bargaining chip, to ensure that we stay relevant."

Why would I say such a thing? I don't fucking know.

Maybe it's the resentment I feel toward my brother for bringing me back and making me realise the life I left behind. Maybe it's because I'm starting to feel things I shouldn't for Rafael. Maybe it's because I'm just so sick and tired of being the good girl everyone wants me to be.

Frances huffs a laugh, completely unbothered by everything I've just said, and I begin to think that maybe I don't know everything that's going on behind closed doors.

"You should have a word with your brother, Nera." I hold my breath as he steps closer to me, his height towering over mine, sending goosebumps down my spine as he speaks into my ear. "Because this night was just as much for *you* as it was for me."

What?

My mind swirls and the anger is back.

He plants a soft kiss on my cheek. "Dante should have told you by now."

Although the lighting in here is dim, his high cheekbones are accentuated when he smiles. He takes his leave through the door on the opposite side of the bar, leaving me with the most rage I have ever felt.

A moment passes and I'm unsure of my next move. Tonight was a bust. I didn't get any of the answers I hoped for. Instead, my trust in my brother and Rafael is now at zero. Groaning from frustration, I take another gulp of vodka when a silhouette emerges by the door.

"So, this is my punishment?" Rafael's voice is hard, and I know he's pissed.

I don't give him the satisfaction of an answer. Instead, I

hold up the bottle of vodka and take another gulp, the liquid flowing down my chin.

His hands flex as he steps into the space, the roars from the crowd now pouring into the Fortress.

"Why are you even here?" I turn around and place the bottle back on the counter, then begin to remove my shoes. "J-Just forget about it." My words begin to slur.

"Forget?" He remains still, watching me struggle with the buckle. "You think it's *that* easy?"

"Yeah." My chest constricts as I say the words. "Watch and learn." Finally getting the last shoe off, I grab them and walk over to him, ramming them into his chest. "Whatever the hell this was," I gesture between us, "it's done."

The Beginning of the End.

Disillusion crowds her face as she presses the heels I gifted her into my chest, and the molten lava inside me bubbles. I don't hold onto them, so when she lets go, they hit the marble floor. Before she can storm off, I grasp her elbow, reminding me of the very first time she saw me again after those years apart.

"Don't fucking walk out on me," I warn her, and she blinks slowly, ripping her arm out of my hold.

"Don't *ever* touch me again." She gets in my face, her perfume like a warm, comforting hug. "You will *never* touch me again." A tear rolls down her cheek and a lump forms in my throat at the reality of our situation.

She pads slowly to the open door, and I forget where I am. It takes two steps for me to get to her and when I do, she's pressed against the glass doors.

"I said don't touch me," she says through gritted teeth, but I don't listen because I *need* to touch her, to be around her, *smothered* by her.

"Whatever he's been filling your head with is a lie."

"Don't fucking insult me," she spits.

"Nera!" My hand curls around her delicate neck, the

urge to squeeze, strong. "Don't make me take your breath away again. This time, it won't be so pleasurable."

She laughs loudly. "This is more like it."

Confused, I release her.

"Look at us, fighting like brother and sister."

"Shut up, Nera."

"Why? Are you scared of the truth?" She pushes me hard, and I falter. "Does it haunt you at night, knowing that your cock has been inside me, that you know what I taste like?"

She pushes further, trying to get under my skin.

"Do you look at yourself in the mirror and feel proud of the big brother that you are?"

There's a silence that lingers in the air, and I let her words sink in before eating up the distance between us.

"This is not over, and it will *never* be. Not while I'm still fucking breathing."

Dante releases his bow tie and unbuttons the first few buttons on his dress shirt. The dim light from the sunrise begins to shine through the office window as he leans back in his chair, clearly exhausted from the night.

"The Casellas are leaving this morning." He picks up his phone to text someone, then locks it, placing it on the desk again as I flick the lighter in my hand and scoff.

"Well, they got their revenge, why would they want to stay any longer?"

He doesn't answer me. Instead, he stares into the distance and opens his mouth, almost like he's about to tell me something, when Nera walks in with fury.

"Tell me," she demands, still dressed in the outfit she wore last night. "I deserve to know *everything!*" she yells.

Dante looks to me, and I wait for his answer.

"It's dawn, Nera. We will talk about this later when we are level-headed," Dante tries to explain, but she pushes.

Taking the medium-sized Jesus statue in the corner of the room with both hands, she hurls it at him. The statue hits the oak desk and shatters into a million pieces. "I want to hear you say whatever you have to say to me right fucking now, otherwise I leave. I don't care if I have to *swim* off this island, I will."

"Fuck," Dante murmurs to himself, pressing his fists to his forehead.

Her eyes find mine and I stand.

"Raf, can you give us a second?"

I brush past her, intentionally grazing the back of my hand against hers. Reluctantly, I exit and wait by the door. Everything in this house is old, making the doors heavier than the ones manufactured these days, and the walls are thick, built from bricks. Sound doesn't travel through this house much, and it's always creeped me out a little.

The silence.

The heavy silence, continuously there as a reminder of the sinister things we do. The purity long gone, leaving only the imminent darkness that awaits us. Being in bed with Frances might be a great substitute for not going without, but for our souls, it's damning.

Voices are raised from within the room as I flick the lighter open and closed, absently running my thumb over the letter. It's been years since I've thought about him, of all the things he's done for me and everything I've done for them. I don't regret it. Any of it. Dante helped me become what I am today. The ruthless, rogue killer. Unafraid.

But it wasn't until she came back here that everything changed. She's made me take another look at myself. A long hard look into how much I've changed from the boy who stole that egg, to the man who's willing to burn down an entire empire to be with her.

If she asked me to, I'd kill anyone. I'd do anything she wanted.

My ears perk up when a loud crash comes from the room. I go to open the door, but Nera's already storming out with tears in her eyes.

"Nera!" I call out after her and grab her hand. Fuck the rest of them. I don't care if they see. "What happened?"

She looks at me, streams of tears on her cheeks as she shakes her head, her brows crossed. "How could you?"

"What?" I turn my head to see Dante with his head buried in his hands. "How could I what!?"

"This whole time. This entire time, you knew what was happening and you still didn't tell me. Do you derive some sick pleasure from it? Huh?"

She tears her hand out of mine and lands a blow on my cheek, the sting making me grit my teeth in anger and frustration.

"How can I fucking know what you're talking about if you don't tell me!?"

"Look at you! Still acting like you have no idea what's going on! I am so fucking done with you. With *all* of you!"

She storms past the main entry and out the door, taking my heart with her, and I have two choices I can make right now. Follow her and get to the bottom of what's making her feel this way and risk Dante questioning my intense actions toward her, or try to probe the answers out of Dante.

Either one, I fear, won't get me what I want.

175

Blood Oaths and Pathetic Excuses.

My stomach is in my mouth as I run barefoot toward the one place I have avoided since getting here. I stop by the shed, my heartbeat frantic as I search for something, anything that'll help me alleviate the way I'm feeling right now. Spotting a shovel leaning up against some gardening tools, I grab it with two hands, the heavy steel making it hard to hold with one.

What did you expect, coming back home?

You knew things would end up this way. You thought about it.

I silence the voice in my head and haul the shovel over my shoulder. I have something I need to do before anything else. It's long overdue and with the way I'm feeling right now, it's very much a necessity.

The hired maids work to get the yard cleaned up, empty glass bottles littered all over the lawn, and I scowl as I walk past them.

I've never hated someone as much as I hate Dante at this very moment, and it's that hatred that keeps me fuelled. Not caring who might stop me, I head up the edge of the cliff, the dark stones of my father's mausoleum now withered from the salt of the sea. It's big enough to house our entire family, and I know this is why he built it. So even in death, he wouldn't be alone.

Selfish prick.

I pull on the gate, the large chain and lock rattling against it. I could have asked Dante for the key, but I couldn't look at him for another second. Taking a deep breath, I swing the shovel where the chain meets the lock.

Again.

And again.

Puffing, I drop the shovel to the floor and scream, shaking the gate as the chains remain in place.

"How could you!?" I sob. "I trusted you, *Papà!*" Wiping the tears with the back of my hand, I take another breath and pick up the shovel, ramming the sharp edge into the chain and it breaks, the padlock falling to the ground.

Discarding the shovel, I enter and take the descending steps one at a time. The dank smell gets stronger as the door creaks open, revealing my father's concrete tomb in the middle.

My lip wobbles, the adrenaline now well and truly gone, replaced by fatigue and exhaustion catching up to me from the night. "I miss you so much, *Papà*," I whisper, running the pads of my fingertips over the carving on his tomb.

Dante Della Torre.

Niente è più importante della famiglia.

Nothing is more important than family.

"I don't think I can do this." I sniff when heavy sounds of footsteps descend the stairs until I'm staring at Rafael, anger and frustration clear as day on his face.

"Tell me why you're upset."

"Leave, Rafael. I don't ever want to see you again." It

hurts to speak the words because I hate that he kept this from me.

"What did Dante tell you?" he asks like he doesn't already know.

"Don't do that!" I smack my hand on the tomb. "Don't pretend like you don't know *everything* that's been going on since the moment we got here. Hell, since you came to the States."

"I—"

"Don't act like you two don't live in each other's pockets!" I face him as he storms over to me, gripping my chin so hard, my lips part.

"Listen to me very fucking carefully." He doesn't give me the chance to speak as he tightens his grip, his fingers pressing into my jaw. "I don't know what Dante told you, and if I was privy to *any* sort of information that would hurt you, I would *never* keep it from you." His eyes sweep over me, and I grip his untucked dress shirt.

"Now tell me what you're so upset about." He releases my jaw, and I swallow, unsure if I should say anything.

Sighing, I meet his gaze. "The revelry wasn't just for Frances."

"What do you mean?"

"Dante knew what he was doing by bringing me back home. He had a plan."

I watch as the puzzle pieces fall into place in his head, the slow realisation creeping onto his face.

"No. He wouldn't."

"He did."

"Nera…" He's lost for words, as am I.

His eyes darken, his hand coming between us to wrap around my throat. "You will never belong to anyone but me."

"Don't, Raf." He doesn't listen to me. His tongue darts out, licking the skin beneath my ear, sending a shiver down my spine.

I moan, lifting my leg to wrap around him. "It's not worth your life to pursue this. Frances will kill you."

"He can have my body," he says in a breathy voice as he sucks down hard on my neck, the pulsing growing stronger between my legs. "But my heart belongs to you."

"We shouldn't do this again," I pant as he turns me around, forcing my head onto the cold stone of my father's tomb.

"Keep telling me to stop, *Principessa*." He hikes my dress up over my hips and tears my panties off, discarding them on the ground. He runs his hands over the roundness of my ass, like he's savouring the moment until one of them lands down hard on my skin.

I yelp, watching the door in fear that someone might see us like this. He grabs my face and turns me around to take my lips with his, stealing the air right out of my lungs as his tongue dances with mine.

I can't breathe as he consumes me, *all of me* until I don't know right from wrong anymore. Until I can't see the line in the sand, the grey now morphing into pitch black. His bruising grip on my thighs makes me moan as he lifts me atop the tomb.

"Open your legs," he demands, and I spread them wide open.

He removes his dress shirt. The hard ridges of his muscles are perfectly sprinkled with dark hair, his buff chest moving up and down as he devours me with his eyes.

"Tell me you're mine."

I purse my lips, not wanting to hear myself say the words because once I do, we pass the point of no return.

Guiding my hand to my inner thigh, I slip a finger between my lips, my pussy now wet for him, giving him the answer he's searching for without having to say the words. Slipping my fingers inside, he palms his cock, watching me, making me hungry for his length inside me.

"No. Because it'll never be true."

He lunges at me, his hand now fisting my hair and yanking it back, forcing me to meet his gaze. "Say it," he repeats, but I refuse to do what he wants. "No?"

With his hand still gripping my hair, he unbuckles his belt and undoes his pants, pulling out his cock. He snaps my head up, aligning himself with my pussy. "Then watch, *Principessa*, watch me *take* you for myself."

He makes sure I'm watching as he eases the tip in, my flesh stretching around him as he goes deeper.

"That's it…" he coos. "Are you watching the way you open for me? The way your pussy eats my cock?" He jerks my head. "Now say it before I lose my fucking mind."

I smile and he rams into me, my gasp audible inside the near-empty mausoleum.

"Make me," I whisper and the fury he's been holding onto finally comes out in waves. He slides out of me and forces me down, my knees hitting the ground with a thud as he shoves his cock inside my mouth.

"I think you want to be taught a lesson."

He thrusts into my throat, hitting the back, and I gag. Without a second to catch my breath, he does it again, pinching my nose as he wedges me between him and the tomb, his cock pushing further down my throat.

"You're going to learn that there's no one else on this shit pile of a planet that will feel for you like I do."

My lungs burn as they beg for air and I push his thighs, but they've become immovable objects. Digging my nails into them, I gag again when he pulls out completely, the room now filled with my heavy breathing.

"Oh, you think we're done?" He smirks, grabbing his belt from the floor and buckling it around my neck. Once fastened, the leather cinches my skin as he yanks it up, forcing his cock down my throat again. My eyes tear up from the lack of oxygen.

He runs his hand over my face, smearing my makeup as he thrusts into the back of my throat, the saliva dripping down my chin and onto his boots.

"How do you taste, *Principessa?*"

He doesn't give me a moment to catch up as he wrenches himself from my mouth and rubs his cock over my face. Tears pool in my eyes as I realise how aroused I am, and I clench my jaw shut.

"Open," he demands, and I shake my head.

Smiling, he repeats himself and I open my mouth as he leans over me. His saliva dangles off his tongue and slowly drops into my mouth.

Twisted. Sick and fucking depraved.

I moan, grinding my hips into the air, wishing it was his cock.

He loosens his hold on the belt. "Get on your hands and lick the remnants of your pathetic excuses off my boots."

My heart jump-starts at his degrading request, but I do it anyway. The leather of his boot is smooth on my tongue as I gather the saliva in my mouth, my pussy now throbbing with need. I *want* him to take me, to make me his. In this moment, that's the truth.

I *am* his.

Licking from the toe of his boot to the top, I make my

way up his leg, until I'm staring up at him, his large cock filling most of my vision.

"Say it," he demands again.

I open my mouth to speak, to tell him there could be no one but him, but instead, my voice is taken away by the thought of my life being promised to someone else. That promise was made by my father right before he passed, setting the burden of Falcon's Keep onto his children. There was never a possibility of Rafael and I ever sharing a life together. Now, my family has made sure of it by promising me to Frances.

CHAPTER TWENTY-ONE
Rafael

The Sting of Reality.

Fierce, striking, and remorselessly beautiful. Those were the exact thoughts that ran through my head when I saw her get into that Uber in the States. I knew she'd changed. I knew she wasn't the same girl who left Falcon's Keep. What I never thought was how much she'd crawl under my skin, and make me crave her touch, her smell, her company. It's like she's the Earth and I'm the sea, being drawn to her magnetic pull no matter how many other planets surround us.

My cock strains as she smiles beneath it, her tongue darting out, gliding from my balls, along my length, and to the tip of my cock, drawing a groan from deep within my chest.

"I will never let them have you, *Principessa*." Guiding her up by her elbows, I kiss her with everything I have. I grip her by her hips, driving her back into Dante's tomb as I grind my cock into her belly. Removing the straps of her dress, it pools at her feet, revealing her perky breasts. I want to run my tongue all over her body just to be able to say I've tasted every fucking inch of her because that's how much I desire her.

She bites her bottom lip, still refusing to say the words I

need to hear, but it doesn't matter if she says them or not because the reality is: I will never let her be with anyone but me. I will gut them all if I have to. One by one until there's none of them left.

"I don't think I can ever open my heart to anyone else," she whispers as a tear rolls down her cheek. "Not like I have with you."

Scooping her up with one arm, I rest the back of her ass on the tomb as I enter her. "Don't think about anyone else right now, Nera." I slide deeper into her warmth, fighting the urge to roll my eyes back into my skull from how good she feels. "It's me and you."

She nods, and I grip the belt still fastened around her neck, pulling her to my lips, and our tongues perfect our tango. Mine, fighting for a chance for her to choose me. To realise that it's me she's meant to be with, not him. However, I think she fights for the one thing she's been thinking about ever since arriving on this island.

The States.

Maybe she thinks she can escape her fate by marrying the rich cunt and fleeing without a care in the world.

Maybe…this is what she *wants*.

My chest sinks as my head takes me places I don't want to fucking go. My heart still calls her name as she bites my lip, pulling me deeper into her as I thrust, our skin slapping against each other.

"Rafael." Her moans sound like desperate pleas. For me to save her, to save us from this destiny. But all I can think about is the way her pussy squeezes me tighter the harder I fuck her.

I pull the belt tighter, and she digs her nails into my back, rolling her hips against mine. I stare into her stormy eyes filled to the brim with tears, and it makes me burn with rage, a fiery hell whirling inside me, just waiting to be released onto Falcon's Keep.

She closes them, freeing me from torment as she nears her release. Her thighs are secured around my waist like heavy chains, but I keep my eyes on her, watching her body react to my touch.

There will not be a life without her in it. Not now, not ever.

I groan when her pussy clenches around my cock, the sweat on her body mixing with mine as I continue to fuck her against the tomb, slamming into her, jolting her body back with each thrust.

The pleasure surges from beneath my spine and ripples through me as I come inside her, my forehead pressed to hers. When she opens her beautiful blue-grey eyes, the corner of her lips curl ever so slightly as she places her hand on my cheek.

"Don't ruin everything you've worked for just for a shot at something the world will *never* see as normal," she whispers, placing a chaste kiss on my lips.

The earth is pulled from beneath me as she gently draws herself away, slips on her dress without another word, and walks out the door. She leaves me with my exposed heart on the tomb, the oxygen surrounding it like acid, corroding the flesh agonisingly slow.

I needed sleep. My head was pounding after the one I gave Nera and considering how sickeningly sober I was at the revelry, my mind needed a damn break. A break from Dante Senior's words echoing in my ear every six minutes about keeping Falcon's Keep safe from outsiders. Sometimes, I rue the fucking day I was swept up onto these shores. Maybe I should have just drowned, perhaps it would have saved me from this excruciating hurt in the middle of my body. The constant pull from one direction and the other is giving me hardcore vertigo, but this afternoon, after the sleep I just had, I somewhat feel better.

I stare at my hands as I sit up on the edge of the bed, the veins now protruding more than they did years ago, the scars from countless knives and burns covering my skin. Even when they're clean, all I see is the thick, red blood—a constant reminder that no matter where I go, or who I try to become, I'll always be this.

Sighing, I head over to the connected bathroom and step out of my briefs. The water hits the floor of the shower as I step in, the cold shocking my system before it begins to heat up. I haven't heard from her since last night, and it's making me question if she ever wanted it. I knew it would be hard for her to admit the way she felt about me, but I never thought I'd be second-guessing that she ever had those feelings to begin with.

It can't be it.

Not like this.

There's a knock on my door and my hand curls into a fist. I just want to be left alone. For one whole day, I just want to exist.

"What?" My voice is harsh.

"We're leaving in half an hour, just wanted to say bye." Darcy's voice travels through the door.

"I'll be out in ten. I'll meet you at the dock."

Finishing up, I head out the door after getting dressed, into the cool breeze. The ferry rocks as the waves hit the wharf, the entire Casella family waiting to take their leave.

"You call me if you need anything." Ezra faces Dante, his arm placed on his shoulder, and my body tenses as I watch the exchange.

Dante nods. "What will you do?"

"Well, I'm looking forward to the birth of my son any day now," Ezra says with joy in his tone. Funny, didn't think he was capable of such feelings. "And Nicholas…"

"We're leaving in a few days. Starting a new life." Nicholas smiles at Darcy and although he makes my skin crawl, I wouldn't choose anyone else to take care of Darcy.

"You're here!" Darcy smiles as she strides over and into my arms.

Jackson extends his hand and I take it. "Thank you. To both of you." He reaches for Dante and they shake hands.

Darcy places her hand on my cheek as the others begin boarding the ferry. "If it's worth fighting for, don't let it go so easily," she whispers. "Don't make the same mistake I did."

Without another word, she takes Nicholas's hand and boards the ferry.

"Don't forget, brother, you will always have a place in London." Ezra nods as Darcy waves.

The loud horn of the ferry hums as it departs, and Dante takes his place beside me.

"I take it you heard about Nera?"

The blood runs hot in my veins at the mention of her name. He's not the brother I once thought him to be.

"You signed her fucking life away," I say with contempt.

"There's so much more to it that you don't know."

I turn to face him, keeping my violent urges at bay. "How could you do that to your own flesh and blood?"

He laughs, running a hand through his thick hair. "You have no idea what it takes to keep a family safe."

Something freefalls inside my chest, the words aimed to cut, slicing me deep. "Because I don't have one, right?"

He stares at me, unwilling to clarify what he meant, and the red smoke clouds my vision as my fist charges into the air, cracking through his jaw. I climb on top, taking out my rage I was desperately trying to curb and unleash it on the person I once called my family. Lifting him by his collar, I ram him back onto the wharf, hitting his head, the blood trickling from the wound.

He coughs, the red liquid spraying onto my shirt as he pushes me off. He gets to his feet, wiping the blood from his mouth with the back of his hand. "Don't act like you haven't done some heinous things in your life, too!"

"I would never—"

"That's the difference between us, brother. I would go to the ends of the fucking earth to save my family."

"By signing their lives over to the devil!?"

"Better the devil you know than the one you don't."

CHAPTER TWENTY-TWO
Nera

Whispers of a Broken Empire.

I haven't slept. Not a wink since Dante told me what my future has in store for me. I stand here, staring at the suitcase on my bed, my phone beside it, and I wonder how I can possibly stop this from happening. Every scenario I put together in my mind ends with me dead or imprisoned by a signature on paper. I close my eyes to take a breath, the exhaustion now taking over as I steady myself on my dresser.

What the fuck am I going to do?

I won't go through with it. I'll pack my things and leave. That's what's going to happen. Impulsively, I open my purse and count the cash I brought with me from the nights I spent at the strip club.

Eight thousand.

That'd be enough to get me off Falcon's Keep and into another country. I'll be fine as long as I find a cash-paying job and stay hidden.

I shake my head at the stupid thought.

Who are you kidding, Nera? They'll find you.

I take a shower to calm my nerves and change into a cotton black dress. Gathering my hair, I tie it high on the crown of my head, the strands still wet. The obvious darkness beneath my eyes does nothing to hide my exhaustion and I don't care enough to cover them with makeup.

My phone lights up as it beeps, the floorboards creaking as I pad over to pick it up.

DANTE

Need to speak with you.

My grip tightens around my phone and I shove it into the pocket of my dress. The prick thinks he can order me around after telling me he basically signed me over to the Lucchese family? I scoff, ramming my clothes into my suitcase. I haven't completely dismissed the idea of running, so I'm preparing a contingency plan in case the one I'm currently carrying out doesn't work. Stuffing the money into the side of the suitcase, I cover it with a toiletries bag, then close the suitcase and zip it up.

There's a knock on my door as I hide the suitcase in my wardrobe and I step out right before my door flies open.

"*Venite subito! Dante sta sanguinando.*" My mother charges into my room, her hands flailing beside her face.

"*Mamma, calmati per favore.*" I try my best to calm her, but she grabs my arm, pulling me out of my room, down the stairs and into the main foyer.

"*Sta per morire!*" She motions to the middle of the empty room, tears in her eyes as Dante opens the doors to his office, hearing the commotion. My heart breaks for her as she stands there, covering her mouth, clearly revisiting the memory of seeing my father on the floor.

"I'll take her," Dante says, stepping forward, but I stop him.

"No." I place my hands on her shoulders and look into

her eyes. "*Mamma, Papà non c'è più. Se n'è andato da anni.*" I explain to her that *Papà* is no longer with us, and hasn't been for years, and she wraps her arms around herself, the tears flowing freely down her cheeks.

"*Mi manca...*" she whispers, and I hug her tight, wishing I could take away all her pain. Gently, I take her hands and guide her up the stairs, back into her room.

There's always one thing I fear more than dying, and that's forgetting who I am and the life I've lived. There's nothing crueller than nature deciding your memories are not worthy, and wiping them out entirely. Only allowing you to access them once or twice each year.

After a few minutes of calming my mother down, I convince her to read the book on her table, the same one my father bought her for their anniversary. The first edition of *Romeo and Juliet*. She's probably read this a thousand times, but she doesn't remember, so each time she reads it again, she experiences it for the first time. Even before her memory loss, it was her favourite tragedy.

Dante's presence looms into the room and when I look up at him, I know I'm going to regret stepping out of my mother's room. He leaves, waiting for me outside and I place a soft kiss on my mother's cheek. "*Ti voglio bene, Mamma.*"

Closing the door, I try to move past Dante and avoid whatever the hell he has to say when he grabs me by my wrist. "Frances will be waiting for you in the greenhouse tonight. He's requested to have dinner with you."

"Do you really think this is going to work?" I tear my wrist from his hold and face him. "He's a killer and a madman."

"And you think we aren't?" he questions, towering over me. "You think we got here by exchanging pleasantries and donating to charity?" He shoulders past me and pauses before the staircase. "It's your turn to pull your weight for the safety and security of this family, Nera."

The portable crates that were in the middle of the greenhouse are now pushed to the side, freeing up space for the table and chairs now neatly placed in the centre. Two candles, plates, cutlery, and glasses on top. My stomach churns as I take a seat, staring at the two muscled men standing by the door.

Frances clears his throat, setting his phone on the table, smiling as he pours me a glass of red wine.

"This isn't a hostage situation." I move my hair behind me, glancing from him to the men at the door. "Are you afraid of having dinner without protection?"

He waves at the men and they leave. "I've seen a lot of things in my life, Nera." He begins pouring himself a glass of wine. "I've met a lot of people in my line of work. Some of them happy to go about life without ever experiencing more than their backyard, others thirsting at the opportunity of a sliver of wealth or power. But none quite like you."

I roll my eyes and lean back in my chair. "Is this the part where you tell me I'm not like the others?"

He smiles, bringing the wine glass to his lips. "You tell me. Do you want any of those things?"

"Power and wealth come with more baggage than I'm prepared to be burdened with. Especially when it's given by someone like you." I do my worst, because what else is left besides my pride? If I can make him hurt, I will.

He chuckles, unmoved by my insult and takes a sip. "Do you know why I asked for you?"

I stiffen in my chair, waiting for his next words as he fixes the cuffs on his suit.

"Because you just can't stand seeing my family happy?"

"No, Nera, because your father owes me."

My brows furrow. "I thought that debt was settled."

"The souls we send here are not the settlement. That was the price of our agreement, to let your father keep Falcon's Keep afloat." He takes another sip and places the glass on the table, resting his hands in his lap. "The price to settle was you."

Bile rises to the base of my throat as my whole life as I knew it is being unravelled in front of me. Everything filled with lies and deceit.

"I'll never love you," I say through gritted teeth, wrapping my hand around the handle of the knife at the table.

"I'm not after love, Nera. All I want from you is your cooperation."

"And what if I don't give it?"

He sighs, pulling out his phone and placing it in front of me. The blood rushes to my head at the sight of my two brothers tied up with guns pointed at their heads.

"Nino and Santi," I whisper. "You've had them this entire time."

"Welcome to the real world, Nera. As long as you do as I say, I won't harm them."

"You're a fucking liar. The minute you get what you want, you'll kill them."

His laugh bellows inside the greenhouse. "I like you. You're smart and admittedly a great judge of character."

"I'll make you a deal…" He stands, placing his hands

in his pockets and steps behind my chair to lean into my ear. "Marry me, and I'll only hurt them a little."

I pause, considering my moves like a chess game, and he has me cornered. No matter what I do, he has me checked.

"What are your terms?"

He waves one of the men over who reaches into his breast pocket to pull out a thick yellow envelope, then walks out.

"Everything is written down in plain black and white. You have a week to decide how you want to proceed."

CHAPTER TWENTY-THREE
Rafael

Jealousy.

The sky is dark and so are the thoughts inside my head as I watch him lean over her, so close to her skin. The same skin I was kissing not long ago. Needles prick my face at the thought of him touching her and I have to hold myself back from barging in there and making him lick his own blood off the floor. He hands her an envelope as I suck in a breath of smoke. It's my third one in fifteen minutes and as soon as this one's finished, I'll light another.

My entire world has been thrown into a pit of nothing. I thought I knew how my life would go. I thought I'd at least have something to hold onto, something that was mine. I'm not delusional, I knew in my heart no one could love me—the *true* me. How could anyone want someone whose own family didn't want him?

But I thought at least one thing would be mine. Maybe, just maybe, I could hold onto Falcon's Keep with the Della Torres and claim a small portion of that for myself. But as I stare at the raven-haired woman, curling her fingers around a knife, I know none of this could be mine because she is the only thing I am prepared to fight for.

She is the only one I want.

You wonder what it would be like, to live in someone else's skin, to be them for a day, a week, a month. At times, I wanted to erase my entire existence from this world, to become someone else. To know what it might feel like to be loved and cared for by a mother.

Angrily, I swipe the lone tear from my cheek, the truth too harsh to admit to myself. I watch Frances leave, his men following closely behind him, leaving Nera alone.

Why would she pick me, when she has the most dangerous and powerful man asking for her hand? Why would she want a man who hates himself more than he hates the world?

Squashing the cigarette beneath my boot, I head toward the greenhouse, thinking about what I'm going to say to her and all that comes to my mind is that I love her.

Dammit, Nera, I love you so fucking much. Your tenacity, your pure heart and soul, everything from your sour attitude to your bratty little mouth. I don't think I'll ever be the same without you.

How can I say these words to her? I can't.

My heart is yanked from my chest when I walk in to see her wiping tears from her face and my first instinct is to saw into Frances's stomach to claw his intestines out and wrap them around his neck.

"Nera?" My voice is low as I kneel before her, softly placing her hand in mine.

She sobs, lifting her head to face me, her eyes now red from the countless tears she's shed. The sight of her like this revives the soulless demon in me as I reach behind me and pull out my gun. I'm about to walk out when she stops me, her hand curling around my wrist as she stands before me.

"Don't," she warns, the laughter and light in her eyes

now dimmed so low I can barely see it. My grip on the gun loosens and she takes it, placing it on the table.

"I have to kill him." I try to explain, that I need to leave and kill the entire Lucchese family, but she won't allow it.

"They'll kill you before you even get the chance at a clear shot."

She places her palm onto my chest and everything within me wants to take her away. Far from here, to a place where only she and I exist.

"I need you to kiss me," she whispers, another stray tear trailing down her cheek and disappearing between her lips. "Please." Her chin wobbles as I grip the base of her neck, pulling her mouth to mine.

She tastes like the dark ocean, chaotic, wild and free. Her hands roam my chest, then reach around my neck as she hoists herself into my arms.

"You said you didn't want this." I don't know why I say it, because I want her—no, I *need* her.

"I know what I said." She palms my cheek and stares into my soul. "Until the day comes when I'm no longer a Della Torre, I want to be yours."

It's different, the way she kisses me. Tender and passionate like she wants to savour the moment. Running my fingers through her midnight hair, I grasp it at the base as I knock over the table with my foot.

"You belong with me, *Principessa.*" I walk her over to the glass and place her on her feet. Her hand slithers down between us to my cock, palming it. "Let me take care of you."

She gives me a broken smile after undoing my pants and pulling my cock out of my briefs. "I can't be saved, Raf." She strokes me from base to tip, my cock growing in her hand until I'm fully erect, a painful reminder that she's the only one who can make me feel this way.

"Make love to me," she murmurs onto my lips, then removes her dress, her round breasts sitting perfectly in her bra. "I don't want to die without experiencing what it's like to be loved," she sobs, covering her mouth.

I wrap my arms around her and pull her into me. "We're going to be okay," I whisper against the strands of her silky hair and plant a chaste kiss on her head. I don't know how I'm going to keep that promise, but I will work it out. I don't know everything that's going on, but before the week is done, I will have answers. I don't care if I have to cross the one person I have called a brother.

Lifting her chin, I taste the tears on her lips as I snake my hand around her to undo her bra, the strapless material falling to the ground. The soft glow of the moon casts its gentle light upon us, illuminating the rest of Falcon's Keep as I gaze over her shoulder at the island—once my saviour from a dark past, now the very place that will seal my fate.

TWELVE YEARS EARLIER

They will all feel my pain. One way or another, I will make it happen. I don't care whose head I have to bash in to get what I want, I'll do it. The pain in my side is a constant reminder of the hurt and betrayal, and it'll be the same for them. I'll make certain of it.

The bandage around my waist is gone, but I still feel it there. Every fucking night, like a phantom. I had it on for a long time. It almost became a part of me. Now the only thing remaining is a thick, ugly scar on my skin, red and angry.

"You better not be exerting yourself," Dante warns as his heavy footsteps sound on the stairs.

Pushing myself off the floor, I take a look in the mirror. I've lost some muscle mass. Given the long recovery period, I know it was expected, but I hate it. I feel weak, unable to take my revenge on the people who deserve it the most.

Sighing, Dante enters my room and plops himself on my bed. We're almost the same age and after spending a few months with him on the island, he's become my closest confidant.

"I know you've been through some shit, Raf, and I know you don't want to talk about it to anyone, but I want to tell you that no matter what happens, I've got your back."

We spent every minute of my recovery playing cards, and chess, and discussing the endless books Dante Senior tasked us to read. I can tell he means what he says because unlike me, he doesn't lie. He'd much rather hurt your feelings than hide the truth and I admire him for it.

"Don't tell me you spend a minute with your mother and sister and you've gone all sappy on me," I jest, wiping the sweat from my forehead as he makes a face and extends his leg in an attempt to kick me.

"You know what I mean."

I nod and throw on a shirt, covering the hideous scar as Nino and Santi appear at my door.

"*Papà* is looking for you," Santi says to Dante, throwing him a basketball, which looks to be as old as him. Santi is lean, as tall as me, and if he ate a proper meal, he'd probably be as big as me.

Dante raises his eyebrows and walks out as Santi makes his way to the corner of my room to look out the window. "Always fucking raining." He sighs and takes a seat on the stool by my bookshelves. "So, what are you planning to do?"

"Are we coming with you?" Nino asks, his smile widening to his ears at the possibility of violence.

"No." I cut it short because there isn't a chance I'm taking innocents into a fucking war that I started. "You're both staying here."

"Oh, come on, man, you promised us!" Nino leans against the doorframe, crossing his arms, his long dark hair resting just above his shoulders.

"I didn't promise shit." I snatch my book out of Santi's hands. "Your *papà* would kill me if I took you along."

"He doesn't have to know." Santi smiles, pulling out a toothpick from his pocket and placing it in his mouth. "I have a good relationship with Giuseppe. I can make it happen."

"No."

Placing the book back on the shelf, I feel a twinge in my side and I wince, covering my scar with my hand.

"Fuck, is it not healed yet?" Nino asks from the doorframe as I take a seat on my bed.

The doctor who was seeing me on the island said it was the scar tissue, still healing.

"Guess not."

"What was it like?" Santi asks, obviously wanting details on the event. "We never asked before because we thought it'd be too painful for you to share or talk about, but is he everything he's revered to be?"

I don't want to answer his question because Enzo is the biggest piece of shit I've ever met and to say that to their faces when I know their father still has a deal with him is the last thing I want to do. Dante Senior saved my life, and I owe him some self-restraint.

"I think I heard Dante calling for you both."

Without lifting my gaze, I stand and lean against the dresser, their boots softly padding on the floor as they slip quietly from my room. I know Nino and Santi mean well. They want to get to know me on a personal level like I've begun to know Dante. I just don't think they'll like what they find.

Would anyone?

Would I ever meet someone who'd love me for me or am I destined to be alone?

Fated to fight alongside Dante as he marries to keep Falcon's Keep afloat, just another brute muscled enforcer to keep him safe from harm.

The thought makes me shiver.

I've been alone most of my life, so it's not like I know what I'm missing, but I can't help wondering what it'd be like to be loved by someone so fearlessly that even in the darkest depths of the ocean, they'd choose you. Even after seeing the blackest parts of your soul, they'd still want you.

I stare at my reflection in the small mirror on the wall and make myself a promise that if I ever encounter a love like this, I'll fight for it.

Until death.

CHAPTER TWENTY-FOUR
Nera

Unspoken Goodbyes & Deafening Regrets.

PRESENT

His grey eyes are filled with chaos and passion as he stares down at me. His lips move as if he wants to say something but he can't. He holds himself back from me and I hate it.

"Just say it," I whisper, gripping onto his arm. "Tell me."

"I can't." He looks away, avoiding the pain he knows we're both going to endure.

"Then show me."

Without another word, he spins me around, pressing me against the glass as he leans into my ear, his hands wandering down to my hips.

"I can't say it because you don't believe it," he says into my ear, his warm breath fanning onto my neck as I part my legs and push my hips back into him. "But I'm going to show you that we belong with each other, *Principessa.*"

Slipping his fingers beneath the material of my panties, he loops them and tugs, the cloth falling to the floor. As he snakes his hand around me and reaches my clit, he presses himself against me, his cock rubbing against my back, making me feverish for his touch.

"I—"

"Don't talk," he commands, slipping a finger inside me. "I want your body to do the talking."

I do as he asks, parting my legs a little more to give him access. He slides another finger in, eliciting a moan from me, my breath fogging up the glass. I don't want him to stop touching me, knowing that my body only comes alive with his touch.

If I'm sick, I don't ever want to get better. I want to stay like this until the end of time…Until the world stops turning and the fire inside the sun dies because that's what it'll take for me to stop loving him.

"Does he make you feel like this?" he asks, slipping his fingers out and coating my pussy in my arousal.

I stay quiet, wishing the throbbing between my legs would ease up just enough for me to hear my thoughts, but it doesn't.

"When you look at him, I want you to think of me." He presses the tip of his cock inside me as I hold my breath. "I want you to feel every inch of me inside you, imprinted in your mind like a song you sing on repeat, over and over again."

He pushes in further, stretching me as I back up into him, pressing myself onto him, needy and desperate. He threads his arm through my elbows and pulls back, gripping my upper arm as he fills me up completely.

"I don't ever want you to forget this feeling. Your nipples hard, pressed up against the glass," he groans. "Holding your breath as you wait for me to fuck you because you know no one else can give you what you want but me."

I take in a breath, finally breaking the spell as he thrusts into me hard, pushing my cheek into the glass.

"You will never belong to anyone else."

Thrust.

"Because Falcon's Keep is ours, *Principessa.*"

Thrust.

"I'll never let him have you."

I moan as he takes me against the glass. Gliding his hand up my stomach, his calloused fingers are rough and hard as he grasps my breast.

"I won't say those three words you're waiting for…" The head of his cock rubs against the one place that makes me see the galaxy. "Not until you're ready to hear them."

I can feel the pressure building up inside me as he slips his hand between my legs, pressing two fingers against my clit, and I buck against it, the sensation becoming too strong. My body rides the wave as he fills me up with his cum.

We stand here panting, with his cock still inside me as I lean back into his embrace. Tonight may not be the first night where I've wondered if there was something wrong with me, but it is the first one where I know I'm in the arms of someone who would die for me.

The paper weighs heavy in my hand as I stare at the crumpled edges of the yellow envelope, the creases a stark reminder of what's going to become of Falcon's Keep if I sign the agreement. I don't know what else to do. I'm cornered and caught like a deer in headlights. There's only one way everyone I love gets out alive and it's if I play my part, keeping everyone safe from the monster by becoming his wife.

It's ironic, the deal my father made to keep Falcon's Keep afloat even after his death. By burdening his children just like he was when he was alive.

Wouldn't he want a better life for us?

Wouldn't he want us to be free of this life?

My grip tightens on the envelope as I stomp out of my room and head to Dante's office. It's been the same ever since the revelry. He shuts himself in there day in and day out, smoking, probably hoping his lungs will collapse.

I don't bother knocking as I enter, slapping the documents on his desk. His gaze remains on the oak, not having the balls to face me.

"Is it done?" he asks, taking another drag of his cigar.

"Did you know he had Nino and Santi?"

He remains still, and then his eyes burn through mine, confirming everything I already knew.

"And you said *nothing*," I whisper as my heart shatters at the betrayal and lies from my own blood.

I trust my brothers with my life, as I have done the entire time I've been alive…like my father told me to, but now, that trust is buried beneath the deception.

"It was the only way to save Falcon's Keep."

"To save the island, or to save the Della Torre name?" I scoff, shaking my head at his excuse.

"Nera—"

"Don't."

"I can fix this…" He tries to placate me, but I know better now than to trust what comes out of his mouth. "Marry him, and I'll share my plan with you."

"I can't trust you, Dante."

Visible hurt flashes in his eyes and he looks away, his

jaw clenching rapidly. A beat passes before he speaks again. "When *Papà* told me about the plan, I was against it."

I purse my lips, unsure if I want to hear what he has to say.

"I told him to undo it…I begged him to dig us out of the hole he dug." He leans against his desk with his elbows, placing his head in his hands, and his voice shakes. "I never wanted this fate for you, Nera."

Tears begin to form, but I fight them back as I swallow the lump in my throat.

"If there was something else I could do, I promise you I would have done it in a heartbeat." When he looks up at me, there are unshed tears in his eyes as he silently pleads for me to believe him. "I have no choice," he whispers, his voice barely audible, the words laced with a quiet desperation. "If we remain here under their control, we will never get to live a proper life. If we have him backing our move to the mainland, we can put this island behind us." His chin trembles and a single tear breaks free, trailing down his cheek as the image of my big brother—so tall, so strong—shatters before my eyes, crumbling into something unrecognizable.

The silence is piercing as the skin on his hands blanches from his grip. I pace around the desk and place my hand on his.

"No more lies."

He stands and wraps his arms around me, the crushing hug a desperate plea to keep me close and maybe an unspoken goodbye.

"No more lies," he echoes my words, a promise I hope he keeps because if we are to make it out alive, we need to be able to trust each other.

I lean against the desk as he wipes a tear from his

cheek, fidgeting with his rings as he contemplates what to say next.

"Did Rafael know?" I ask, my heart almost skipping a beat at the anticipation of his answer.

His brows furrow, wondering what this has to do with him. "No."

I nod, relieved as I take out the stack of papers from the envelope and hand them to Dante.

"His terms."

He flicks through the pages until he comes to the section of terms clearly listed in bullet form, and the remorse in his eyes is replaced with rage. I flinch as he swipes the top of his desk clean, the items clattering onto the floor.

He points to the papers now in a bunch. "This is *not* what I agreed to."

"It's done. He wants the wedding in a week, and I've already signed it."

"Fuck," he breathes in disbelief.

I feel numb as I gather the papers off the floor, the words on the pages blurring as tears fill my vision. Handing them to Dante, I walk out without another word.

CHAPTER TWENTY-FIVE
Rafael

Between Saving & Letting Go.

I'm stuck.

In limbo, like a ship in the sea, fighting the waves until the boards beneath me rot and give way. The endless blue swallowing me whole, the pressure collapsing my lungs and decomposing my body agonisingly slow.

How are you meant to find a sense of belonging when your parents were never meant to create you?

The thoughts that have plagued me for years continue to eat at my black heart, withering it down day by day. My brothers, the Casellas and the Guerras, never once had to worry about the things I did and I envy them for it. Not having to concern themselves with when their next meal would be, or if one day, those who held them captive would call on them to slaughter on their behalf.

It wasn't until I met Dante that I saw what it was like to be part of a family.

He saw me.

He took me in and raised me like a son amongst his own.

What better way to thank him when he's six feet under than by lusting over his twenty-three-year-old daughter?

Except it isn't lust anymore. It's turned into something

I cannot explain. Something I've never felt before. It's all-consuming and anxiety-inducing, like if I'm not with her, the delicate organ inside my chest will suddenly stop or spontaneously combust.

I always imagined what it would feel like to be in love, but I could have never thought it would feel like this. Wrong and right all at the same time and fucking confusing.

Is this the way it's meant to be?

I don't know.

All I know is I love her.

I've searched for her all over the island. The greenhouse, the mausoleum, the waterfall, and she's nowhere to be seen. Not knowing where she is makes me irrational.

Footsteps sound, getting louder as they get closer, and I don't bother to look up to see who it is because no one besides her is my concern anymore.

"It's going to storm tonight," Dante speaks over the waves.

The grey clouds smother the light from the sun, like a warning of imminent danger. I used to love the stormy nights. It helped me sleep. Now, all it does is make me think.

About her.

The way her brows crease as she comes for me.

The way her curves feel beneath my hands and the way she says my name.

Everything about Falcon's Keep reminds me of her and I hate that I can't escape it even in the place that saved me from me. Now she's the only thing that can stop me from burning it all down.

The crutch of it all is that I'm never going to get the

girl. I'm not the person she thinks I am. I'm not the hero. I won't sacrifice her for the greater good. I'd rather shatter the sands of time and live this life in an endless loop than save the world from its own Groundhog Day, because my version is simply her—and to me, that's heaven.

"What was the deal you made for Enzo's life?"

I know he won't confess to it, but if there is a chance for me to save this brotherhood between us, I owe his father to try.

He takes a seat beside me, twisting the large ring on his index finger, the one passed down from his father, the symbol of their family's crest engraved on it.

"I did that for you."

I shake my head. "I didn't ask you to."

He sighs, his dark hair slick back, unmoving even as the wind picks up speed. "I know. I thought it was the one thing I could do for you after everything you did for my father and my family."

"I never did any of those things without the want inside my heart."

He nods, the notch in his throat bobbing up and down as he swallows. "And that's why I'm struggling, Raf. I hate that I haven't been honest with you."

"Then start."

"If I shared everything with you, you'd try to stop it."

I clench my jaw, my mind going to places I don't want it to. "We don't do this, Dante. We don't get into bed with the ones who bring the heat. Even your father knew this. He's the one who put distance between us."

"I had no choice!" His tone is veiled with frustration.

A beat passes before either of us speaks.

"I'm sick of it…of being pushed around and them forcing my hand at every turn—"

"And you think this is going to stop with the new deal you've made with him?"

He purses his lips, knowing I'm speaking the truth. "I'm cornered."

"With what!?" I run a hand through my hair, the irritation now setting in. "*Merda*! Just fucking tell me so I can help you."

"This is *my* problem and I'll fix it."

Raising my eyebrows, I shift my body to face him. "You'll fix it…" I chuckle and shake my head, pulling out a cigarette to calm myself. "The only thing you're doing is binding Falcon's Keep to the one person whose only goal is to dominate the criminal playground around the world." Lighting my cigarette, I take a drag and get to my feet. "I can't help if I don't know what's going on, and if you don't tell me soon, you might as well dig the graves yourself."

Sifting through this mountain of paperwork on Dante's desk is like looking for dust in a pile of sand. I don't know what I'm looking for, but I know I'm determined to find out about this fucking deal. I shuffle through a bunch of old photos, some of me and Dante, his brothers, and I pull out one of Nera. She must be ten or eleven in this photo, sitting with Dante Senior on a picnic blanket, watching the sunset beneath the large tree at the back of the property. His arm is draped around her, watching her closely as she smiles and points out to the horizon.

She deserves to be happy, Raf.

The *stronzo* voice inside my head attacks me when I'm already on the edge, and I push it aside, stuffing the photo into my pocket as I continue to dig through the desk drawer. Nothing in the top or the middle.

I yank at the bottom one.

Shit.

Locked.

If I know Dante, and I think I do, he wouldn't keep the key on himself because he's afraid of losing anything sentimental to him, so he keeps everything within reach. Everything has a home, and I don't doubt this key does also. And it's somewhere in this room.

The bookshelves are out of the question. He hasn't touched those books since we were teens. I cross my arms, thinking about where he might have stashed the key, when my eyes lock on his father's portrait hanging behind his desk.

Lifting the frame, I glide my hand between the wall and the frame when metal clatters to the floor. I stare at it, the voice in my head begging me to put it back.

No, we're past that. We are done with blinding loyalty.

Sliding the key into the hole, I take a breath and open the drawer to find a yellow envelope. My heart sinks as I pull out the thick papers, the words on the pages echoing through my mind as I read.

Marriage contract. Frances Lucchese and Nera Della Torre.

I grip the end of the table, unable to stop reading. Sweat beads at my temple as I flick through the pages, each word jabbing deeper into the already open wound, when I reach a page titled: *Terms and Conditions.*

1. Transfer of Ownership:

All parties hereby consent to the transfer of ownership of Falcon's Keep to

Frances Lucchese, granting full rights of its use for business and trade purposes,

with no financial consideration exchanged.

2. Severance of Ties:

All parties agree that Nera Della Torre shall sever all personal and professional associations with Falcon's Keep and the Della Torre family. Nera Della Torre further agrees to reside exclusively within the United States of America for the remainder of her life.

3. Forfeiture of Personal Rights:

All parties acknowledge that Nera Della Torre hereby irrevocably forfeits any and all personal rights, claims, and interests in Falcon's Keep to Frances Lucchese, with no further entitlement to ownership, control, or decision-making authority over the property or related matters.

4. Freedoms:

All parties acknowledge and agree that Nera Della Torre grants her full consent to comply with all requests made by Frances Lucchese, whether pertaining to business or personal matters, without limitation or reservation.

Over my dead fucking body.

Slamming the papers on the desk, I will my body to calm down but everything warps into a tunnel of red rage and opaque hate.

A roar tears apart my throat as I slam my fists onto the desk, knocking the objects onto the floor. Wasting no time, I fist the papers in my hand, denting the pages as I storm out of the office, down the stairs and out the door.

I've never felt this kind of rage before, not when I was left for dead in the sea, not when I found out my own blood had abandoned me, and not when I saw the one father figure I had in a pool of his own blood. If this is what Nera agreed to, and Dante allowed it to happen, I'll bury this island beneath the goddamn sea where it belongs before I stand by and watch her take his hand.

Do your worst, Frances, because I'm coming for you.

The Chill of the Thrill.

Lace, satin, silk, and other materials lay before me, sprawled out on the large round surface of the table in the dining room. The skin around my nails stings as I pick at it, tearing the thin paper-like skin, careful not to draw blood.

It's not about security or power. For me, it's never been either of those things. I lived in the States like a ghost. No one knew who I was, and I preferred it that way. Now, my signature on those papers changes everything about my future and what I thought it might look like. All that's left for me to do is accept it.

How can I when all I want is someone I can't be with?

"Miss Nera, this one would look great as the base," Olga says softly, picking up the ivory lace and laying it on top of the satin material. She arrived yesterday, at Frances's command, to help with preparations for the wedding. I want to hate her but her kind nature and understanding words have only brought us closer.

Scrunching my nose, I pick up both fabrics between my fingers. "Seems a little excessive." My eyes fall to the pure white silk on the table. "Maybe we go for something a little less…over-stated?"

She catches my gaze and smiles, picking up the material and laying a small part of it over my shoulder.

"What style are you thinking?"

Anything. I don't care. I don't want to marry him.

"I haven't decided yet."

My phone vibrates in my pocket, and I'm surprised it has reception. It's usually in and out because the signal is constantly choppy on the island. I expect it to be from Elodie, but I stare at Rafael's name on the screen. Hesitant to open it, my finger hovers over the message and with one tap, my heartbeat soars.

RAFAEL

Meet me where I first tasted you.

Shoving it back into my pocket, I consider his words, afraid that if I do meet him, it might set a precedent. I've never experienced something like what I have with Rafael before. It's like this energy surrounding me, lifting me, pushing me toward something unknown. It's terrifying and exhilarating all at the same time. It's not fair to me or to him to want this. It's shameful to even think about wanting it when both my brothers are locked up.

But I *do* want it.

I want it to be *him* that I walk down the aisle to. I want him to be the one kissing me, touching me…*fucking* me. I want it all to be him and nobody else.

"*Bella,* what do you think?" Olga's words pull me out of my thoughts and I nod. I didn't hear a word she said, but I'm sure whatever it was, it relates to my betrothal to Frances, and *that* I do not care about. I'm not sure I want to pursue a revenge tactic or scheme because with the power he holds, he would smell it coming from a mile away and kill everyone I love without blinking.

A loose cannon like him cannot be underestimated.

My phone vibrates again, but I don't want to check it because the more I think about Rafael, the easier it will be for me to give in to him. My hand betrays my thoughts as I stare at another message.

RAFAEL

Wear that black dress.

I do my best to hide the smile on my face as I turn to face the door. Olga tidies things up in the dining room, and I head upstairs to get changed into his favourite outfit. When I reach my closet, all I see is the same box he left for me before the revelry. Opening it, I hold the shoes in my hands.

I don't regret what I did.

Whether he deserved it or not, our fates do not meet at the end. That I know.

I shake my head and put them back into the box then rest my back on the wall as I stare at my phone beside me.

Picking it up, I type out a message.

ME

Let's not keep hurting each other.

The three dots appear as he types, then disappear and reappear again, my heart skipping along with the dots.

RAFAEL

Those that try to keep me away from you
will be the only ones who end up hurt,
Principessa.

ME

Just let it go, Raf. It's done.

RAFAEL

It'll never be done, not when I still breathe
the same air as you.

ME

I'm tired.

RAFAEL

Stop making up excuses as to why you
think it won't work. Meet me and I'll show
you exactly why you're wrong.

I think about it longer than I should because I already know I'm going to meet him. I shouldn't. I should fight it because if Frances were to catch us, he would turn Falcon's Keep upside down and we'd all be buried beneath it.

The dress is like a soft hug, hanging over my hips and dropping to just above the curve of my lower back. I know why he likes it. He thinks it makes me look fearless and unstoppable, but he couldn't be further from the truth. I'm none of those things.

Slipping my shoes on, I curse myself for giving in because I know how badly it can end.

No, how it *will* end.

I'm lost in my thoughts as I leave the manor, careful to make sure I'm not being followed as the day turns into night. When I make it to the building, the gates are open, almost inviting as they rest upon the brick building. I take a deep breath and straighten my dress as I step in through the double doors. I take in the room, a silver table in the middle, freezer drawers on the left, and medical equipment lined up on a tray at the back. Its instantly cooler in here, the temperature raising the hairs on the back of my neck.

"Raf?"

The wind rustles the trees outside and I jump as the

door thuds closed, strong arms curling around my chest, and cool steel pressing against my throat.

"You thought I wouldn't find out?" His breathing is ragged as he presses the front of my thighs against the steel table, jolting the locked wheels from the force.

"W—"

"Shhh…" Leather clamps over my mouth as I struggle beneath his hold. The sting of the steel on my neck turns into a burn as warmth trickles down between my breasts. He forces his thickness against the curve of my back, pushing me down onto the cool steel table.

Terrified, my thoughts become a haze as I lock my fingers around the table.

"Tell me, *Principessa*…"

Instantly, with the use of his favourite pet name for me, my body relaxes.

"Do you really not have any faith in me?"

A yellow envelope thumps onto the table next to my face and I know why he's angry.

"Let me explain."

He whirls me around, the steel of his eyes wild and filled with rage. "Explain how you signed your life and your *body* to someone like *him*!?"

"I had to," I whisper, the reminder of every detail listed in the contract seared into my brain.

"*Fanculo!*" His fists come down hard beside my face, rattling the table and my chest thumps wildly out of control. "I'll kill him."

"No." I revel in the prickly texture of his beard as I run my fingers through the hair. "You need to stay out of it."

"How can you ask this of me?"

"The same way you want to save me from it."

"Nera…" His cross dangles in front of me, and I grab hold of it to pull him closer.

"You know there's not much you can do. So just let it go."

"*Perché?* Because you've started to get a taste of his life?"

His words sting, the venom in them threading through every inch of me he's previously kissed. I shove him off with all my might and he stumbles, shifting from one leg to another.

He's been drinking.

Fury burns inside me as I take a step toward him.

"He has Nino and Santi!" I yell, hoping my words make it through to him. "If I don't marry him, my brothers are dead!"

He shakes his head and stares at the floor, unwilling to believe anything I'm saying.

"I'll get them back."

"How!? We have no one to back us. Not the Casellas, not the Brayfords…The fucking Guerras are now with them, too. Who do we have left, Raf!?"

His jaw tics, knowing I'm right. When my father died, so did all our ties. My brother tried to make things right, to reach out and make alliances, but no one wanted to work with him because of who our father was.

"Don't stand there and pretend you can make this right or save me from anything because no one can. No one but me."

His hand curls around my throat, ramming me back down onto the table.

"You don't get to decide who your body belongs to, *Principessa.*" His hold tightens, the blood rushing through to my eyes as I claw at his hand. "You gave that to me when you let me fuck you over your father's tomb."

When he loosens his hold, I choke on air as I pull it into my lungs, my vision pulsing as I work to regain composure. The skin around my wrist prickles as something is fastened around it, then the other follows before he's standing at my feet, separating them and fastening them to the table.

"If you're so adamant on marrying him, let me show you that you're a liar."

I pull at the restraints, and they don't budge in the slightest. "Untie me."

He pulls out a large hunting knife, the black steel glinting in the harsh light of the room and I swallow at the sharp tip now running along my skin, up my thigh, and into my G-string. He severs the material, leaving me bare.

"Don't do this," I warn.

"Why?"

I rest my head on the table, my hands in fists as the cool metal slips through my middle, building a cold sweat on my skin.

"Because you're afraid you'll enjoy more depravity?"

The coldness of the knife disappears, and when I look up, I should feel fear, but instead, it's curiosity as I stare at him with a revolver in his hand. He opens the chamber, the bullets clattering to the ground as he places one back in and flicks it closed.

I purse my lips as he gently traces the barrel over the inside of my leg. "I'll make you admit it, *Principessa*…even if you don't want to."

"Untie me."

A smirk plays at the corner of his lips as he leans into me, the tip of the revolver dangerously close to my core.

"Your mouth says one thing, but your body begs for another."

I yelp as my dress is yanked open, my chest spilling out. A hot flush overcomes me as his mouth closes over my nipple, his tongue twirling and sucking. His teeth graze my skin, raising the hairs on my arms as he reaches my neck. My eyes bulge when the barrel fills my vision beside his face.

"Open."

When I hesitate, he pries my mouth open, stuffing the barrel inside and cocking the gun. Tears brim my eyes as terror builds inside me.

"Suck."

The sharp and bitter taste of the metal is all I can think about when the light touch of his hand trails down my body and in between my legs. My muscles tighten in anticipation of his next move as he slips his finger inside me.

"Do you need reminding of how to suck?" He forces the gun deeper into my throat and I gag, the tears spilling down my face.

I suck the cold barrel and work the gun in my throat.

"*Brava ragazza.*" He chuckles when I whimper, slipping in another finger as my arousal smothers his fingers.

"That's it…" he purrs as I continue to suck. "Make it nice and wet, ready for your desperate pussy."

His fingers are buried inside me, his knuckles working to massage the perfect spot. My hips move on their own, my body pleading for more of his touch.

My saliva drips over my chin and down my neck as he pushes further, the sounds of my choking echo through the room. Removing the piece, he waits for me to regain my breath as he inspects the gun, now glistening in the light.

I feel the loss immediately when he removes his fingers, but it's not for long.

"Now take a deep breath," he commands and I follow. The cool metal fills me up as I moan, expelling the air out of my lungs. "Tell me you're going to marry me."

I catch his stare—possessive, obsessed, and out of his mind.

"No?"

The gun clicks, sending a jolt through my entire system, and I yelp, the restraints tightening around my wrists at the rush.

"What the fuck!?" I breathe.

"Don't make me repeat myself."

"Who *are* you?"

"A man who will *never* let someone else have what's mine."

His words should terrify me. I can feel the intensity vibrating off him and through me as the gun clicks again, sending my mind into a tornado of spiralling thoughts. But all the thoughts are of him.

"Only four left, *Principessa.*"

"You'd kill me?" I ask, needing a reason for his madness as I fight the urge to rock my hips against the piece inside me.

"I'd follow you to the grave, Nera." He smiles, gripping my hair at the top of my head, his bourbon-filled breath strong and sweet. "Having you now isn't enough. I need to know you'll be mine."

"What then? We sail off into the sunset?"

The chamber of the gun enters me as he pushes deeper, stealing my breath.

"No. You're going to promise me you're mine, then you're going to come all over my gun..." He kisses the tears gliding down my cheek. "Then, I'm going to shove this gun so far down Frances's throat so he gets a taste of you before I pull the trigger. His last thought will be that he's never going to have you. You hear me?"

I can't focus on his words. My nipples harden as he works the gun inside me, the hardness of the pistol creating a deep hum within my body.

"No one can keep me from you. Not your brother, or the unforgiving waves crashing onto the shores of Falcon's Keep, and certainly not death."

I give in to everything—the moment, the heat, the possessiveness—and rock my hips into the gun, moaning with pleasure as his hand curls around my neck. I want to say everything he's asking of me, to tell him I don't want anyone else and that he already owns my heart and soul. But how can I tell him this and marry someone else?

"Please," I pant, unsure if I'm begging for him to give me more or to stop asking me to tell him I'll be his.

"I won't stop, Nera."

I rock my hips again and again, chasing the sweet release I'm desperately craving at the hands of the one person I've come to love.

It's twisted.

All of it.

One thing is certain. A heart that loves is a heart that bleeds, and mine is bleeding out for him.

The Announcement.

Why would the world be so cruel as to give me everything I ever wanted in someone I shouldn't be with? What kind of god allows their sons and daughters this suffering? I know loving her will only bring me death.

But I'm ready to die.

I'm ready to give it all up to be the one she loves.

Without her, I wouldn't taste the salt of the sea on my lips or see the green in the trees. Everything would remain in black and white.

I curse myself for letting her touch me and for knowing what her skin feels like beneath my hands. For a minute, I'm lost in the thought of what it would be like to spend a lifetime together, to grow old and watch our children run in the wind of Falcon's Keep. As my gaze lands on the thick envelope now on the floor, every bit of hope I had of living that dream fades.

"Raf…" Her beautiful voice surrounds me like a trance, snapping me back into the room.

"Are you ready to tell me what I want to hear, *Principessa?*"

My fingers are covered in her arousal as I continue to

work the pistol inside her, careful to keep my index finger from the trigger.

"I-I'm so close." She takes a deep breath, her eyes rolling into the back of her head as her collarbones rise from their resting place, her body shuddering around my gun. The sight of her coming undone, bound on the same table I almost bled out on, makes me tent my pants.

Leaning into her ear, I take in a breath of her luscious scent, my cock growing harder. "You hide like a sin, afraid if you revealed yourself, you'd be seen as dirty, weak, and unworthy."

Her chest rises and falls, whimpering as I remove the gun from her pussy and bring it up to my mouth. I taste her sweetness, groaning as I gather the traces of her lies from my gun. She watches me with hooded eyes, still working to come down from her high.

"Please, Raf," she whispers, gently tugging on the restraints.

"Tell me," I demand, my voice hard as I flick the safety back on and place the gun down on the bench behind me.

"How?" Her lip wobbles as tears gather in her eyes, one of them falling down the side of her face. "Please don't make me say something I know can never happen."

My jaw aches, the hurt in her voice waking the beast I've caged.

Her soft curls wring themselves into my fingers as I bring her face to mine. "Listen to me carefully, *Principessa*."

Another tear falls, the inferno inside me now as hot as how I imagine hell to be.

"I will find a way."

"Even if you do, Dante will *never* let it happen."

I swallow the razor blades and take her mouth with

mine. I can't hear another word about how the world is against it.

Against *us*.

I won't.

A frantic energy surrounds us, her lips tasting of frustration and longing. The kiss is rough, like we're trying to prove something to each other. Our breathing increases and I wish I could erase all her pain and torment.

I'm afraid the suffering is just the beginning of the hell we're about to endure.

"I need you," she whispers onto my lips, and I give in.

She looks the other way when I climb on top of her, and there's a sting right inside my gut. I want her, but I don't know how I can have her. It'll take a lot of guns, men, and betrayal to get what I want. I must be ready for it all.

The blowback from something like this will incinerate us all.

I place my hand on her wet cheek and pull her eyes back to mine. They're everything I could ever need in this life, filled with desire and mixed with stoic heartache. The world is on her shoulders and all I want to do is take the weight of it from her.

Tearing her dress with my knife, I watch it drop on either side of the table, baring her completely to me, just like I've done for her.

"Look at me."

She purses her lips, another tear riding its way down her already damp face. "I'm so sorry," she whispers, cutting her invisible knife deeper into my gut.

"No, *Principessa…*" I unbuckle my belt and unzip my pants to pull my cock out. "Never apologise when your hand was forced."

Her deep moans send shockwaves to my cock as I enter her and almost lose my mind.

"They will be the ones to apologise, right before they stare down the barrel of my gun."

I thrust deep into her, her warmth enveloping me, inviting me down a dark cave I'll be happy to never emerge from again.

The chains rattle against the table as she reaches for me, her head jerking back as I ram into her again and again. I watch her breasts bounce as she bites her lip, her hands curled into fists. I could watch her like this for the rest of my life. Just like I'd love to watch the world burn if I can't have her.

Grasping her soft curls at the top of her head, I hold her head up, her eyes hooded as she watches me enter her.

"Fuck," she breathes.

"You think anyone else could ever give you what I can?"

Snaking my hand to the restraint, I free one of her hands as I roll my hips into her. Freeing the other, she wraps them both around me, pulling me in closer to her.

We become one, moving in a rhythm we've found together, her beautiful, pleasure-filled sounds right beneath my ear.

"I love you," she whispers and it's all I've needed to hear. One second, I'm like a god, untouchable and omnipotent, until she takes it away in the next. "But I have to marry him."

Her eyes find mine and I decide against the harsh words that have sprung into my head. Instead, I make sure this moment is everything it can be.

Me and her.

"I promise this isn't it, *Principessa.*"

I move against her, thrusting into her again and again, the metal table shifting beneath our weight. Freeing both her ankles, she locks them around my waist and buries her face in my neck, her kisses making my cock harder than ever.

"Nera."

She moans, kissing her way to my lips, the last tear cascading over her cheek as she whispers, "I love the way you say my name." She gives me a small smile as I hold myself back from bursting inside her. "Say it again."

"Nera," I drawl as her soft lips rest on mine, her pussy clenching around me. Her eyes roll back into her head with a smile on her face. My cock pulses inside her and I groan, filling her up as she caresses the stubble on my face.

"It will always be you," she murmurs against my lips, sending my mind back into a frenzy over how I'm going to get her out of this mess.

Helping her off the table, I give her my dress shirt and she buttons it up, the ends falling to her knees. Her midnight hair tumbles down her shoulders and past her breasts as she stands in the heels I gifted her.

"Don't come to the wedding."

"There won't be one." I stuff myself back into my pants and she looks around the room.

"Will you tell me what really happens here?"

I hesitate for a moment, unsure if I should share it with her, but decide to anyway. I just hope she doesn't judge me for it.

"Where should I start?"

She steps into me, placing her hands on my chest and I know I'm not leaving Falcon's Keep because I'll either be with her or I'll be buried here for trying.

"Nothing good has happened here since your father made a deal with the Lucchese family."

Threading my hands with hers, she looks up at me, ready for the truth.

"We ferry the lost souls here to either break them or kill them."

She looks to the freezer drawers. "Why do you have those?"

"In case their families pay their debts. Then they get their body shipped back to them."

"And what happens if they don't?"

I swallow, looking away, not wanting to expose her to this side of Falcon's Keep, but I fear she's already seen more than she's bargained for.

"I gut them. On this very table. Dismember them and dispose of them on the other side of the island."

She pauses, eyes wide, clearly not expecting what she's just heard, and I wait for her response. I check over her face for an insight into her thoughts, but she gives nothing away.

"What does Frances give us?"

"Protection and financial aid to work off a debt. A lifetime of servitude for a stupid fucking thing I did when I was young, angry, and impulsive."

"But my father was already indebted to Frances before he met you…"

"No, he wasn't. He cleared that and set up here to get you all away from it. He fucked it all up by taking me in. I stole from Enzo. A possession that belonged to the Lucchese family."

"What was it?"

I smile, remembering the first time I held the Fabergé

egg in my hands. Something small and seemingly insignificant that could feed most of Italy's homeless.

"A Fabergé egg."

Her eyes widen and I explain exactly what I had to do to get it, how close I came to losing my life to prove a stupid fucking point.

"I get it…why you feel like you're indebted to my family."

"No, Nera, I am. Your father didn't have to help me. He could have handed me to Frances, but instead, he made a deal so everyone could keep their lives. That's when I promised I'd give Falcon's Keep all of me. Blood, sweat, tears, and everything in between."

She gives me a small smile and weaves her arms around my neck as she rises on her toes.

"I release you, Raf. You no longer need to be tied to Falcon's Keep if you don't want to be."

I hold her closer to me, my lips tracing hers. "You can release me from Falcon's Keep, but I'll forever be tied to you, *Principessa*."

The house bustles with activity. Multiple people run around as I lie on my bed, staring at the ceiling. I've never once felt this powerless in my life. I consider the choices I have and I can count them on one hand. Either way, this is going to turn into a bloodbath. I just have to decide how to reinject the blood that's been poured back into Falcon's Keep so we don't bleed out.

There's a shuffle at my door, then a shadow disappears as I notice an envelope on the floor that's been slid into my room. It's emerald green, my favourite colour. The words on the front are enough to explain the contents, so I don't open it.

You're invited…

Throwing the envelope onto the dresser, I dig out my phone and scroll through my contact list. All ten of them, until my thumb hovers over the one name I swore I'd never contact again.

Erhan Kara.

I take a breath and hit call.

There's a long dial tone before he answers.

"Never thought I'd see your name again." The other end of the line is quiet as he waits for my response.

"I wouldn't be calling if there wasn't something in it for you."

"I'm listening."

"I need your cavalry. Might also need your doctor."

His chuckle is deep. I have second thoughts about involving Erhan, but the only other person who can take on Frances is someone who isn't afraid of dying. Someone who has governments in his pocket and on speed dial.

"I'm sure Dante has his own doctors for your fever."

"It's the black plague and Dante is dead."

I swear I hear him smile with his response. "When?"

"Two days."

The line clicks followed by beeping when he hangs up. I stare at the screen, hoping I made the right choice, then dial Darcy's number.

She answers after a few rings.

"Raf! Hope you're calling me to tell me something good."

It's so nice to hear her voice. The sister I sometimes wish she was by blood.

"I just called to say thank you."

She laughs at something Nicholas says. "What? I didn't catch that."

"Take care of yourself, Darcy."

Hanging up, I shove the phone back into my pocket after switching it off.

Let's go to war.

CHAPTER TWENTY-EIGHT
Rafael

The Wounds Within.

My cigarette hangs from my lips as I take in the early morning sunrise, her silhouette bathed in the orange and yellow glow as she slips out of the water. She's been keeping her distance from me. Hasn't responded to any of my texts or calls, constantly keeping herself in others' company so I won't approach her.

I don't mind watching her for now, waiting until the moment is right for me to take her for myself.

Her slick hair sticks to her back as she stands in the water, staring out into the sunrise, and all I can see is me and her exactly like this, every single day of our lives. Putting my cigarette out, I make my way to her, the sand soft beneath my feet. The water is ice cold as I step in, sending a chill down my spine as it passes my waist.

When she turns to face me, every single worry about the future fades because I see it right here in front of me.

It's her.

She wanted to set me free, to shed my ties with Falcon's Keep and to her family, but the truth is, the wounds of Falcon's Keep run deeper than a knife ever could. I'll never forget everything I've done here. The lives I've taken, the promises I've made, and the days I've spent with the Della Torres.

"Old habits," I whisper, taking her into my arms as she wraps herself around me.

"I think it's the most refreshing thing to do to start your day. Someone even told me it was healing."

I smile at her words, remembering our conversation at this very beach.

"Salt water is also extremely corrosive."

She takes my lips feverishly, holding onto me like she's going to lose me, and I give her every deep stroke of my tongue to remind her I'm not going anywhere.

"Not as corrosive as this disease that's taken my family hostage."

She places her forehead on mine, water from her lips falling onto mine.

"I miss you," she whispers.

"*Principessa…*" I drawl. "I'm not going anywhere."

Holding onto me tighter, she lifts her head, fear in her tone as she whispers, "And that's what I'm afraid of."

She sniffles, tracing her fingers over my brows, the water from her hand running down my chest. "I'm scared, Raf."

I close my eyes, willing my heart to find its regular beat again as she expresses her fear, but all I want to do is take it from her and bury it deep beneath the abyss of the sea.

"I promise, you won't be marrying him," I whisper onto her lips, trying to comfort her with my words as the sun continues to rise, shining new hope onto the island. She doesn't know I'm prepared to turn the world upside down to have her, even for five minutes before we enter the earth together. I wasn't lying…I'd follow her to the grave.

And if the world doesn't want to see us together, then maybe we could create our own world in another life.

"We have rehearsals today," she breathes, running her fingers through my hair as my cock begins to rise at the sight of water entering the cavity of her breasts. "I don't want you there."

"I'll be there. Front row, *Principessa*."

She releases me and stands, twirling her hands into mine in the water. "Don't do that to yourself, please."

I chuckle, appreciative of the hurt she's trying to save me from. "What do you think it'll look like to Dante if I didn't show up? I need to be there, Nera."

She bows her head, resting her head on my chest, then places gentle kisses on my pecs.

A beat passes, both of us just enjoying the water, the silence and the comfort of each other's presence before she speaks again.

"What are you going to do?" she asks with hesitation.

"You don't need to know the details, *Principessa*. Just know I won't let him take you from me."

The shirt feels tight on my skin but it might just be the unsettling feeling of knowing I'll be watching her with him tonight. Watching her walk close to him, be next to him. It makes me want to throw out my entire plan of waiting until I have back-up, to toss him to the floor and pound the shit out of his face until he's unrecognisable, or my knuckles shatter. Either one will do.

My phone pings on my bed as I stare at myself in the

mirror. Even the fancy suit I have on won't disguise the terrible person I am beneath.

Are you sure this is going to be good for her?

Maybe she's better off with him.

At least he has the wealth to give her anything she ever asks for.

My thoughts rattle around in my mind and I grip the pistol in my hand tighter.

You can't afford to do this on your own. You need Erhan.

I close my eyes, wondering how the fuck I got here. One moment, she was Dante's annoying, sassy younger sister and now she is the sea that crashes on the shores, the sun that shines through the glass of the greenhouse, and the rain that gives life to parts of me I never knew existed. She's the last hope I have of becoming who I want to be.

A better man.

A worthy man.

But how can I be better when I want her to myself?

How can I be worthy when I'm willing to watch Falcon's Keep burn?

My mind is at war and I'm afraid the casualties to suffer will be me and Nera.

Placing my revolver in my holster, I check my phone.

ERHAN

My terms are steep, Rafael. Are you sure you're ready to meet them?

I stare at the message. He's giving me a chance to back out, to rethink my choices, but I've already made up my mind.

ME

Be here in forty-eight hours. I accept the terms.

I take one last look in the mirror as Dante's words ring in my ear.

Better the devil you know than the one you don't.

The Fortress has been transformed from coked-up rich kids to prim and proper gangsters, pretending to have morals. I watch them, lifting their glasses, cheering to whatever the fuck they are. Lifting my whiskey glass to my lips, I pause when she walks in. Her champagne dress hugs her every curve, the silk material falling effortlessly around her body, and I don't hide my staring. Tipping the glass up, I enjoy the sting the alcohol leaves behind as I watch her chatting with some of the guests.

They arrived yesterday. No doubt all of them related to or invited by Frances. It's intimate, with only fifteen people on the guest list. The Casella brothers were invited but Ezra's wife, Aries, had gone into labour last night, so they are preoccupied with a new member of the family entering the world. That kid will be one lucky boy.

Her eyes meet mine for a millisecond before she smiles at Frances, and my glass shatters in my hands, the slick blood now covering the crisp white tablecloth, stealing everyone's attention.

Fuck, Raf. Nice way not to be noticed.

Discarding the glass shard, I wrap a napkin around my hand and get to my feet. Maybe I can't do this. Maybe I can't watch her with him.

A hand lands on my shoulder and clamps down. "Don't be reckless."

Dante steps beside me as I grip the napkin tighter and clench my jaw.

"Everything is done. There's no going back now."

Sorry, brother, but you're wrong.

"He's going to hurt her."

"He wouldn't do anything to harm her, not when I'm still alive."

I shake my head as the sound of clinking glasses pierces my ears, and her eyes clash with mine before Frances has his arm around her waist.

The red-hot rage is back and it's angry, pounding on the door I've shackled it behind, demanding to be let out. All I want to do is let it wreak havoc. I take a deep breath as she moves her focus to him and gives him a peck on the cheek. Relief only lasts a moment before he pulls her in for a kiss, angering the beast inside me. My nails dig into the wound on my hand and I can't look away as his tongue darts inside her mouth. My lip curls into a snarl. Before I have the chance to reach into my holster, two of Frances's bodyguards fill my vision.

"There will be a shipment tonight, before the wedding," one of them says, and when I look back, Frances is now seated with Nera beside him.

"How many?"

"Two men. In their fifties."

"And what are their crimes?" I ask, not out of curiosity but out of habit.

"One of them started a rebellion against the Lucchese family and the other cannot pay off his debts."

I nod and they leave. Another thing to add to my already growing to-do list. More bodies to gut and toss means less time to prepare for the wedding.

"I've called Nicholas, but I don't know if he will be coming," Dante says as he pulls out his phone to check it.

"He won't come…" My eyes follow Nera as she lifts the

champagne glass to her lips. "He hates me for what happened with Darcy."

There comes a moment in life when you're forced to choose between something that will keep you in your circle of comfort or take you out into the trenches of the unknown. Ninety percent of people choose comfort because it's what they know and it's how they've always lived their life. The other ten percent that step out of it have a new sense of self, a new reality upon which they can determine their worth and their future.

For most of my life, I've tried to live in that ten percent, but somewhere along the line after Dante saved me, I became part of the ninety percent. I forgot what it was like to have control over something as simple as thought and choice.

Not anymore.

Rising Tides.

The only way to give up something you love is to watch it die right in front of you. If it lives, breathes, and moves, you're tethered to it and there's nothing that could pry it out of your reach. That's what I thought before I came back here. Before I was signed away to be bound to Frances Lucchese. The dream of a degree or a quiet life away from here died as soon as I stepped foot on this island. Like any and all dreams do as soon as they reach these shores.

The music is muffled inside my head as my life flashes by, bending and breaking at his every command, by his side like some trophy wife that he won in a bidding war. The guitar warps as it comes back into focus when Frances speaks.

"Don't forget your promise to me."

"How can I when it's seared into my brain?" I seethe, smiling as I lift the champagne glass to my lips.

"Don't forget why you're doing this."

"You promised you'd let them go as soon as I signed the papers. Where are they?"

He swirls the drink in his cup beside me, his watch glinting in the low light of the Fortress.

"You don't need to worry about your brothers. They are safe. Until you are married to me, they will remain in America."

I take a deep breath, the alcohol flowing through my bloodstream, slowing everything down. "If you renege, I'll kill you in your sleep."

He huffs a laugh. "Do you know how to hold a gun, Nera?"

"I know how to hold a knife and there are plenty of those around."

Our eyes meet and he smiles at me. I don't expect him to say anything further but then he surprises me.

"Maybe in a different world, you would have found me as alluring as you do him. Maybe even more."

My brows furrow at his words and I pause.

"It's impossible to miss the look of a man filled with rage at the sight of another kissing the woman he loves, wouldn't you agree?"

I purse my lips, unwilling to speak, so he continues.

"Maybe if you had continued your degree, we would have eventually met and you would have given yourself to me."

"I'd never love someone like you."

He brings the glass to his lips and polishes off the rest of his drink, then leans into my ear.

"And yet, you'd risk it all for someone like him."

He stands to leave, some of his men taking him out toward the back of the Fortress, and I search for Raf inside.

This is utterly fucked in so many ways.

When I come up empty, my heart starts to race, my chest almost constricting as I stand abruptly, clutching at my throat.

What the fuck is going on?

I stare at my glass, wondering if I've been poisoned as I struggle to get air into my lungs, my chest burning with the need for oxygen.

Oh my god, I'm going to die.

My cheeks become wet with tears as I claw at my throat and clutch the end of the table, my vision dimming slowly.

"Miss Nera," Olga's voice sounds from behind me, but I can't turn around or move at all, my entire body is focused on trying to breathe.

"R-Ra…" I try to speak but the onyx wave pulls me in and a small rush of calm makes its way through me.

I've always wondered what it'd feel like to die. Do you see a bright light? Is there some mystical creature that hovers over you as it sucks your soul out of your body? I guess I won't be finding out today because as soon as I open my eyes, I'm surrounded by people I've never met making a fuss over me like they've known me my entire life.

"I'm fine," I say with disappointment. Maybe it would have been easier to escape all of this and watch from below as Falcon's Keep met its unavoidable fate. It doesn't matter anymore because I'm alive.

Strong hands clasp around my waist and pull me up.

"You gave us a scare, Nera." Dante's voice is filled with concern as he walks me out of the Fortress.

"Sorry, didn't mean to make it all about me." I chuckle and he reciprocates. I want to ask him where Rafael is but I need to trust him. My head spins as Dante walks me back to the manor and I wonder what could be making me feel this way. I'm not sick, I never get sick.

"Are you okay?" I know Dante's question comes from a place of brotherly concern and even though I don't think I could ever forgive him, he's my blood.

"I think I just need to lie down and rest."

He walks me up the stairs and helps me sit on my bed, making sure I don't pass out again.

"I need to ask you for something."

"I don't think I can say no to you considering…well…" He gestures with his palms facing up. "Everything."

"I need you to call Olga and ask her to bring me a glass of water."

"Sure."

I pull my phone out of my purse and lie down on my side as he steps out, closing the door behind him.

I pause my thumb over Rafael's name, then lock my phone and toss it over my shoulder. Taking a deep breath, I try to relax my thoughts because I know I'm going to be expected back at the Fortress to continue our charade, but the more I want my mind to relax, the more it accelerates. Not only does it conjure some wild thoughts, but it causes my anxiety to heighten to a level I've never experienced before.

"Miss Nera, it's me." Olga knocks on the door.

"Come in, Olga."

She steps in carrying a tray with buttered bread and a glass of water, and I smile at her attentiveness. I sit up as she places the tray on my bed, then stands to the side, watching me bite into the bread.

"Miss Nera, maybe it would be good for you to see a doctor."

I shake my head, my mouth full of bread as I chew.

"I can call Mr Lucchese's doctor. She can be here tomorrow morning."

Swallowing, I look up at her. "I'm fine, I just think it was a panic attack. I'm okay, really." I reassure her because I'm already beginning to feel better after some bread.

"Should I call Mr Lucchese?"

"Absolutely not. I don't want to see him."

She looks at the floor, considering if she should say what she wants to.

"Go ahead, Olga, say what you want to say."

"Pardon me, Miss Nera, but I saw you with Mr Guerra by the beach in the morning and I can't help but wonder why you want to marry Mr Lucchese when I don't think your heart is in it."

My mouth goes dry and I reach for the water, biding my time so I can think of a response to handle the situation. Does everyone know? Were we that careless?

Yeah, fucking your adopted brother any chance you get and ogling him whenever he walks past would surely get noticed, Nera.

Before I can speak, she sighs.

"You're young, Miss Nera, I just want to see you happy."

"Happiness is overrated."

She purses her lips, knowing she's not going to get anything out of me, and turns around to walk out. Before she does, her hand lingers on the door as she looks back at me. "Sometimes, we might think we're doing the right thing but instead we're enabling all the wrong things to continue."

She leaves with her words hanging in the air, making my stomach churn. As soon as she shuts the door, my balcony doors open, slamming against the wall, making me jump to my feet. Rafael stands there, his crisp white shirt stained with dark red liquid, his hair a mess and his eyes filled with concern and rage.

"I'm okay."

He rushes to my side, lifting my chin delicately with the crook of his finger as he places a gentle kiss on my lips.

"Tell me what happened."

"Honestly, I'm fine, I think it was just a panic attack."

He checks me over. "Did he do something to you?"

I shake my head and whisper, "No, but he knows about us."

"What?"

I rise to my toes and wrap my arms around his neck. "I don't think we were as subtle as we thought we were."

"How can you expect me to be when you walk around in those short dresses?"

I can't help but smile at his words as I hold him tighter, resting my cheek on his shoulder as the silence surrounds us, a reminder of the imminence of what's to come.

"I have to go back."

He steps back and heads toward my walk-in robe. I wonder what he's up to as he rummages through my things and steps out holding my suitcase.

"Pack your things."

I look at him with confusion. "Why?"

"Be ready, Nera. Pack your things."

When I don't move, he opens my drawers and begins stuffing my clothes into the open suitcase, the urgency now on the rise.

"You're scaring me."

He whirls around with a pair of my panties in his hands. "You were right, *Principessa*, except you had it twisted. It's not that *you and I* were not worth fighting for…" He drops my panties inside the suitcase and leans into me, placing his hand on my cheek. "It's Falcon's Keep that wasn't worth the fight."

CHAPTER THIRTY
Rafael

Desperation of a Forbidden Love.

I wonder when things changed for Dante. Was it when his father died? Was it when his mother no longer remembered his name? I watch the way she pretends like she's having the time of her life and I wish she was. Above everything else, that's what I want for her. Happiness, safety, and security. The freedom to be happy in herself and in the plan for her future. Maybe I can still make that happen, far away from Falcon's Keep. Maybe she won't end up hating me for taking her from here.

What are you going to do when she eventually does?

The voice inside my head can be the cruellest of all at times and in this moment, I want to silence it. For a split second, I wonder if this is what Nicholas went through on a daily basis, and it makes me regret not nurturing a relationship that we could potentially have had as brothers.

She smiles at Olga as she places the champagne flute on the table, talking about something that makes her eyes sparkle, and I wish I was the one having the conversation with her.

After changing, I returned to the party, not because I wanted to but because I needed to be next to her even if that meant I had to watch her from afar.

Every hair on my neck stands when a heavy presence makes itself known beside me as the chair scrapes on the marble flooring.

"I heard you took care of the twin issue tonight." Frances places his gun on the table, a clear sign of aggression.

"Not to piss on your parade, but you throw one boring fucking party." I shrug. "Decided I could entertain myself."

"Come on, Raf. I know we don't know each other that well but it's hard to miss the way you stare at her."

I clench my jaw, watching Dante now talking with some woman beside Nera. I grip my thighs harder as I fight the urge to throw my fist into his mouth.

"Was it not enough to have Dante bow to you? Why are you doing this to Nera?"

He sighs audibly, reaching for a cigar he's left on the table, and I watch him pat his pockets for a lighter as mine burns in my pocket, the heavy burden left behind by the one person who would know exactly how to navigate through this.

"Have a light?"

Reluctantly, I reach into my pocket and hand it to him. He lights the cigar, handing the lighter back.

"I'm not interested in Falcon's Keep."

I remain silent, trying to work out what the fuck he's after if he doesn't want the island. What could he possibly need with Nera?

"I know how you're feeling right now—"

I scoff. "That's very fucking unlikely."

He sits upright, his elbow now resting on his knee as he leans forward. "Let me make this clear for you. If you try to stop the wedding tomorrow, all it takes is one phone call and Nino and Santi will be dead by your hands."

It's like molten lava is flowing through my veins as he speaks.

"Do you think Nera would ever forgive you for that?"

My jaw aches from how hard I'm clenching, and he smiles, like a sick fucking psychopath.

"Great. Glad we had this chat." He pats my shoulder and stands. "I expect you there, front row."

Tomorrow. Fuck. The wedding isn't supposed to be for another day.

When he leaves, I slip my phone out of my pocket and send a text.

ME

You need to be here tomorrow.

I wait to see if he's read it when a minute passes, then two, and three before I mutter under my breath and light a cigarette as I follow Frances with my gaze. He reaches Nera, and she doesn't make it obvious, but I can see she's uncomfortable.

The music stops and a slow ballad begins as he takes her to the middle of the dancefloor, whispering something into her ear as his eyes clash with mine. My hand twitches with the desperation to put the entire chamber of bullets into his fucking head.

Like a car crash, I can't turn away as I watch him put his hands on her waist, where mine were just moments ago, and it incites a war within my body.

I can't be here.

My chest cracks as I rush out the doors with Dante on my tail.

"Brother!"

His footsteps follow me, but I don't stop.

"Raf!"

I whirl around.

"*Vaffanculo!*" I yell, all the bottled-up emotions now spilling out of me.

He raises his hands and takes a step back as I point my revolver in his face.

"Rafael…*Che succede, fratello?*"

"Don't call me brother! I'm not your fucking brother! I never was and I won't ever be!"

"Just—"

"Dante! I'll put a bullet in your head if you take a step closer."

He remains still, unsure of my next move, and if I'm completely honest, neither am I.

How the fuck am I supposed to save her when I can't even get past my differences with my own blood? How in the world is she supposed to love me when I can't give myself the grace I deserve to admit that I no longer owe the Della Torres anything?

A rush flows through me as I let it all out. "I love her, Dante!" Dropping my arm beside me, I reveal every single emotion that's been killing me ever since I saw her smile.

"I know I shouldn't and I know she deserves someone better than me, but I don't think I can live without her. I need her…"

He swallows but I don't let him speak. I need to tell him…to tell someone before I die.

"I didn't plan it, any of it, but I know it's real and what fucking luck I have that she's marrying someone else."

I snarl as a tear rolls down my face and I dry my cheek with my shoulder.

"All this island has been for me is a lifetime of bad fucking luck. I thought I could do it, to forget about her, maybe move on from here, countries away, but it's too much to bear knowing she doesn't want this."

I take a breath, the silence weighing heavy.

"What are you going to do?"

I don't answer him as he stares into my soul. He knows me better than anyone else so I know he can probably guess what my plan is.

"I'm going to take her."

"Then what? Jesus, Raf, have you thought this through? Frances will kill you where you stand. We have no choice!" He takes a step towards me. "Don't do it. If you love her, don't put her in that position."

"I can't let him have her."

"We will figure something out, I promise you. Let's take some time to think about this. Maybe call Ezra and Nico—"

"We don't have time, Dante! The wedding is tomorrow. Then he's taking her to the US, and I'll never see her again."

I begin to retreat as he stares at me, his brain ticking away, trying to find a way to reason with me.

"Don't get in my way," I warn.

"It's fucking suicide!" He gestures at nothing, the desperation clear in his voice to get me to see his view.

"Good thing I don't believe in God."

Checking my phone has become a new tic within the last eight hours. Erhan never responded to my text and now I'm wondering if he's going to leave me alone in this. I barely got any sleep last night, thinking about whether I should visit her or not. I told her I would, but I never showed up. Instead, I spent the night obsessing over conjuring up different scenarios of how this would go.

The hot shower helped to relieve some of the tension in my shoulders, but it's not my muscles that ache, it's the damn toxic thing in my chest. I want it out. I want to reach in there and remove it like I do for those lost souls.

I stare at myself in the mirror, at the dark circles surrounding my eyes and my hair mimicking the mess inside my head. The noise inside the house adds to the fucking chaos as the preparations for the wedding begin. The bile churns in my stomach, knowing what I must do.

I check my watch.

One hour.

Sighing, I gather what's left of my sanity and promise myself to keep it together. I ignore everything happening around the house and make my way to the church, heavily armed.

People might believe that war is about determining who is right. They're all wrong.

It only means they're dead and you're not.

CHAPTER THIRTY-ONE
Nera

Signed in Blood.

I imagined it differently. Everything from my dress to the location of my wedding, down to the person I'd be promising my forever to. Unfortunately, what I imagined doesn't matter anymore, not when I'm wearing this dress, in my home, about to marry the one person I wanted to avoid at all costs. On top of everything, I'm carrying something inside me that will only complicate things further, for everyone.

"Miss Nera," Olga says, taking a deep breath as she steps into the room on the side of the church. "I've got it." She hands me a pill along with a glass of water before checking if I'm okay.

"Thank you. I'll be fine."

She nods before stepping out and I clasp the pill in my hand, the woman in the mirror staring back at me, calling me a coward.

"I won't do it," I whisper to myself. "I can't." I try to hold my tears back when the door opens. Hiding the pill behind me, I place the glass on the table beside me when the lock clicks.

"Why didn't you come last night?" My voice is barely

over a whisper as he steps towards me, his dress shirt unbuttoned, his face looking completely unravelled.

Was he having second thoughts?

"Please tell me you found a way to stop this."

When he doesn't answer me, the contents of my stomach swirl in a frenzy and I brace my corset as it crushes my lungs. The terror begins to build, the slow realisation creeping in that this is no longer a ruse. It's real and it's going to happen.

I take a deep breath, fighting the tears as he wraps his arms around me.

"I'm sorry," he whispers, his words breaking me in a way nothing else ever could.

"No, no, no…" I press my lips on his, my hand on his face as I speak. "None of this is you."

He turns his head away from me, but I guide it back, the hurt in his steel eyes like the blood on his shirt last night. Thick, stained, and permanent.

"Kiss me," I ask, begging him to love me one last time, and he doesn't waste a moment, almost tearing my dress as he lifts me. Pinning me on the table, he devours my mouth. The pill is knocked out of my hand as I brace myself, his passion and desperation taking over the moment he lifts the layers of my wedding dress and removes my panties. We fight, gripping, scratching, and bruising as the inevitable looms over us.

"*Principessa*," he whispers.

The clank of his belt is followed by a groan as he slides into me.

I let the tears fall, allowing myself to feel everything.

"I love you," I whimper as I curl my leg over his hip, pulling him deeper as he buries his face into my neck.

"I won't ever be the same without you, Nera," he says

as he peppers kisses from my throat to my wet cheek. "I will keep my promise to you."

My head spins as he thrusts into me, his fingers intertwining with mine as our breaths become one. Threading my nails through his unruly hair one last time, I begin etching it into my memory, so I don't forget what it was like to be truly loved by someone. I vow to myself to keep the raw intensity, passion, and devotion of his love inside me until I die.

His soft lips fit like a glove over mine as he claims my heart forever. I know I won't ever feel like this for anyone else in my lifetime and that's okay because I don't want it to be anyone else.

I want it to be him, even if I need to travel into my memories to feel this love again. I'll do it every day so I don't forget.

His hips slam into mine as his grip grows tighter on my hand.

"I'm…"

Thrust.

"So…"

Thrust.

"Angry."

The helplessness he must be feeling is likely drowning him from within, and I can sense the anger that's pouring out of him and into me.

I swallow back the tears as I clasp his cheek. "It's okay, *amore mio*," I whisper. "I will be okay."

Lifting me, he drives my back into the wall with the passion I fell in love with in the very beginning. My legs fasten around his waist, gripping him to me as he moans, entering me to the hilt.

The breath is pulled from within me as he fills me

completely, powerless to the arousal and desire that's constantly coursing through my body with his proximity. He sets my world ablaze as he drives into me again and again.

A cool rush flows down the base of my spine as he bruises my hip, bouncing me up and down as the deep timbre of his moans makes my nipples tingle.

Shutting my eyes, I fist the material of his dress shirt as I clench over his cock, rocking my hips back and forth, riding the high of my orgasm.

"Nera fucking Della Torre," he drawls, and the way he says my name has me shuddering again, extending the waves of pleasure rolling through me.

"Think of me," he breathes as he nears his climax. "Think of me when you're walking down the aisle. Think of my cum running down these thick, beautiful thighs just as you're about to say I do."

He thrusts deeper and I struggle to keep my legs around him. "Don't ever stop thinking of me. I want to live inside your mind like a fucking cancer, metastasising until your body eventually gives in, the thoughts of me covering every inch of space inside your head."

The calluses on his hands are like a velvet scarf around my neck as his grunts fill the space inside the small room. I work to catch my breath as he holds me against the wall, his cock still deep inside me.

"Keep us alive, *Principessa*," he pleads.

The lump in my throat is back, as are the tears as he slowly pulls himself out of me and lowers me until my feet touch the floor. As we stare into each other's eyes, I see the memories I don't want to lose and the wound inside me grows bigger as I watch the tears build in his steel eyes. Unnerve settles into the air as I think about everything he's said to me and I step into him, twisting both my hands into his collar to pull him closer.

"What are you going to do?"

He doesn't answer, which only causes my unnerve to rapid-fire into dread.

"If you do anything stupid, I swear—"

"Don't worry, *amore mio*," he says softly, the back of his fingers brushing the runaway tears on my cheek. "Just promise me you'll keep us alive."

My bottom lip quivers as I try to speak, his devastatingly handsome smile gracing me for what seems like the last time. A spear-like force hits me right in the chest as he drops his hand and steps out of the door, leaving me to my inescapable fate.

The rain patters lightly on the roof of the church as I take a few deep breaths, clutching the small bouquet in my trembling hands. I contemplate running, but it'd be futile. I can't escape this fate and even if I tried, Frances would hunt me down and kill off my family one by one to get to me.

The doors open and the guests turn to face me. I'm grateful for the lace veil, shielding my red eyes from the crowd as I take a step forward.

One step at a time, Nera.

You can do this.

You have to do this.

Frances stands at the altar with his brother beside him, and Dante opposite them. I don't check to see if Raf is here because the pit in my stomach tells me he's left.

Flashes of the moments I spent with him fill my mind. The more steps I take towards my fate, the more I feel the remnants of our passion gliding down my thighs.

"Keep us alive."

His words echo in my mind, and I grasp the bouquet harder as if it can somehow help me keep my composure. When I reach the altar, I beg myself to switch off, to disassociate from everything that's about to happen. If only there were such a thing.

If only we could switch off our minds, our hearts, and our emotions.

"Nera, you look phenomenal." Frances plays his part far too well, and it makes me rage inside. I stay silent because if he's going to own my body, the only thing that's left to me is my voice and my thoughts.

The deacon clears his throat without taking a second glance at me and opens his book.

"Frances Lucchese and Nera Della Torre, have you come here to enter into marriage without coercion, freely and wholeheartedly?"

I take a breath as Frances answers first. "I have."

Forcing the words out through my teeth, I focus on the statue in the back. "I have."

"Are you prepared, as you follow the path of marriage, to love and honour each other for as long as you both shall live?"

"I am." His responses are quick and sharp like he wants this to be over.

"I am," I repeat after him.

"Are you prepared to accept children lovingly from God, and to bring them up according to the law of Christ and his Church?"

My mouth goes dry and I second-guess my decision not to take the pill Olga gave me.

"I am," Frances responds, and I am forced to follow.

"I am."

"Since it is your intention to enter into the covenant of Holy Matrimony, join your right hands, and declare your consent before God and his church."

My breath shakes as he reaches for my hand, taking it in his, and the reality becomes far too much to bear as he begins to state his consent.

"I, Frances Lucchese, take you, Nera Della Torre, to be my wife. I promise to be true to you in good times and in bad, in sickness and in health. I will love you and honour you all the days of my life."

I hesitate, the cold sweat now taking over my entire body.

"I—"

The doors of the church ricochet off the walls as my eyes clash with Rafael's.

"No! Don't!" I yell before he raises his revolver and storms through the church. My veil is torn off and cold steel is pressed against my temple, the fear now multiplying inside me as I stare at the man I love with multiple guns aimed toward him.

"Let her go," he demands. "Let her go and you can have me. I'll do whatever you want."

Frances chuckles beneath my ear, his arm wrapped tightly around my shoulders as he presses the gun harder into my temple. "What makes you think you're more valuable than her?"

He reaches into his pocket, pulling out something I never thought I'd see in my life. "Because I can give you this." The small egg-shaped item shimmers in the dim light of the church.

"Drop your weapon," Frances orders as I struggle in his hold.

He lowers his weapon slowly, the guards immediately descending on him the moment he places it on the floor. He grunts as they take him, pushing him down onto his knees.

"It's worth more than Falcon's Keep. Just take it and leave," he implores.

Frances loosens his grip on me and steps in front of me, eyeing me, then eyeing him. He expels a long breath with a slight chuckle to his tone when he speaks next. "I guess they never told you, huh, princess?"

The corset slowly crushes my ribs as I struggle to breathe again. "Tell me what?" I glance at Dante, and he shakes his head like he doesn't know what Frances is talking about either.

Frances pulls a knife from his pocket and motions for his men to grab Dante.

"What the fuck is going on!? Frances! We didn't agree to this!" Dante exclaims.

The blood rushes through my neck and up to my head as the sharp blade cuts through my corset and I stumble to the floor.

Fuck. Fuck. Fuck.

I stare down at my hands, now covered in my own blood as Frances kneels before me.

"Nera!" Rafael's screams bellow through the church, mixing with the memory of us just minutes ago.

"If you see your father again, you can blame him for all of this." He yanks the blade out and tears open my corset, sticking the knife back into my scar as he cuts his way into me. My cries tear through my throat at the searing pain.

I used to think about the moment of my death and how it would happen, how old I would be, and where I'd be. Like everything in life, nothing is black and white. All I see before me is the grey, the murky grey filled with lies and betrayal until it gets darker, the pain now fading into the distance as I admire the rain glistening on the stained-glass windows of the church.

Finally, I surrender to the depths of Falcon's Keep, the pull of its tide too strong to fight.

Reaper.

My world darkens and my arms burn as I watch helplessly, restrained by Frances's men. The dark red pool of blood runs down the steps of the altar. Dante is pulled back as he lunges to get to Nera, and everything I believed in has now withered into dust. I stare at the love of my life lying in her own blood, cut open as Frances reveals the item he's pulled from inside her.

"I was willing to do this the more humane way, with anaesthetic and such, but you left me no choice when you barged in and showed me I could triple my money." His sadistic smile spreads wide as the rare blue diamond shines, even when it's covered in her blood.

"Nera!" Dante yells, the deep sorrow in his voice matching my internal anguish.

"I'm going to kill you," I say through gritted teeth as I struggle, with four men holding me captive. Then the guests shriek in horror and begin exiting the church as a shotgun is fired into the space. Freeing myself, I charge at him, toppling him over as I release every single ounce of rage I've held onto for months.

"Frances!" Tommy calls out to him as we tussle on the

floor of the church, my only goal to get to my revolver. Reaching out, I inch closer to it as he lands a blow on the side of my face.

"Don't think I'm going to make this easy, Guerra," he seethes, his arm curling around my neck and locking in place, the air thinning inside my lungs. Extending my arm further, my fingertips almost touch the handle of my revolver when another blast is set off inside the church. My ears pulse, every sound now muted as I choke on the minimal air left inside my lungs. His grip loosens a touch, allowing me to wrap my hand around the gun and fire into his leg.

I gasp for air as it enters my mouth, sucking it in, desperate for my vision to return to normal as I turn and face him. He groans, clutching his leg, and I take advantage, still unaware of what's happening around me. Hell-bent on getting my revenge. Climbing on top of him, I slip the barrel past his lips and force it down his throat until he chokes.

"I keep my promises," I say as his eyes widen. My finger rests on the trigger and I take a deep breath as I pull it, the bullet spraying through his brain and out onto the floor. The struggle stops, and when I look up, my heart tears itself out of my chest to join her.

"Nera." My voice shakes when I rush to her side, lifting her head off the floor as delicately as I can. "Breathe, *Principessa,* breathe…please," I beg as she fights to keep her eyes open, her hands clutching her side.

I press the extra material of her dress onto her wound, desperate to stop the bleeding, and when I look up, Frances's men have been detained, along with Tommy.

Erhan Kara towers over us, the stark white streak in his

hair noticeable by anyone who's crossed paths with him before.

The warm blood from Nera's hand rests on my cheek as she tries to speak.

"No. You're not saying goodbye. This is *not* the end for us," I whisper onto her lips, my tears mixing with the blood now smeared onto her face.

"My doctor is waiting in the morgue. If you want her to live, you need to take her there now." Erhan places the Fabergé egg into his pocket. "I'll be here to sort out our agreement when you're ready." He clicks his fingers, and his men begin slaughtering the others.

"You're all going to pay for this," Tommy threatens as he's pulled out of the church doors.

"Stay with me, okay?" I lift Nera into my arms and cradle her into me.

Dear God, if you're listening, if you're watching, I beg you to save her.

She tries to speak again and I lean in as I rush her out of the doors and into the thick forest. "I-I…" Her voice is hoarse as the tears flow from her beautiful eyes.

I know I said I'm a non-believer, but if you're there, please…I'm begging you…please don't let her die in my arms. Don't take her from me.

I'll do anything.

Just don't take her…not yet.

Give me a chance to love her.

Please.

Her body goes limp in my arms as I burst through the doors of the morgue and lay her on top of the silver table, and it's like a sick, full-circle moment. Every single person in this fucked up family has now been on this table.

Slipping my hand through hers, I crumble at the sight

of her closed eyes, the stark white of her dress stained with thick red blood. "Don't leave me, *Principessa...*" I choke back tears as the doctor and his assistant rush to get ready to operate. "Keep us alive," I whisper against her cold skin.

"You need to leave. Now," the doctor demands as Dante rushes through the doors. "Get him out of here."

Dante stares at his lifeless sister on the table and runs his hands through his hair. "It's all my fucking fault."

"Get out! Both of you!"

Reluctantly, I step out into the night with Dante behind me, and the doors are shut after us.

"What did you do?" Dante speaks softly, the both of us standing side by side, trying to make sense of everything that's transpired in the last hour.

"I did what I had to do."

"You've traded one devil for another."

I'm wounded, tired, and broken. I have nothing left to lose if Nera is no longer part of my world, and I'd be happy for the ocean to swallow this godforsaken island.

I take in my white shirt, tainted with her blood, and it's like someone's shoved their hand through my stomach to grip my organs from within.

If she dies, I'll drown Falcon's Keep along with myself.

CHAPTER THIRTY-THREE
Rafael

Comatose.

I've been through every scenario of this. Through a negative lens, a positive lens, and an outsider's lens, and the only way we can move on from this is through a lifetime of servitude to Erhan Kara. It goes against everything Dante Senior wanted for his family, but I think he should have thought of this when he decided to cut his daughter open to shove a rare blue fucking diamond inside of her. I know why he did it, to ensure some sort of security in the future for his family. It's barbaric, unconventional, and disregards all human choice, but that's just the world we live in.

De Beers.

The rarest diamond in the world, probably worth over fifty million dollars.

The monitor beeps rhythmically and the softness of her skin reminds me of everything we have a chance at being. Real, calm, and *happy*. I know it will come at a serious price, but I'm willing to pay it. Whatever the cost, I'm ready to cover it, as long as she gets to live her life.

She hasn't opened her eyes since that night, and something inside me frantically worries that she won't ever again.

It's been days since that awful night. Days since she looked at me, touched me, and spoke to me. I'd fucking give anything to hear her say my name again. It's pure agony, counting the hours, minutes and seconds, not knowing if she's ever going to wake up.

Her room is now decorated in flowers. From her dresser, down to the last shelf on her makeup desk. I stare at them as they wither away slowly and flick the lighter open to watch the flame dance.

Loyalty.

What does it mean to be loyal, anyway? It's just a sick way to get you to act blindly, afraid if you don't, you'll be shunned and cast aside. Well, I was already cast aside.

No one wanted me.

Not even my own mother.

The metal clanks shut, my knuckles blanching as I grip the lighter in my hand.

"No one but you, *Principessa,*" I whisper, the lump now back in my throat as the machine continues to beep by her side. "Please," I say softly, unable to look at her, the image of her with tubes inside her mouth and nose already seared into my mind. "Wake up. I can't live this life without you."

I grit my teeth, fighting to hold back the tears when her door creaks open.

Dante doesn't say anything as he takes a seat at the foot of her bed with his back to me.

"Erhan is waiting." He fixes her blanket, covering her arm as he rests his hand upon hers. "We need to end this."

"I'm not doing anything until she wakes up."

He nods, clearly already knowing what I was going to say.

"Well, there's someone else here to see you."

As I lift my head, Darcy walks through the door,

followed by Nicholas and Ezra. My heart sinks as I stand. I wasn't expecting to see them again, but they came.

Darcy's expression is filled with sorrow as she sees Nera lying there.

"Oh, Raf." She wraps her arms around me and I hug her back.

"I did this." My voice falters as I speak. "She's not going to wake up because of me."

She pulls away and it takes me a second to register what just happened, the sting residing on my face as she grips my collar. "Pull yourself together. She needs you right now."

She's right. I should be out there, fixing this, doing everything in my power to make sure everything is perfect for her when she wakes up.

"What are you doing here?" I ask, surprised to see them all.

"I didn't get a good vibe when you called me last. So when I couldn't get through to you again, I asked Ezra and Nicholas to come, too."

I can't say I love the fact they're here, but in my books, actions are louder than anything else could ever be. It's hard to admit it, purely because I've hated them for as long as I can remember. Being the one who was left behind, the one who had to fend for himself for years without a mother or a father, my hatred for them ran deep.

"Above everything else, if there's one thing I pride myself on, it's that family always sticks together." Ezra leans on the door frame.

"Not your body count?" Nicholas jokes, trying to lighten the mood.

"What's the plan?" Ezra asks, waiting for me to respond.

I take a breath, my original plan of taking Nera far away from here now dissolving right in front of me. There will be no escaping Falcon's Keep and I won't ask my brothers to bear this burden because of me.

"I did this. I'll fix it."

"Erhan Kara isn't just going to give you a free pass." Nicholas weaves his hand through Darcy's as he speaks.

"Leave him to me," Dante says as he stands. "I'll—"

"Erhan wants *me*." I glance back at Nera, her beautiful raven hair covering her pillow. "No one else is going to get hurt because of me."

"You don't have to do this alone." Ezra steps forward and places a hand on my shoulder. "You have *us*."

"*Lealtà*," I whisper, the constant reminder of my unwavering loyalty to the Della Torres always in the forefront of my mind.

"Fuck loyalty," Darcy says, smiling. "Make him an offer he can't refuse."

CHAPTER THIRTY-FOUR
Rafael

Debt for Debt.

THIRTEEN YEARS EARLIER

It's not every day that you decide you no longer give a fuck about your life or anyone else's. A year ago, I made a decision that changed my world. It took everything I had left, no matter what little I did have. Everything was taken from me and I was ready to take some power for myself. I was desperate to feel some of the control I thought was stripped from me when my family didn't want me, and that led me to this moment.

"Where is it?" Erhan leans back into his chair, resting his ankle on his knee as he lights up a cigarette.

"With Dante Della Torre." I come clean because I have nothing left to hide.

"Hmm." Smoke rings fill the air as he lets the silence linger and the longer he's quiet, the more scenarios I make up in my mind of how he's planning to skin me alive.

"I'm sure we can come to an arrangement," I barter, knowing he holds all the power over me. If he decided, he could end my life right now and I couldn't do anything to stop him.

He motions his two men to come forward and they pat me down in search of the item.

"It's not here, Erhan."

"Forgive me for not taking your word. Being in this business, we all have some trust issues. I'm sure you can understand." His curly hair is raked back and a few strands fall onto his face on each side, his piercing blue eyes almost glowing in the dark night.

"I washed up on the shores of Falcon's Keep by accident. I didn't plan it."

"Yes, but you decided to stay. Why?" He looks at me with intrigue, not understanding why I would stay with strangers. Although I didn't know the Della Torres, they've become closer to me than I could have ever imagined. I consider every single one of them my family, regardless of the blood we don't share.

"I didn't see a point in spending my life alone."

The cool breeze of the night brushes past me, sending a shiver down my spine as the low hum of the horn of the ferries in the harbour sounds beneath us. Lights from the Hagia Sophia mosque twinkle in the background as I wonder how I'm going to convince Erhan to keep me alive.

"Why did you tell me to take it?" I ask, wondering what his end game is, but all he does is smile.

"A magician doesn't tell the crowd how his tricks are done, Rafael." He takes a drag of his cigarette, blowing the smoke into the air. A bead of blood trickles down my face and I let it. At least I know I'm still alive.

"I did what you asked but you weren't there to receive it. Given I almost gave my life for this *thing*, I think I deserve some grace."

He chuckles at my response and stands before me in his perfectly tailored suit, a stark contrast to my outfit.

"Let me make this clear," he speaks softly, but his voice is so deep that anything he says comes across as a threat. "You're breathing because I'm allowing it."

"Just name your price and let's be done with it."

You can't barter with a soul who's continuously been denied compassion, love, and empathy because when they find it, they'll never let it go.

"Keep it."

Shock and disbelief are the first emotions flooding me at his words.

"What?"

"The item will always belong to me, but given the war you've incited, I believe you're going to need my help, and with the trade I'm running through to the Russians, I can't have all my eggs in one basket."

I scoff. "You're trusting me with an asset worth millions of dollars?"

Flickers of embers dance on the ground as he drops his cigarette, stepping over it as he checks his watch.

"Trust is a fickle thing. Let's call it a debt for a debt."

"Meaning?"

"One day, you might wake up and realise you have no one in your corner and that day, you might decide to call an old friend." His blue eyes darken as he extends his hand to me. "And I might just be the only one to take your call."

CHAPTER THIRTY-FIVE
Rafael

Check Mate.

PRESENT

I t's easy to hate. But it's harder to crave the touch of the one person deemed forbidden by the world. Even when it makes you feel more alive than ever. If there is something to take away from the events that have unfolded over the past few months on this island, it's that loyalty isn't given blindly to anyone who asks for it.

Loyalty is earned.

A currency, like loyalty, might get you somewhere you've wanted to be your whole life, but you have to know the risk you take when you sell yours. You must prepare for the inevitable moment where that loyalty you gave away so blindly can end you.

"If you want me to bend the knee, it's not going to go the way you want."

"*Lealtà,*" Erhan whispers, a darkness growing behind his eyes. "Funny how the one thing you all pride yourselves on almost got you buried beneath six feet of dirt."

"Let's finish this."

Erhan stands, and I feel my brothers' support as they

wait behind me. Erhan's men surround us like a lion circling its prey before tearing into its jugular.

"Let's think about how this will end if you continue." Dante attempts to diffuse the intensity in the room.

"I'm sure we all know how this ends." He reaches for his pocket, as do I, ripping my pistol from its secure spot. I've never felt the adrenaline thicken in my blood as much as I do now.

Guns raised, we all wait for the defining second of the first shot fired, but no one takes it.

"I have an offer." I can almost hear everyone's neck snap as they look to me for an explanation.

Erhan pinches the cigarette between his fingers, intrigue practically glowing in his eyes as he waits for me to continue.

"What the fuck are you doing, Raf?" Nicholas steps forward, aiming his gun at Erhan.

"Thinking about someone else other than myself for the first time in my life," I whisper.

"Don't leave us in suspense. I'm wondering what could possibly be worth more than your life in my hands."

I smile, lowering my gun and motioning for my brothers to do the same.

"How about a lifetime of not only my life in your hands but the fate of Falcon's Keep as an asset that continues to provide?"

"What the fuck?" Dante mutters beneath his breath and Ezra laughs, catching on to my plan.

"Erhan, we're all businessmen here." Ezra turns the safety back on and lowers his gun to his side. "Let me paint a picture for you…" He takes a step forward, the two now face to face. "Let's say you kill us right now…What support do you have to take on the Lucchese family?"

"Not to mention, you'll also have another war on your hands if you kill the Casella King," I add.

Check. Fucking. Mate.

He came to Falcon's Keep, thinking it would just be Dante and I, not knowing my brothers would also be here, and now he's stuck choosing between the possibility of death or certain death if he takes the path he's been frothing over since I called him.

Some believe being in this business is kill or be killed, but the longer you live in this world, the more you learn to use the cards you have in a way that serves you in the long run.

It's easy to kill.

It's harder to think ten steps ahead and see the opportunities that can be leveraged.

Erhan's jaw tics and he nods, his men now lowering their guns to the ground, and one by one, they walk out of the office. As the door is shut behind them, Erhan takes a seat in Dante's chair.

He chuckles, the expression on his face resembling fascination. "I have to say, boys, you've come a long way since Dominic's reign."

"Well, we're meant to learn from history, not repeat it, right?" Nicholas places a cigarette between his lips as he takes a seat on the lounge by the bookcases.

"What's the offer?" Erhan asks, flicking the ashes from his cigarette onto the floor.

"We run your cocaine trade through Falcon's Keep to grow your business through to France and Spain."

His eyes widen, the sparkle returning as he envisions the growth of his business.

"You have Istanbul's port. All you have to do is run

your shipment through to Falcon's Keep and we distribute it to our contacts in France and Spain."

"In exchange for?" Erhan asks, glancing from me to Ezra. "What's the fine print?"

"You swear your allegiance to both our families, and the drug trade through Falcon's Keep dies with me. I'll run your trade through Falcon's Keep until I take my last breath, but nothing of this world falls onto anyone else. I'll bear it all as long as we have your financial aid as well as your allegiance."

"Interesting." He hums, leisurely grazing the cigarette side to side between his lips.

"I can triple your yield with the years I have left. By the end, it'll be worth more than that pathetic diamond in your pocket."

"You drive an interesting bargain, Rafael, but there is one thing I can't seem to move past." He stands, the ash on his cigarette lighting up as he takes in a drag. "With Frances gone, the empire in the States remains open. Their allies in France will retaliate, so how do you plan to fight your way through that?"

"We don't."

His brows knit, obviously wondering what my angle is.

Why do people retaliate? Why do people get mad? Why does anyone do any of the horrible things we've done?

Because they've been wronged.

They've been crossed.

"We make sure their ties to France are severed before the news even hits them about Frances." I give him a moment to think about it.

Ezra chuckles. "Might be time to brush up on your history, Erhan."

"What is more effective than an external war that's brought to their door?"

Erhan's smile is slow as the plan finally starts making sense to him.

"A civil war."

CHAPTER THIRTY-SIX
Rafael

Severance.

You can obsess and worry about what's going to happen tomorrow, the next day or in a year's time, but the fact is, you can't fucking change any of it. What's going to happen will eventually happen.

Does that mean it's fate?

I find it hard to believe events are predetermined by a supernatural, all-mighty being, but it makes you think. It makes you question if you had done something different, no matter how small the action would have been, would it have altered the outcome?

I've lived my life wondering what if?

What if I hadn't been abandoned by my family?

What if I hadn't stolen that fucking egg?

What if I hadn't let her touch me?

What if I hadn't stepped foot into that fucking alley?

The what-ifs are the biggest killers because they take you from the moment.

The one that matters the most.

You're in it.

You're living it.

Why fucking bother wasting your energy, time, and

effort on thinking about all the what-ifs that most likely won't happen?

Humans do it to themselves. They make themselves sick with worry about outcomes that are out of their control, and maybe that was my problem. I won't do it anymore. I won't let the venomous thoughts ruin my life anymore.

It's up to me now to turn it around for all of us. The first action was to bring Santi and Nino home. It paid to keep Tommy alive because he was the key to making sure they were breathing when they arrived. All it took was a phone call from Tommy asking a couple of men to bring them to Falcon's Keep, and as we held him under pressure, he had no choice but to do it.

The rate at which human flesh rots will always be remarkable to me. When the blood runs through our veins and our hearts pump it through our bodies, it vitalises us, nourishes us, and when it stops flowing, we die. Our skin rots, almost as if the body begins eating itself. The smell doesn't bother me so much anymore.

Frances's body is on the silver table in the middle of the morgue, the flesh turning brown at the top of his head, mixing with his dark hair. Throwing on my overalls, I cut through his clothes, removing the arm of his blood-stained suit, his hand now stiff as I hold it down. The machine in my hand whirs as I press it just above his wrist. If he was alive, the fresh blood would have splattered all around me, but the only thing covering my overalls is rotten flesh. I meet some resistance as it hits his radius bone, so I push harder, forcing the chainsaw down until it saws through, cutting into the tendons, then meeting his ulna. Finally severing the last bit of meat, I lift his rigid hand and place the chainsaw on his chest.

The door creaks open as footsteps echo through the concrete space.

"Is that going to be enough?" Nicholas asks, covering his mouth and nose with the crook of his elbow.

I hold up the hand and point to the tattooed crest. "How many people do you think have the same tattoo?"

He gags. "Fuck man, no gloves!?"

"I'm not afraid to stain my hands with my enemy's blood."

"Jesus, you and Ezra are so alike, it's fucked." He hands me a box and I take it. "We're waiting in the pit. Let's finish this so I can get off this sludge-covered island."

Placing the hand inside the box, I tag it with a note.

THE DuPONTS WILL RISE AGAIN.

Capitalising on the feud between the DuPont and the Lucchese families is the best way to attack this. If we were to attempt to take on the Luccheses alone, we'd be better off digging our own graves.

As I enter the pit, I notice the way Tommy looks around the space, probably afraid of what his end is going to look like. Ezra twiddles his knife, a bored expression on his face, as Nino and Santi take turns laying into Tommy.

"The package is ready." The box thumps as I drop it on the table by the door. "It's just missing one more piece."

"You're all going to eat your own fucking flesh." Tommy spits, the sand now red beside his feet. "I'm going to fucking bury you and your beloved fucking island so deep below the surface, you'll have your own personal hell in the Earth's core."

"Hold his arm," I demand, and Nino and Santi pull his arm taut as I approach with the chainsaw. "This is going to hurt. A lot." Holding the chainsaw just below his elbow, I press down, forcing it into his skin as his screams tear through the space.

"Fuuuuuck!"

"Hold him still." Fresh blood splatters onto my hands and face as the chain breaks through his bones, severing his forearm. His head hangs forward, surprisingly still awake and aware of his surroundings.

I throw the forearm with the Lucchese crest to Nicholas and he doesn't make a move to catch it, the lump now covered in sand.

"Why would you throw it? I'm not fucking picking it up."

Ezra rolls his eyes and picks it up to inspect it, the blood running down his fingers and arm. "Clean." He admires the stump, before dusting off the sand and placing it into the box.

"Are we sure this is going to work?" Erhan questions.

"It will, as long as we eliminate our survivors," Dante says, pulling out his gun and aiming it at Tommy. He fires, the bullet sinking into his temple. It's a precise shot, ending his life in a second.

The chainsaw remains heavy in my hand and the only thing I want to do is head back to Nera. Handing it to Nino, I head to the exit. "I don't want to be bothered until it's done."

Blood drips from my fingers as I head to the manor, passing the memories we've made through the thick trees.

It hurts to see her in the exact position I left her in as I walk into her room.

"Come back to me, *Principessa*," I whisper.

Taking a seat beside her, exhausted, I lean back into the chair and watch her chest rise and fall. Minutes pass before my eyes begin to weigh heavy, overtiredness settling in until I let sleep take me in the hopes that I might get to see her…even if it is in my dreams.

CHAPTER THIRTY-SEVEN
Nera

Under the Brightness of the Moon.

The tingles in my fingers pull me from the dark, calling out to me, desperate for me to notice it. There's an echo from afar, a pinging noise as I struggle to open my eyes. I try to swallow and almost choke on something obstructing my throat. My eyes jolt open as the panic shocks through my body, tears beginning to pool in my eyes as the terror intensifies.

"Nera," a familiar voice sounds beside me as my vision clears. I stare up at Rafael with worried eyes. "Don't speak," he says softly before screaming, "She's awake! Get the doctor now!"

My pulse thumps at the base of my throat when I take in the several machines beside me, the needles in my hand, and the searing pain in my side. A man rushes past Rafael, pushing him out of the way before he presses a stethoscope to my chest.

"Miss Della Torre, you're okay. Please try to stay calm. I'm going to take the tube out of your throat now."

I squeeze my eyes shut as he unfastens something, the plastic tube now moving, scraping the inside of my throat. As soon as it's withdrawn, I gasp, gulping the air into my lungs.

"Rafael," I cry as his hand curls into mine.

"I'm here, *Principessa*."

"Nino…Santi…" My voice sounds croaky as I squeeze his hand.

"Everyone is okay," he assures me and I open my eyes to be met with his steel gaze. "You're okay."

I have so many questions I want to ask, so many things I need to know, but I can't speak. Instead, I focus on breathing—telling myself I'm still alive as the memories of that night begin tearing through the wall inside me.

I want to forget, to erase it all from my mind.

"Why?" I whisper.

"Don't do that to yourself, Nera. I'll tell you everything, I promise."

My gaze travels down to his shirt and further down to his hands, the dried blood stuck on his skin like a blemish.

What did he do?

When I meet his eyes again, he smiles. "I missed you so much."

We stay like this for a while, just holding each other, hoping the weight of the world can wait for just another day.

He saved me.

I don't know what he did, but I know in my heart he did what he could to keep us all alive like I knew he would.

"Raf, I have to tell you something."

He waits for me to speak again but when I stare into his eyes, I don't have the heart to tell him.

How can I?

How can I explain to him that I was holding something within me…something that could have changed the trajectory of our lives?

It seems like a waste now trying to explain it. Why have

him spend his energy and emotions on something that's likely not going to be reality anyway?

"I know." The low rumble of his voice is soothing as he leans forward.

My breath hitches and I pause.

"I know about the baby," he whispers, and I fear for what he's about to say next. Before I can fall apart, he places his forehead on mine. "*Our* baby is okay."

I sob. I didn't expect to hear those words since I watched the knife plunge through me.

"I'm so sorry I didn't tell you." I sniff. "I-I didn't—"

"It's okay, *Principessa*." His soft lips grace mine. "We have time to talk about it all. I just want you to rest now."

I nod as footsteps enter my room and when I look up, I blink twice, my mind working to catch up to the image in front of me. Nino and Santi stand before me, smiling as the tears I've been fighting finally fall.

"Nez," Santi says, taking a seat on my bed as Nino covers his mouth, warring with his own emotions. "What a mess, hey?"

I chuckle, tears rolling down my jaw. It's been years since I've seen my brothers and as soon as I stepped foot on Falcon's Keep, I knew something was wrong when they weren't here. Seeing them now, I don't want anyone to be apart anymore.

I finally understand my father's vision.

"*Niente è più importante della famiglia*," I murmur.

"Nothing is more important than family," Dante echoes as he steps into the room.

I've found a new respect for my family and all that we've endured. Regardless of our differences, my loyalty doesn't depend on anything but the love I have for them. When people say they can't choose their family, it usually comes from a negative place. I'm thankful we don't get to choose because I wouldn't have chosen mine. I wouldn't have had the joy of growing up alongside my brothers, learning from them and seeing the steadfast devotion they have for the ones they call their blood.

Dante places a stack of papers on my lap and smiles, holding my gaze. Glancing down at the dark letters on the first page, I see my name with a space for my signature on the deed to Falcon's Keep.

"It's all yours, Nera. Take care of our home."

CHAPTER THIRTY-EIGHT
Nera

Blood is Thicker Than Water.

"I'm so sorry, Nera," Dante says as he sits on the other end of the long dining table, avoiding eye contact. There's no question what he did was despicable, but the true guilt rests with my father. I understand why he did it.

I recognise it all.

Being amongst it for the past few months, I see why this world is not meant for those who fold too easily. It was a contingency. Sometimes it's necessary to swap one evil for another to get by, and that's what my father did, thinking the evil he was swapping to was the lesser of the two. As I saw it, if I were to continue hating my father for making the decisions he did, I'd spend my entire life in misery.

I don't want that.

I want something better for myself and for my family.

"I know why you did it."

His bloodshot eyes meet mine as he twists the rings on his fingers out of habit.

"You thought it was the only way out."

"I should have—"

"No, it's done now. I just want to move on," I plead.

Rafael tightens his hand on mine beside me, letting me know it's okay to leave if that's what I want.

"I just need to know one thing…" I shift my gaze to the glass on the table, unable to look him in the eyes, afraid of what his answer will be. "When did you find out?"

It's the question that's been playing on my mind since I watched Frances pull a diamond from the place my kidney should have been.

My healthy kidney.

"I found out when *Papà* died. No one else knew but me."

I thought I had endured just about enough betrayal and hurt within the last few weeks but as it turns out, there was more to come.

"And you didn't say *anything,*" I whisper, choking back the tears. "You're my *brother.*"

His knuckles blanch when I look up, his face contorting with anguish. "If I could do it differently, Nera, I fucking would. Sorry is not enough."

"No, it isn't."

The silence lingers like a fucking plague, cementing the memories into the walls.

"I'll leave—"

"No." Standing, I make my way to his side to place my hand on his shoulder. "Our family has been separated for too long." His soft sobs echo through the dining room as he gently covers my hand with his.

It takes a lot more to be a good person than a shitty one. As much as my heart hurts right now, I just know it would be a lot worse if I were to watch my brother leave Falcon's Keep.

"This is our home."

He stands and pulls me into him, the familiar spice of

his perfume like a comfort blanket. The memories of us hanging around the bonfire we used to light just before Christmas, huddled up together, playing rummy, run through my mind. My mouth twitches in a smile as I wrap my arms around him.

"I want you to promise me something."

"Anything." He rests his chin on my head.

"Promise me our family will always be together for the holidays. I know I can't stop you from leaving Falcon's Keep, but I want everyone to be here for important events."

His deep chuckle vibrates through me and I look up at him.

"I wouldn't miss it."

"And promise me you'll take *Mamma* to a better place. Off this island and get her the proper care she needs."

I want our mother to live the rest of her life the way she was supposed to. Surrounded by her friends she once had back on the main island. Cared for and loved.

"But…"

"The more she's exposed to Falcon's Keep, the more she'll remember the things that haunt us all at night." I know when she remembers, it's never the good moments. It's always the ones that send her into a spiral. The further she was from here, the better it'd be for her.

He takes a moment before he answers me. "Done."

"And Dante," I pause, his arms still around me. "Make sure you seek your own happiness too."

RAFAEL — ONE MONTH LATER

For the first time, this foreign emotion creeps into my soul. It's been so long since I've shaken hands with it that I hardly remember what it's like. The sweat, the jitters, everything from the excitement to the euphoria, it's unsettling.

I was so terrified Nera would see me through the lens I view myself, that I never stopped to think about what it would be like to at least try to see myself through her eyes. As I stare at myself in the mirror, dressed in a tuxedo, I see a man worthy of love.

Not the love most people would come across in their lives, no.

The dark and twisted love that only lives in our world.

When you settle for a level of love you believe you deserve based on what you've done or who you are, you close yourself off to the possibility of experiencing the true definition of it.

It's endless.

It doesn't care what you've done in your past or what you'll do in your future.

There's no judgement.

What matters is that you do it with your whole fucking soul.

"It's done. They have the package." Nino turns the page of his book and steals a look at me in the mirror. "I just hope this plan works the way you want it to."

"There's one more thing—"

"It's done." He closes the book, placing it on the table beside him. "The fake Fabergé egg has been planted in one of their warehouses and the Luccheses have been tipped off anonymously."

"And how does Erhan feel about it?" Dante pipes up, blowing a cloud of smoke into the air.

"He's probably counting the endless cash he's about to make through Falcon's Keep instead of inserting himself into a war." Nicholas flicks my lighter open and the flames spark before he snaps it shut. "I'd say he's pretty fucking chuffed as he gets to not only keep the De Beers diamond but also have his iron grip over this island."

"It was the only way." Straightening my bow tie, I look at myself one last time in the mirror.

"You did what a leader would do," Ezra says.

"You're only saying that because he practically gave Frances an unconventional lobotomy, which is probably what you wanted to do to Ray but Aries beat you to it." Nicholas snickers and Ezra tries his best to hide his smirk.

"Right, before you both take out the ruler and start measuring, get the fuck out. I want all of you to make sure everything goes perfectly today. One of you head to the greenhouse, and as for the rest of you, make yourselves useful and see if Nera needs anything."

"I haven't seen you this nervous since…well…ever," Nicholas pokes again.

"If you say one more word, I don't care if we're brothers, I'll sell your bike for parts."

"Aw." He steps toward me and pats me on the shoulder. "Did you just call us *brothers*?"

Shrugging off his hand, I roll my eyes, and he chuckles as they all file out the door one by one.

NERA

It's been tough recovering as I figure out how to run this place. It's all on me now. My brothers said they'd stay for as long as I needed them to, but eventually, they said they'd move on from Falcon's Keep. Santi and Nino decided they'd stay until Christmas and then move to the mainland to begin a new life. Although Dante said he'd move, I know in my heart he wants to stay. I just don't think he's prepared to watch his adoptive brother marry his younger sister and carry out a life together.

"Are you sure you want to wear this?" Elodie holds up the dress I had ordered, the black lace flowing over the black satin with sheer lace arms. "I mean, it doesn't exactly scream *wedding*."

"No, it doesn't."

"Why are you smiling?" she asks as I take the hanger from her.

"Because I don't want to wear white *ever* again."

Shrugging, she enters my wardrobe and tosses out some boxes, a single shoe falling out from each one. I didn't tell her about everything that happened on the island, but she knows whatever went down wasn't good. She arrived on Falcon's Keep two weeks ago to help me plan for the wedding and ever since we were reunited, she basically recounted all of the gossip that began to circulate. From the teachers who were flirting with their students, to the news of Frances's death.

"So, what are you planning to wear on your feet?" Her voice is muffled behind the wall.

"They're in a green box." I raise my voice a touch so she can hear me.

After a minute, she comes out with the box Rafael gifted me, and I'm back in the moment again—innocent, free, and nervous. She places the box on my bed and lifts the lid, her jaw dropping to the floor in an exaggerated expression as she pulls out one of the shoes, the jewels twinkling in the daylight.

"Oh. My. God." Immediately, she removes her shoes and tries them on. My face hurts from smiling as I watch her parading them in front of my mirror. "They're stunning, Nera!"

She pauses, admiring them when her face changes.

"I know you said *need to know basis*…and I don't ever need to know anything about what happened here, but there is something I have to ask you." Taking the shoes off, she places them back into the box and closes the lid. "Is this what you want?"

I give her a small smile, admiring the true concern she shares for me. The moment I met her, I knew she and I were going to become close friends. "It's everything I didn't know I wanted."

"Because, you know…if you don't want this, I'm so ready to google how to operate a ferry." Elodie grins and I laugh at her absurd suggestion.

"You'd probably kill us before starting the engine."

She scoffs. "I'll have you know, I'm an excellent driver."

"Operating a ferry and driving are not the same."

She laughs as she reaches for my pillow and throws it at me. "Get dressed! You're going to be late to your own wedding."

I always wanted a small wedding. There's just something about an intimate setting with your nearest and dearest that makes a wedding mean that much more. Is it necessary?

Absolutely not.

I would be happy with the love we have for each other. Having Rafael with me on Falcon's Keep and getting a chance to live our lives together would be more than I could ever ask for, but it's what he wants.

You will be my wife.

His words echo in my head as I slip into my dress, pulling the silk and lace over my hips. Elodie zips the back for me and I take a deep breath to steady my nerves. I take the rollers out of my hair one by one with Elodie's help when Darcy walks in.

"Are you not ready yet?" She purses her lips, unimpressed. "They're already at the greenhouse, waiting."

"She'll be there when she's ready," Elodie huffs, handing me the crimson dahlia bouquet. "Are you ready?" She aims her question at me as I watch my reflection.

"Let's do it."

Everything happens so quickly, from putting on my shoes to heading to the greenhouse, that I hope I haven't forgotten anything. I did my own makeup, so now I'm wondering if I've put mascara on. Elodie senses my nerves and does an excellent job at calming me, like she always has.

"Hey, do you remember that drunk man by the Dunkin Donuts?"

I do my best to ignore everything else around me as I stand outside the greenhouse, the doors covered with black cloth to keep the groom from seeing the bride.

"Yeah," I snort at the memory of Elodie tripping over her laces and spilling her hot chocolate everywhere.

"He was such a dick."

"At least he made us laugh."

"You look stunning," Elodie says as she holds my hands in hers. She stops, the comfortable silence now falling in between us. "I'm *so* happy for you, Nera."

She kisses me and places my hand in another's. By the chunky rings against my fingers and the smell of spice, I know it's Dante. Elodie slips through the door without opening it fully, shielding me from everyone else.

"You don't have to do this."

"*Papà* would want me to," he responds. "Plus, I might not get another chance to see Rafael in tears."

I huff a laugh, secretly hoping he does shed a tear or two.

The doors open and immediately, his gunmetal eyes clash with mine, sending a rush down my spine as I step down the makeshift aisle toward him, the greenery surrounding us. Rafael never let me worry about the smaller details. After proposing by the beach, he said he wanted to take care of everything and all I had to do was say yes.

Nino stands beside Rafael with Santi next to him as Dante and I reach the end of the aisle. Placing my hand in Rafael's, Dante takes his place alongside my brothers.

As I look up at Rafael, the unshed tears remain in place, his emotions causing mine to war within me.

"You're so beautiful it fucking hurts," he whispers as he places a chaste kiss on my cheek.

I feel my cheeks heat at his words when Nino clears his throat.

"You're officiating?" I ask Nino and he nods, smiling. "Does that mean we can skip the boring stuff?"

The greenhouse fills with soft laughter.

"Well, we all know you've come here willingly, so I don't see why not." Nino reaches into his jacket and a green box with a white ribbon emerges. He opens it and hands it to Rafael.

I catch a glimpse of the emerald in a high-setting ring and I fight with my memories. I was so sure I had lost it that day at the beach. My mother was so angry with me, but Dante said he searched for it from dawn to dusk for five days and found it sitting on a rock by the cove. Ever since then, it had been placed in the safe.

"Nera, I don't want to live another second without calling you my wife. I want you to be a part of me as much as Falcon's Keep is a part of you. I vow that I will never leave this place. I will never leave you until I take my dying breath."

He places my mother's ring on my finger, the weight of it almost as heavy as Falcon's Keep.

"I don't ever want to know a life without you."

A piece of cool metal slides into my hand and I realise he purchased his own ring. Guiding it onto his finger, I take in his weathered hands, the scars protruding from his skin, and I mark it into my mind.

I never want to forget.

"I now pronounce you—"

Rafael takes me roughly, slamming his mouth onto mine, dipping me, and carrying me further into the kiss as he enters my mouth with his tongue.

"Husband and wife."

Cheers and applause resound off the glass walls and surround me as we pull away from our kiss.

"Finally." His deep chuckle is like my favourite song.

And I'll never get sick of hearing it.

Light Again.

The right wing of the manor was never used, locked up tight like a fucking stronghold because nobody wanted to enter it. Everyone was so fucking terrified of Dante Senior's ghost that they barricaded the entire wing and left it to rot. When Nera was recovering, I spent the time restoring it. Gutted the entire thing from the inside, removing the black cloud that seemed to rest upon Falcon's Keep. Now it looks more like a home, a place where Nera and I can spend the rest of our lives away from the judgement of the rest of the world.

"You did all of this when I was laying in bed?" she asks, astounded.

"Among other things."

She enters our bedroom, her black dress following behind her as she takes in the oak bed frame.

"Did you make this, too?" she questions, caressing the wood at the foot of the bed.

"As much as I would love to take the credit, no. But I did modify it." Stepping beside her, I raise the wood, the three holes now more obvious as to what they are.

Her eyes widen, and fuck, I love how her face reddens when she's thinking of me fucking her.

"If you think I'm putting my limbs in that—"

Crowding her, I inhale her perfume, sweet just like her. Brushing the back of my fingers against her back, I revel in the way her body responds to my touch. "Do you want me to *make* you, *Principessa?*"

Moving her raven hair out of my way, my lips are on her neck and her reaction is instant. "Or maybe you want to play roulette again?" I whisper just beneath her ear, and she moans, making my cock tent my slacks. "Do you remember how you felt as I made you come with my gun?"

She leans back into me and my hands snake around her front and down into the top of her dress.

"First," she breathes, gathering her composure as she reaches behind her to unzip her dress. "I want you on your knees." Turning to face me, her dress drops to the floor, revealing her gloriously curvy hips, dressed in a barely there lace G-string, and her breasts bare.

"For you, *amore mio*, I'll live my life on my knees." There's a thud as I drop to the floor, her hands in my hair, guiding my face to her stomach.

"After you make me come with your tongue, I want you to fuck me."

"P—"

"Shh." She places her finger on my lips. "Tonight, I want to feel nothing but pleasure."

Your wish is my fucking command, Principessa.

Hooking my fingers in her underwear, I guide them down her legs slowly, admiring the smoothness of her skin and the beauty in her eyes as she looks down at me.

Parting her legs, I don't break eye contact as my tongue has another taste of her, her head dropping back at the contact. Sucking her into my mouth, her hips rock forward and back, and I pull her in, gripping her hips, wanting to cement myself in this moment with her pussy over my face.

If I died, I'd die a damn lucky man. I'd want them to put it on my fucking gravestone.

'Died by pussy asphyxiation.'

I leisurely devour her, spending some time on her clit, then move down and back up her pussy, making up for the lost time I didn't have her taste on my tongue.

She giggles and I smile, unable to speak, still working to come to terms that she is my wife.

Mine.

"Your beard tickles."

Coming up for air, I make sure to lightly graze the hair on my chin over her clit. "I'm not attached to it."

She looks down at me with a mix of lust and adoration in her stormy eyes. "No, I like it," she whispers and I move back to my position.

You're about to like it even more.

Standing at full height, I tower over her, lowering my wet beard to her mouth. "Do you remember the first time you ever left your mark on me?"

She huffs a laugh, her mischievous eyes meeting mine. "Remember it? It's the one moment I constantly think about."

"So you enjoyed it. Like I knew you would."

Her tongue darts out, lapping up her mess on my chin, and I can't help the smile on my face. "More than you know."

"I knew you were trouble, *Principessa.*"

"One you most gladly took head-on." She runs her hands down my chest and to my pants. Unbuckling my belt, she lowers them, along with my briefs. Without breaking eye contact, she cups my balls and everything within me buzzes with need.

"But I'll let you in on a little secret," she speaks softly, luring me into her as she strokes my cock. "I wanted you first."

Something inside me does a fucking pirouette at her confession and I want to sink my cock into her to the hilt. I'd be happy to live there, inside her warmth, until she had enough of me.

Maybe not even then.

"Don't play with me."

"Why not? I think I deserve a little play." Ever so softly, her fingertips graze the crown of my cock, making me twitch as she spreads my precum over the head.

"Nera," I groan, grinding my teeth as she wraps her hand around my cock, my length hardening even more with her touch. "I want to be inside you," I whisper like a pathetic man reduced to his base desires, and the gleam in her eyes screams power and victory. She knows she'll get whatever she wants.

And I know I'll give it to her.

Hard.

She strokes me as I lower my lips to her perfect breast, her nipple hard in my mouth as I swirl my tongue around it, memorising the taste of her skin. My need outweighs everything else within me and I grip the hair at the base of her head.

"I can't take much more of this, Nera."

She moves her hand a little faster, and I move my hips to her motion.

"I think I kind of like being in control."

Her raven hair falls just above her beautiful, round ass as she guides me to the bed with her hand still secured around my cock, like a fucking dog on a leash, and I follow like a lost puppy.

"We should make up for lost time."

If this is what my life is going to be like, I can't wait to live it with her. I'm ready. So fucking ready for my life to finally start.

"Tell me what you want, *amore mio*, and I'll do it."

The bed dips as she presses me down onto it, and one by one, begins to undo the buttons on my shirt.

"I could just tear it off," I say, still admiring everything about her, from the way the corners of her eyes crease when she smiles, to the way she fucking blinks.

She ignores me, both her palms now beneath my dress shirt, running all over my chest as it lays open when she stills over the falcon tattoo.

Holding her hips, I watch as something passes over her thoughts. "What is it?"

She hesitates for a moment before climbing on top of me and wrapping herself around me.

"I had this terrible dream when I was in that bed," she utters, her face buried in my neck.

I stare at the wall in front of me, a thousand and one things going through my mind. "Over and over like a nightmare."

"It was…"

"Just a dream. I know. But it was something else, Raf. It was more than a dream." When she finally looks at me, there are unshed tears in her eyes.

"*Principessa,* you're scaring me."

"What if I forget?" A tear falls and so does my heart.

"Forget?"

"In the dream, I couldn't remember anything. I was talking with someone who seemed very familiar, I had a feeling I knew them, but I just couldn't remember how. What if…"

She trails off and I know exactly where her sentence was heading.

"You won't." Her cheeks are soft on the backs of my fingers as I wipe away another tear filled with fear. "Because I won't fucking let you forget."

Her lips collide with mine, full of hunger and urgency, mixing with my own desperation for her. I haven't had her since the blood wedding, and I hadn't even thought of it until a week ago when she was starting to feel like herself again. Even though she wanted to, I couldn't do it. Not when she wasn't better.

My hands find the curve of her back, pressing her body flush against mine, skin on skin. The sensation of her softness against me makes everything else fade away, leaving only us. The urgency of the kiss consumes us as we both lose ourselves to the moment, every part of my body coming alive with her touch. I'm lost in her when she lowers herself onto me, her warmth coating my cock, and I blow out a breath as her pussy takes me whole.

She grinds over me, my cock smothered in her warmth, transporting me to the only heaven I know.

Gripping her to me, I look up at her. "I'll always remind you, *Principessa,* in the quietest moments and in the loudest ones, of just how unforgettable this is."

Grasping her hip in a tight hold, I follow her movements as she arches her back to allow for my hand to find her clit. She moans at the contact, her nails digging into my neck as she holds on, rocking her hips back and forth, chasing her high.

She rides me faster and faster, her moans getting louder and louder. We're in the right wing so there's no chance anyone will hear us, but even if we weren't, I wouldn't care.

She is my *wife*, and tonight is our wedding night.

I will consummate our marriage as long as she wants, however many times she wants.

The salt on her skin lingers on my tongue as I glide it up between her breasts, the taste of her electric and intoxicating, like the true essence of her blasting in my mouth all at once. I can feel she's close when her grinding slows and her pussy begins to tighten. Helping her to ride the wave, I run my tongue from one nipple to another and take it in my mouth, making a popping sound as I release it.

"Now the fun really begins."

NERA

I said I wouldn't be put in this thing, and yet here I am. My arms and my neck are in the holes of the foot of the bed, and I'm completely naked, staring at his cock in front of me.

"Seems like you can't get enough of my mouth."

His cock jerks at my words and I smile, satisfied with the knowledge of how much I affect him.

"It's true." He caresses my cheek, the throbbing between my legs growing stronger the more he leaves me untouched. "But tonight, I want to explore something else together." The light glints off the silver item in his hand and my eyes widen in shock and excitement.

"Open," he purrs, and I do as I'm told. The cool metal fills my mouth and I suck on it, priming it for myself. "Looks like I've taught you well."

He moves around the bed and it dips as he kneels

behind me. I'm exposed to him and there's nothing left to hide. Not in this position. I hear the sound of a bottle opening before a cool, water-like substance drips between my legs, coating my ass first, then dripping down my pussy.

"Fuck," he hisses. "I can't make up my mind if I want to fuck your ass first or your pussy."

"Why don't we start off slow?" I suggest, my heart in my throat. I haven't done it before and I'm slightly terrified that I might enjoy it.

"Anything you want, *Principessa.*" The cool metal pushes into my ass, and I fist my hands at the foreign feeling. "Shhh," he coos, stroking my back as he pushes further. "Take a deep breath and let it in."

"I can't." I panic and get all in my head when he leans over me, his mouth now beneath my ear.

"Stay with me, Nera. You can."

I take a deep breath as I'm stretched and once it's in, there's a constant buzz inside me, the core of the intensity coming from my pussy. It's sensitive when his fingers slide between my lips, a whimper escaping me.

"I want to give you the most pleasure you've ever experienced," he groans as he enters me, the feeling of being full taking me by surprise.

He lets out a deep, guttural moan when he fills me up completely with his cock. He grips either side of my hips, and I have a feeling I need to brace myself.

Luckily, I'm already secured.

He thrusts into me hard and I scream, the intense pleasure ploughing through me at a rate I didn't know was possible.

Do I like this?

I feel his front to my back as he hovers over me, thrusting in and out like a man ruined with need. I can sense his passion as he drives into me, his hand grasping the skin on my ass forcefully. There's something about letting go of your control and giving it to the person you trust the most. It's knowing that they have the power to hurt you, but you know all they want to do is consume you.

"I'm torn," he breathes into me when I moan, unable to hold on much longer. "Torn between the need to fill you up with my cum and bring you to tears with pleasure."

He tugs lightly at the plug, and I whimper as his hand snakes around to my breast.

"I want to make you cry out my name as I watch you take everything I give you. Pain and pleasure," he murmurs as everything around me blurs. The only thing I feel is intense euphoria as I cry out his name with his cock still inside me.

"See, just like that."

His hold becomes bruising as he rams into me with the force of our emotions tied together as one, my thoughts scattering into a million pieces.

His hips drive into me again and again as he chases his own release, and there is nowhere else I'd rather be.

His pleasured moans spur more desire within me, sparking my body up again, refuelling my craving as he gives me everything he's been holding onto.

I take it, breathless, the cold thrill coursing through me again, and instead of pulling away, I embrace it. Because even in the midst of all the fucked up shit we've been through, there was no other place I'd rather be than tangled up with him in it all, wrapped in the raw, undeniable force of what we are.

CHAPTER FORTY
Rafael

The Work.

THREE YEARS LATER

Surprisingly, this arrangement with Erhan Kara has been smooth. With anything, it takes a little work to get everything set up and running. Once we worked out the kinks, like who would watch the shipments and who would exchange the cash, everything was almost perfect. Of course, you'd have a few hiccups, like some dead bodies, but it wasn't something I was new to. It comes with the territory.

"Where do you want the palettes?" Some young chump got stuck with shipping from Istanbul and is wearing his disapproval on his face.

"Under the shed, and keep the fucking powder dry."

Erhan's men move the palettes under the shed we constructed as I check my watch. It's two in the afternoon, meaning Nera will be putting Stella down for her nap. Just as I'm about to head back to the manor, a siren-like voice calls out to me.

"You promised you'd let me take this one." She steps down onto the wharf and I smile. Her hair is now always in a messy bun, high on the top of her head because she refuses to cut it. Since she gave birth almost three years ago, Erhan has given us more than what we need in terms of carers, cooks, and cleaners. Nera wants to believe it's out of the goodness of his heart, but I know he wants our full attention on the trade.

"I just can't stay away." It's a lie. All I want to do is get this done and get back to my girls.

"Well, Stella is asleep." She runs her hands over my chest, stepping into me, her allure still as irresistible as the first time I saw her again in the States.

"Mmm, and what does that mean?"

"Means we have about an hour before she wakes up." Threading her fingers with mine, she pulls me in the direction of the forest.

"I have to stay until they finish loading the shed."

She sighs, turning to face the man on the machine moving the palettes. "Hey!" She rolls her eyes when he doesn't hear. "Hey!" she yells louder, now gaining his attention as he turns off the motor.

"Yes, miss?"

"You're in charge for the next hour. If even one brick is missing, my husband will ensure you have a permanent resting place beneath the sea."

My cock instantly hardens beneath my pants at her demeanour. "*Principessa.*"

"I haven't had you in days. I'm losing my mind, Raf."

I don't think I've laughed as much as I have since being with Nera. She brings out the happiness I've always yearned for. Something I believed to be lost for me.

Sweeping her off her feet and onto my shoulder, I tap her ass lightly. "I can definitely fix that."

Laughing, she wriggles in my hold, still every bit the fighter I know her to be. "Where are you taking me?"

"To see Venus."

I carry her through the forest to the greenhouse, the plants thriving now under her care. Placing her down, she walks in and I follow behind her.

"I think I know why this is your favourite place." Turning to face me, she removes her cardigan, letting it pool on the floor. "It's not about being able to see planets."

I watch her remove another item of clothing, her shirt now discarded.

"Do tell."

"It's the serenity this place brings you. The comfort of knowing you can be in silence with yourself amongst other living things that cannot judge you. They hold your secrets."

She's now completely bare before me. When I saw her scar again after the incident, I couldn't bear to look at it, and although it's become a little easier, it's still difficult for me.

"Maybe." I close the distance between us and tug at the tie in her hair, the curls now flowing down her chest. "Or," I whisper, weaving my hand into her hair beneath her scalp, "maybe Venus is not a planet."

Turning her around, we both face the window, our reflection looking back at us.

"She may have started as a planet but I think the true Venus stands before me."

Tilting my head, I lower my mouth to the skin on her neck. "Tell me, *Principessa*, how would you like to be pleased?"

The corner of her mouth twitches. "Play with me."

My beautiful wife wants to be my toy…

There's a hot rush of blood to my cock, the head now throbbing with the need to be inside her. "As you wish."

Parting her legs with my foot, I guide her to her kneel. "Open your knees wider."

She does exactly as I tell her to, clearly wanting to let loose. She's been wound up, stressed over the constant shipments we've been making before winter comes and some of the ports close due to the weather. Now it's my duty to relieve her of that stress.

"Don't hold back," she requests.

Huffing a laugh, I crane her neck back. "It sounds like my wife wants to be degraded and used."

She smiles like the confident woman she is, knowing exactly what she wants as I caress her smooth cheek, watching as her body comes alive at the lightest touch. "Is that what you want, my twisted little whore?"

Licking her lips, she nods.

There are so many ways I want to make her come. With my mouth, my fingers, and my cock, but right now, I want her to see how divine she looks when she comes for me.

"Place your hands on your thighs and wait for me."

Heading over to the other side of the greenhouse, I roll over the object I purchased just for her. A little anniversary gift I know she'll enjoy.

When it comes into her view, she looks at me, puzzled. "What's that?"

"Don't speak. Get on top and straddle it."

Her eyes clash with mine, the same recklessness still present within her. Then she stands and throws one leg over the bondage horse, straddling it as I move behind her.

I'm about to make you cry with pleasure.

"Hands behind your back."

She does what she's told with a smile on her face and an excited flush on her cheeks.

Securing her wrists with rope hanging off the horse, I push her down hard and she giggles. *Fucking giggles* like I'm not the one in control here. Undoing my belt, I run it over her smooth skin, revelling in the way she rocks her hips as she watches me through the reflection of the windows.

"Look at yourself, *Principessa*," I whisper, wanting this moment to be all about her. "Watch how your eyes gleam when you think of me fucking you."

When she goes to speak, I swiftly bring my belt to her cheek, tapping her smooth skin, and making her flinch. "I said don't speak."

She heeds my warning and closes her mouth. Strapping her down to the horse, I reach for the collar at the end and secure her neck. My cock twitches at the sight of her before me, the control she willingly gives me is unlike anything any man could experience. It's not for everyone, and only a lucky few get to experience their partner giving in to them completely. For me, it's the blind trust to know her limit. To know when to push and when to let her come. For her to trust me with that is one thing I will never take for granted.

I know her body like she knows mine. I know where her curves meet, where her scars run deep, and where she wants to be touched.

I know her like I've come to know the sand on the shores of Falcon's Keep, and it's because of this that I know the rest of our lives will be spent loving each other without fear.

Without judgement.

She is mine and I am hers.

Until death.

CHAPTER FORTY-ONE
Nera

The Affliction.

TWENTY YEARS LATER

I don't know when it began or how I stopped remembering. All I know is one day, I woke up and everything around me was different. The people, the island, and even the air seemed different. It's dry when I try to swallow down the lump in my throat, but the desperate feeling is still there with me. It's like I'm living in a nightmare as I try to focus on the words. But they feel like they're being spoken *at* me instead of to me.

"Signs of early-onset Alzheimer's," the voice echoes in my head, fading into the fog constantly waiting for me in the back of my mind. The words don't make sense, because how can they? It can't be real.

Everyone's heard of it, and as much as I hoped I wouldn't hear them, it was like an ominous fate, waiting for me.

I blink the blurriness away, Dante's desk slipping in and out of focus. Is it the lighting, or is it me? I'm anxious to know what he said earlier, but the words evade me, scattering into the air like a puzzle missing its pieces.

"Do you understand what this means?" his soft voice, intended to keep me calm, infuriates me.

Of course I understand what it means. I've seen it happen to my mother.

My mother. Will I forget her too?

Alzheimer's.

It can't be. This can't be it. I can't accept it.

I open my mouth and nothing comes out, the fog pressing down on my thoughts, trapping them, making everything in my mind harder to reach. It's like walking into a room and forgetting what you're there for but instead of a room, it's inside my head and I'm supposed to know me. I've lived with me. I've grown into me.

How is this happening?

I nod instead, unsure if I'm agreeing or if I'm in a trance, like a robot on autopilot.

His lips continue to move, the words floating into the air, landing around me. It must be a dream. I must be inside a nightmare because this can be the only explanation. I pinch myself, desperate to wake up, but I remain seated in this room, the walls slowly closing in on me.

Memory loss.

Gradual decline.

My throat closes up and my chest tightens as my hand is taken in another's. Frozen, I remain in place, staring at the desk, then up at the doctor, trying to make sense of the sympathy in his eyes.

So what do I do now?

What drugs will help me?

I want to ask him, but my lips refuse to move and even if they did, I'm not sure I want to know the answer, or if I'll even hear it.

Glancing around the room, I spot a photo of me and Dante, me in a beautiful black dress and him in a suit. I want to remember, to know something for sure, something that will hold me in place, but I struggle to keep the memories locked down.

Why don't I remember that day?

I know in my heart I enjoyed that day and that it probably held a massive significance for me but the static distorts the images in my head the more I try to focus. I grip the arms of my chair, growing frustrated the more I try to dig into my memories.

I know I've been forgetting. It was little things at first, like where I placed my coffee mug or what I had for breakfast. But it wasn't like this.

It was never like this.

Squeezing my eyes shut, I listen to the deep thumps beneath my chest.

Please, let this be a nightmare.

Wake up.

Please.

Wake. Up!

But I don't.

When I open my eyes, I want to beg the doctor to help me.

Please. Fix me! Please help me! Don't let me forget!

"I'm sorry." His voice fades as he stands, and there's a sudden wave of frustration. I want to leap from my chair to stop him, to shake him and beg him to do something.

He leaves, his footsteps soft in the hallway outside and if it weren't for Rafael sitting with me, I would be beside myself.

Shakily, I grip the edge of the chair for support and look down at my hands, with his on mine. For a second, I don't recognise them. They're mine, but they're not. I can't bear to look him in the eyes, so I stare at my trembling fingers. The memories I try desperately to cling to remain as fragments inside my head. Even those that once would have meant the world to me.

What are you left to do when the world is pulled from beneath you?

How do you move on with your life knowing you'll forget the things that made you who you are?

How do you accept a fate like this?

"My dream," I whisper.

"I'll always remind you, *Principessa*," he says as he clutches my hand tighter. Leaning into my space, he lifts my gaze to his. "In the quietest moments and in the loudest ones."

RAFAEL

I knew in my heart the moment she uttered those words on the night of our wedding that it was a possibility. I'd never admit it to her, but I knew something was wrong before she even said anything. Her eyes were different.

Distant, like she was looking at me from afar. When she smiled, it didn't reach her eyes and the tightness of her mouth, I'd seen it before, after she'd had a stressful day, and for a while, it had been permanent. It reminded me of the weight I shouldered when I carried the secret of my birth. A secret too heavy to be burdened with alone.

I felt her body tense the moment those words were spoken and I knew instantly she wasn't hearing him. I don't think *I* even heard him the first time.

I keep my hand on hers, a small touch to remind her I'm never fucking leaving her. She's my entire world and right now, she's breaking in a way I'll never know how to fix.

"I don't want to forget." Her voice is vulnerable as she stares back at me, a flicker of something in her eyes. Hope or trust I can't be too sure, but it's enough to know we'll be together in this.

No matter how dark it gets, I'll remind her.

For her.

For *us*.

We've been through too much.

Too much to let this break us.

I know I have to come to terms with the fact that she'll forget me because it's imminent. It's going to happen.

The silence lingers once again but this time, it doesn't feel as suffocating. Her hands tremble in mine and as she tries to pull them from me, I don't let her. I'm not ready to let her go yet.

I don't think I'll *ever* be ready to let her go.

"I don't know what to do," she whispers, her voice barely audible, as if she's afraid to speak the words. "I don't know how to fight it."

Breaking my gaze, she stares down at our hands entwined together.

"You're not going to be fighting it, *Principessa*. We're going to live our lives like we vowed we would the day we said I do. I'm going to love you and you're going to love me."

When she looks back at me, I see a strength in her eyes that I fell in love with. "I don't want to forget you." Her voice cracks, tearing apart my insides.

The thought of her forgetting me, us, and our lives together is one thing that could kill me. But I'm never going to let her know.

"I won't let you forget me. Ever." Bringing her knuckles to my lips, I place a chaste kiss on her skin. "I'm going to remind you in every way I know you'll remember."

We look at each other for a long moment and the way her eyes soften, even in the slightest, is enough to calm the storm within me. Resting my forehead on hers, I curse whatever fake god sits in his all-mighty chair, looking down on his so-called children in suffering.

"I'll be here," I repeat. I want to say it's for her, but I do it more for me.

She nods, a silent promise, the looming uncertainty now muted and distant, like it doesn't matter in the face of what we have together.

Maybe tomorrow will bring more hope. Maybe the days ahead of us will be harder than our past, but whatever happens, I know we will endure it together like we've done before. Desperate to stop the aching in my chest, I take her lips with mine and it's different to all the kisses we've shared in our past. This is slower, softer, like we are trying to memorise the moment before it slips away.

When we finally pull away, the space between us is equally as painful as it is peaceful. That's when I see it in her eyes, the quiet acceptance. No matter how much time we have left, we'll wake up tomorrow and won't waste a second more worrying about the inevitable.

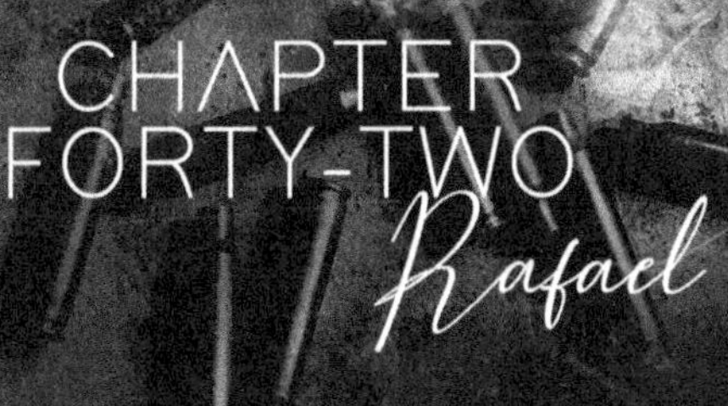

The Final Chapter.

I've walked these halls countless times, covered in blood, battered and bruised at times, too. But even those times would have hurt less than this one. The manor feels different, not the walls or the heavy doors, but the silence that hangs heavier than it did all those years ago. A still, quiet desperation mismatched in the space with twinkling lights and the scent of cinnamon. Even the tree in the corner of the living space, perfectly trimmed, might as well have been a mirror looking into a life we could never return to.

I stand here on the threshold, unable to tear my gaze from the tree, the table set for dinner, everything looking like usual, to feel like how it did before she began to lose herself to the disease. Before life began to shred the last fucking pieces of what we want to pretend we could still be.

I hated it. The pretending. It was harder than being stabbed or shot. Harder than I ever imagined it to be.

"Raf?" Nicholas's voice echoes from the empty hallway, breaking the silence. I turn to face him, standing there, his posture stiff, his usual light-hearted mask slipping.

"Yeah?" I say, not bothering to hide the exhaustion in my voice.

"She needs you, brother." His gaze is distant, despondent like it was years ago when he struggled with himself. The truth was there: no one at Falcon's Keep was the same anymore. But tonight isn't about us, it's about her.

Forcing my feet to move, I make it up the stairs and toward the right wing, down the hall and to our bedroom. I know she needs this. She wants to see us all together again before her memory is stolen from her.

But I don't know which one to agonise over, the fact that this is now a reality she will forget or that I will watch it happen.

Pushing past the door, I see her sitting in her armchair by our large window overlooking Falcon's Keep, an eerily similar sight. She rests her feet on a small round seat, staring out of the glass with her laptop in her hand, the soft light from the sunset casting a glow over her beautiful features. Her gaze flickers to me as I step closer, and she smiles.

"Raf," she whispers. "I'm so glad everyone could make it."

By everyone, she means my brothers, Ezra, Nicholas, and Jackson. Her brothers have been here since her diagnosis. It's what she wanted and without a thought, they all came.

"Just like you wanted." My voice cracks, my heart in my throat. There's nothing I can say to make this better. There's no fixing this, as much as it kills me to admit.

There's no curing Alzheimer's.

"Great," she says through the visible sadness in her eyes. "I just need another minute." Her smile falters, sending a knife through my stomach as I close the door behind me.

We all knew things weren't ever going to be the same. There was no need for an explanation. We all saw it and felt it.

The slow erosion of the woman we all love. The way she would ask the same question twice and how she would trail off mid-sentence, forgetting what the end of it was. As I make my way down the stairs, the living room is now full of voices, but all I seem to focus on is the soft crackle of the fireplace.

"*Papà?*" Stella's voice breaks me out of my trance, a mirror of her mother at a younger age.

"She'll be down in a minute." I force a smile and guide her into the lounge room, Ezra's son and daughter on their phones on the opposite side, waiting to unwrap their gifts, unaware of the heaviness in the air.

Footsteps enter the room and everyone continues as I watch her take a seat between Aries and Darcy. It's a version of normal that doesn't feel normal at all anymore. But to Nera, it didn't matter that we were all afraid of the future because, for her, she needed this. One fucking night where we weren't shipping drugs into the sea, a night where we could all be a family.

Before the secrets and lies.

Before the violence and pain.

And for one night, we will be.

For her.

THE END.

EPILOGUE
Nera

FIFTEEN YEARS LATER

The sea breeze stirs the hair behind me as I watch the tide rise. It should be soothing. It always used to be…at least I *think* it used to be. But now, as I watch the water wash over the wet sand, I feel unsettled.

I know this place.

I try to remember the last time everything felt *right*, but the thought slips from me before I can catch it. I take in the expanse of the shoreline, the sand stretching out, golden and endless. It's completely empty, with no one in sight and I wonder if I'm in the right place.

I can't remember.

I look down at my hands, the skin on my fingertips like the skin of a prune, wrinkled from the salt. How long have I been here? I carve out the inside of my mind, searching for an answer, but it remains out of reach. I've watched the tide pull in and out countless times, the rhythm comforting, but today, it feels strange, like I shouldn't be here.

"Here you are," a deep voice says.

I blink, turning toward it. A man, tall and masculine, stands before me.

Who is he?

"*Amore mio*," he whispers, smiling. "Let's head back." He reaches out to me to take my hand and I hesitate for a second before something inside me calms at his touch. His face is familiar…but I don't know why I feel this way.

I stare at my hand in his, the scars rough and his hold so sure, but…I can't remember when they've held mine before.

"I…" The words don't come. I want to speak, but my mouth has forgotten how to say the words.

"Everyone's waiting for you." He guides me toward the road that leads up to a large house, the ground soft beneath my bare feet.

Everyone?

I walk beside him and with each step we take, it feels like it's pulling me away from something, like I'm walking into a fog I can't escape. The waves crash louder as I glance down at my feet, the sand between my toes. They look different somehow.

We stop, and he guides me to face him, his beard speckled with white hairs, the creases at the ends of his eyes deepening when he smiles.

Those eyes. I know those gunmetal eyes.

"Are you here with me, *Principessa?*"

I want to say yes, I want to tell him that I know him like I know this sea, but the words are lost…Because I *don't.*

The waves crash again and this time they shatter something within me. I squeeze his hand tighter and I wonder if I'm holding on for him, or for me.

"I'm…I'm *scared.*" I glance back at the ocean, the moonlight reflecting off the dark waves. "I…"

There's a sadness behind his eyes, but he doesn't show it on his face when he smiles.

"In the quietest moments and in the loudest ones, *Principessa*."

I smile back, his lingering words like a key rattling a lock I didn't place there myself.

RAFAEL — ONE YEAR LATER

We take it for granted. Everything. From waking up to taking a breath, especially down to the people we love. We take for granted everything that we know our lives to be and it's just my luck that I ended up on the side where I didn't take what I had for granted. I went for what I wanted and in the end, I got it.

Was it in the way I envisioned? Most definitely not.

Nevertheless, *I got the girl.*

And she was mine. Even if it was for what felt like a moment. She was *mine*.

The human mind is a maze and a constant wonder, but even though hers had begun to deteriorate, mine was still intact. The memories of us are like a reel of film, playing in my mind anytime I want to relive our time together because I remember it all. From the moment she smiled at me on the ferry to the heartache I felt as I watched her bleed out in front of me.

As I clasp her ring in my hand, a cold breeze blows over the mountaintop of Falcon's Keep. I close my eyes as it sweeps beneath me and carries the rustling leaves into the air. It seems dull now, the water lifeless like the waves don't have that same vitality they once did years ago. It's almost like the island itself knew when she drew her last breath, and as much as I would like to join her in the afterlife, there are still ties I have here.

"*Papà*, it's going to storm. Come back inside," Stella calls from behind me.

"I will, *amore mio*."

Her footsteps fade and a bolt of lightning lights up the night sky as thunder follows. She used to love the storms, even among the worst ones, she would pull up a chair by the large windows and watch as the rain drenched everything in sight. She used to call it a cleanse, a purifying and healing of our sins. She had hope, more than I did, that we would end up together wherever she is now, but I have my doubts. I know she's in a better place because she's amongst the good ones. She had everything that made her a good person.

But me…I'm everything she wasn't, and why she chose me still puzzles me today. She was ready to give it all up— no, she did give it all up—for everything she stood against because it meant that we could be together.

Her doctor said it was a matter of when and not if. In those with early-onset symptoms, the disease is a lot more aggressive and progresses a lot faster than in an average person. It eats away at the brain, neutralising it, leaving the person a shell of who they once were.

A part of me will always wonder what my life would be now if I never kissed her or touched her…but I have this intense feeling in my stomach I wouldn't be alive to see this day. I wouldn't have the air in my lungs or the wind in my face, nor would I be able to watch my children grow to make a life of their own. She made me a father, something I never saw myself being. When our first was born, I spent the entire year of her life worrying over her, sleeping beside her crib to make sure she was breathing and thinking about how I needed to get her off this godforsaken island. Eventually, that fear faded as our ties and position with Erhan grew stronger.

"*Papà*," Stella calls out to me again, and I release the ring around my necklace as the rain begins to fall just as I make it to the front of the manor.

Stella smiles, her beautiful stormy eyes the same shade as her mother's staring back at me. It's been a year since her death, and even now, she haunts me in the best of ways through the legacy she's left behind in our kids.

There's a stinging behind my eyes as I watch Ezra and Nicholas teach my youngest how to play rummy as his sister carries my granddaughter in her arms, swaying her gently back and forth.

"Hey, you." Darcy places her hand on my shoulder, and I give her a small smile.

She looks the same.

Well, her smile lines are a little more defined, as is the wisdom surrounding her irises as she smiles back at me.

"I guess we all have our time."

"If you believe in that shit." Nicholas approaches and pulls me into a strong embrace. I hold him for a little longer than I normally would, and he doesn't release me, sensing that I need this more than I ever have. "I'm sorry, brother," he says in a low voice and pulls back.

I don't know what I would have done without my brothers. When I met them, I wanted nothing to do with them, but what they say is true. Blood is thicker than water, and regardless of our loyalties, they never once wavered in theirs upon learning of the fact that we were related. It took time, but we eventually worked through our issues.

"Look at what you both have created," Darcy says softly as we stand and observe the chatter in the room, the laughter from my son, and the genuine smile on Ezra's face.

Dante meets my gaze and nods, acknowledging our shared grief. It's been rocky ever since I admitted my feelings for his sister, but goddammit, Nera's optimistic self has rubbed off on me over all these years. I know even though he hated me, the shared experiences and trauma tie us together, bonding us even further than death.

"Shall we?" Aries holds out a tray of baked goods and we all gather around a table, Nino and Santi standing beside Dante, all my brothers under one roof.

"You all better fucking eat the lamingtons. I swear if there's even one left, I'm never bringing them again." Nicholas points to the lamington cake and Darcy laughs.

Over the years, we held birthdays, anniversaries, and important holidays all together as one messed-up family at Nera's request, wanting everyone under one roof. I know she did it for me.

I knew she understood how alone I felt all my life, and when she began to forget, she didn't want me to be alone again. Fuck, I love her so much for that and for everything she ever was.

"Raf, anything you want to say before we dig in?" Nino asks.

Usually, Nera was the one with the words. She was the glue that kept us together. I spent a month after her death in silence. Locked myself in the greenhouse for days on end, just replaying our life together, shutting out my entire family because I couldn't stand that she and I didn't walk the same ground anymore.

I take a breath and swallow the rock forming in my throat as they all wait.

"Nera was everything I wasn't." I chuckle. "She was

the best thing to ever happen to me. Without her these three hundred and sixty-five days, I've felt like a piece of me was missing. Like a constant pull from deep within, she calls to me even from her resting place. Some nights, I find myself kneeling before her tomb, praying to get an hour just to hold her, to tell her I love her."

Stella weaves her hand in mine as a cool tear glides over my cheek.

"The world saw us as a sin like some sort of abomination, but the only atrocity she saw was how cruel the world and life could be. She saw the good in everyone, almost like she was reflecting a piece of herself onto each person she ever met."

My jaw works as I find the rest of my words beneath all my grief.

"She made life worth living. She was my teacher, my lover, and my best friend. She may have left this world, but she'll always remain right here." I place my hand on my chest, the thumping beneath it reminding me I'm here for a reason.

I've never been this open and honest with anyone besides Nera, and instead of feeling vulnerable or embarrassed for showing my brothers my naked grief, I'm grateful to have these emotions because grief and loss are clear signs of love and affection, of loving and being loved in return.

Ezra raises his glass and the rest all follow.

"The most beautiful soul I've ever had the pleasure of knowing in the most prosperous life I could have *ever* asked for," I add, raising my glass and ignoring the lump in my throat. "To Nera Della Torre."

Thank You!

I can't believe this is it. The three books dedicated to the three brothers who came to me in a dream, their stories officially finished. It's been a wild ride. From the excitement of Ezra, the quiet desperation of Nicholas and the endless heartache of Rafael. I will continue to cherish my boys forever because they are the ones who kept me breathing throughout a hard year.

Hubby, you'll never know just how much you've supported me. From the moment I said I wanted to pursue this, to now, you've been my light in a dark place, my sounding board and the person I go to when that imposter syndrome hits hard.

My friends, for continuing to be the best of friends I could ask for in this industry. Your love, support and friendship continue to see me through the pressures of publishing and I admire you all for being such powerhouses.

Sarah, for always boosting me up whenever I need it most and consistently believing in me. I look up to you and I'm so happy I met you. You're now stuck with me.

My editor, Laura, you've become a dear friend through your love for my books but I thank you for your meticulous attention to detail and comments on my work to help me learn and succeed. EJ from Quirky Circe for her talent in design and formatting services but also her ability to put up with my million and one changes. Lee and Katelyn, my cover designers, thank you for giving my boys the most beautiful covers. Anna my PA for dealing with my neurotic behaviour all year. Erin, for always offering a hand in support. When I said I only had a week to complete Beta reads, she immediately said 'Yeah, give it to me'. My street team, Pyro, Dahne, Nicole, Rose, Char, Jenn, Abbey, Mel, Jennifer, Nahi, Lucy and Michelle for hyping me up and sharing their love for my work. You are my safe space and I thank you for being there for me.

Thank you to all the wonderful authors and bookstagrammers in the community whether you have participated in a giveaway with me or shared your knowledge on something specific, I'm thankful for your honest and open words of wisdom.

Thank YOU so much for loving my Casella boys and for your enthusiasm surrounding my work. You will never know what it means to me that you took a chance on me and added my books to your lists, read them and loved them.

I'm truly blessed to be surrounded by such wonderful people and I cannot wait to meet more of you.

If you're wondering what's next, I have a boatload of stories to share so come follow me on socials to be the first to know when a new title drops.

Love always,
C.B.

About The Author

Welcome to my corner of heaven, where the villains and heroes drop to their knees before strong women. My books will have you clenching your thighs and reaching for the bedside table for your best friend.

If I'm not writing, you can find me chasing my favourite bands in concert, or curled up with a glass of red, reading a filthy book.

To be the first to find out about upcoming titles, you can sign up for my newsletter at
https://www.cbfreyauthor.com/subscribe

Thank you for supporting independently published authors.

www.ingramcontent.com/pod-product-compliance
Lightning Source LLC
Chambersburg PA
CBHW051004180726

48291CB00006B/1965